ISLANDIA

Where there is no God but Om in his house of quiet . . . Where people travel on ponies—and a monorail! Where there is no law, and custom rules through the concepts of *alia* (the love of family, house and land) and of *ania* (the love that wishes marriage and nourishes it), and with proper respect for *apia* (lust) and its creative and destructive powers . . .

Islandia—a strange and compelling mixture of fantasy and fact, of what-is and what-should-be, of Tibet and England—and Oz!

"*A constant fusion of the here with the then, the known with the unknown. We know Islandia does not exist in our world, but the opening scene takes place in a pass discovered during our First World War. And so it goes. . . . Good Reading!*"

—Best Sellers

Other SIGNET Science Fiction
You Will Enjoy

The ISLAR

A Narrative
of Lang III

by Mark Saxton

A SIGNET BOOK from
NEW AMERICAN LIBRARY
TIMES MIRROR

SIGNET TRADEMARK REG. U.S. PAT. OFF. AND FOREIGN COUNTRIES
REGISTERED TRADEMARK—MARCA REGISTRADA
HECHO EN CHICAGO, U.S.A.

SIGNET, SIGNET CLASSICS, SIGNETTE, MENTOR AND PLUME BOOKS
are published by The New American Library, Inc.,
1301 Avenue of the Americas, New York, New York 10019

FIRST PRINTING, MAY, 1971

PRINTED IN THE UNITED STATES OF AMERICA

ACKNOWLEDGMENT

ANY EXPRESSION of my indebtedness and gratitude to Sylvia Wright Mitarachi will be inadequate, but it is a pleasure to make this attempt. Her willingness to read the manuscript of this book and the immense care she took in making detailed comment have saved me from many disasters large and small. Of greater importance, her generosity has given me unlimited access to her father's country. Her determined help in identifying error does not, of course, relieve me of responsibility for such heresies as may remain, any more than my passport to Islandia implies that she subscribes to this version of recent Islandian history. For that matter, any reader is free to suppose events other than those recorded here.

M. S.

FOREWORD

SINCE the American-born John Lang published his account of the events that resulted in the unique gift of Islandian citizenship to him and his wife, no other Islandian has written of his country for a foreign readership. More than half a century has passed between this writing and the happenings my grandfather recorded in his narrative. In the intervening time the world outside Islandia has become incomparably grimmer and more terrible than the one John Lang felt impelled to renounce.

The screen Islandia holds up against the world is effective but not impermeable. As though from an astronomical distance we get signals from the outside, and we try to chart them over a spectrum. To put it another way, what reaches us is diffused and diluted; it is the bluish-white stuff that sprays out of the third spout of the separator after the milk and cream have been spun off. For long years we have lived in a condition of slight malaise, aware that things were not quite right inside the country or beyond our borders, but with never an acute, saving sense of danger from either direction.

To the numerous readers of my grandfather's story, and to the very much smaller number who have also seen Jean Perrier's *Islandia: History and Description,* the most reassuring, perhaps even stultifying, thing about Islandia now would be the apparent lack of change. And in many respects the appearance would be true. Islandians still hold by the old ways and customs. They live as they have for centuries by the concepts of *alia* (the love of family, house, and land over generations); of *ania* (the love that wishes marriage and nourishes it); and with respectful recognition of *apia* (lust) and its creative and destructive forces.

They remain agrarian and conservative and, at least in their own estimation, tolerant, industrious, generous, independent, and agnostic in the skeptical sense.

We are also devotedly and incurably provincial.

In Islandia the key to the solution of almost any problem has always been the word *custom*. It controls a vast range of useful resources and expedients. Recently, however, there have been occurrences to which none of the sanctions of custom apply. They've been irrelevant, not inadequate.

It is clear by now that the texture of our society is not as uniform as we thought, nor is the fabric all of a piece. There are rents in it and holes through it. Reasonable suspicion, if not final evidence, suggests that our neighbors to the north know more about our domestic difficulties than we do. And there are still strong differences among us in spite of the clear emergence of peril at last.*

In the event that I am able to carry the ensuing narrative to a conclusion of my own choosing, the reader should know that this prefatory letter is being written in The City after my autumn visit to Reeves and the Frays.

LANG III

---

* See Appendix I: Historical Note, pps. 213-15.

The ISLAR

*A Narrative
of Lang III*

THE COUNTRY OF

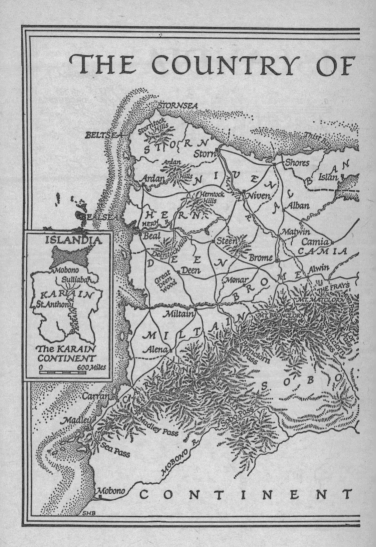

STORNSEA

BELTSE

Storntock Hills

S T O R N

Storn

Ardan
Ardan Hills

Shores

Islan

A L B A N

N I V E N

Thist B.

HERN Hills
Herntock Hills

Niven

Alban

ISLANDIA

Mobono
Sulliaba

KARAIN
St. Anthony

The KARAIN
CONTINENT

0   600 Miles

BEALSE

H E R N

HERN R.

Beal

Deentockhills

D E E N

Great
Deen
Wood

Deen

Steen

Brome

Monar

Matwin

Camia

CAMIA

B R O M E

Alwin

THE FRAYS
MT. MATCLORU

MT. BRONCLORN

Miltain

M I L T A I N

Alena

Falcon
Pass

Falcon
Pass

S O B O

Carran

Madley

Madley Pass

Sobo Pass

MOBONO R.

Sea Pass

Mobono

C O N T I N E N T

SHB

ISLANDIA

NARRATIVE
OF LANG III

SOUND does strange things at high altitude in mist. From where I had chosen to rest for a moment, behind a boulder some thirty feet up the slope from the floor of the narrow pass, the noise of boots on rock seemed directly below me. But there was no one there, nor in either direction within the few yards I could see. After those unmistakable sounds of four human steps there was silence except for the irregular plish of melting snow sliding off the rocks behind me and the low gurgle of ice water working south through the detritus on the bottom of the pass.

My position was good enough. Old, rotten ice and snow, punctured here and there by rock outcroppings, came down in some depth to my own level. Below me was mostly wet shale and smooth stone with ice in pockets and crannies. The narrow place was steaming in the thin air, melting down and raining up. I could see the track of the pass, but to anyone down there nothing existed but a tunnel.

After perhaps two full minutes in which I heard nothing but my own breathing and the seasonal housekeeping of the mountain, a pair of patches in the fog to the south grew darker. Slowly they separated and took shape as humans wearing gray Islandian parkas, long and loose like mine, with the hoods up over their heads. They moved gently, as one does at that height, with a careful respect for the uneasy footing, and also with an impressive sureness and economy.

Passing beneath me, the figures paused on a flat rock slab. The one whose back was fully toward me asked something, eliciting an answer and, for an instant, inside the oval of the hood, I had the impression of eyes, nose, teeth, and a speaking mouth. Again I could hear nothing. From the length of the speeches and the motions that went with them I guessed that the question had to do with the distance still to go, and the reply was to the effect that the divide was near but the border was a considerable

15

distance yet and much lower down. Then they moved on again into the mist, and I determined to allow them five minutes' law.

This near encounter was an unpleasant surprise. I might have challenged the pair. I had the authority, and for a moment I'd been tempted to do it. From coast to coast since the beginning of my own journey all the passes and the upper slopes of the Islandia barrier range had been interdicted. If these men had passed me farther south on the lower slopes, where it wouldn't have been evident that I myself had just been north of the mountains, I might have stopped them.

But here, other considerations aside, the place itself would have persuaded me to do nothing, just as it was the place that made it sensible to climb thirty feet uphill to a resting place. My father had warned me as my grandfather warned him, "Walk through that gully if you can and if you have to, but don't stand still in it. If you must stop, get up one of the sides to a firm place." That was sound advice.

The point was that the track wasn't properly a pass at all. It was a rock ravine, a cleft of varying width and depth, running roughly north and south for about five miles. Under favorable conditions it afforded a high crossing of the otherwise impossible west face of Mount Crask. The place is never safe, but usually each year for a few weeks in late summer a fit and determined man can get through.

The route has no official name, and it isn't shown on any maps of Islandia or the Karain. My grandfather discovered it when he was responsible for the central mountain frontier in the First World War. Islandia was not a belligerent, but England and, more importantly, Germany with Turkish help were stirring up tribal ambitions and animosities in the tropics to the north. There was real danger for a while that some new Sulliab and some Bant chief would patch up their own quarrel and strike south against us.

The importance of Lang's Ladder, as my father called this desolate flume when he first saw it as a boy, is direct passage north and south through the Islandia range. There are no roads in Islandia as Europeans and Americans know them and no motor vehicles in the usual sense, except for one or two ceremonial limousines that decorate the courtyards of foreign diplomats in The City. Individual land travel is by foot, by pony, or sometimes by wagon or bicycle. The regular passes to the north can be negotiated sometimes by pony but mostly only on foot. Three weeks ago when I set out for the inland low country north of the border I had the choice of Lang's Ladder or one of two easier, longer routes. The Ladder saved three days' travel each way over the quickest of them. And it kept my journey secret.

The five-minute delay I had imposed on myself was alarmingly long in passing. The cold steaming mist and the melting ice and snow surrounded me with what seemed to be the essential perfume of naked rock. I had never suffered acutely from mountain sickness, but I had had enough of it to be frightened by it. I am not much good for any length of time at heights approaching 14,000 feet, and this was more than that. Also two weeks in the low, hot river country had cost me some of my tolerance.

I'd been here long enough. I should go. This woolgathering was bad. A singing in the back of my head and a hurting tightness over my eyes warned me. I must get down and go.

With the caution of an invalid leaving his bed for the first time in months, I reached down with my feet and slid off my perch. A bad sprain or a broken leg here would do for me. Ten feet from the bottom I tested a narrow piece of ledge with my foot. It was firm. The motion of my body coming down shifted my weight outward. The lip of the ledge crumbled. I fell, rolled, and slid the rest of the way.

Numb and dazed, I waited for the landslide that would surely crush me. Nothing moved except water flowing under the rocks I lay on and curling and splashing down from the rocks above. A quick inspection showed a series of stone lacerations on the back of my left hand, a cut of some kind under my right cheekbone, and a long, spreading welt above my right knee beneath the torn cloth of my trousers. That seemed to be the damage. I could stand. I could walk.

Moving southward down the steepening slope into Islandia, the thought that racked around with the pain in my head was that only some twenty living people supposedly knew of the existence of Lang's Ladder. And until today just six, living or dead, had ever climbed it. Through the interior noise my choice now seemed clearly right. It was better not to have challenged, and to have seen without being seen.

Later I felt the churnings of nausea my head had told

me were probably coming. Without argument I knelt down to be sick, knowing it would be a slow trip the rest of the long way down to where my pony was pastured.

✠

Of his own accord my pony Tobo came to a stop behind the screen of trees on the high meadow northeast of my father's house in the southern Frays. Tobo cocked his pointed gray ears back at me, and I rubbed his neck along the line of his jaw while I leaned forward to try to see what was happening. There were people moving around in front of the house. Some seemed to be going inside. To be where they were they must have arrived on foot, or more likely by the carriage from Fraysedge.

It looked like some kind of official party, or delegation, from The City or from Reeves. It was late morning and that would be the right time for a visitation. Aside from fatigue I was feeling well again, but my appearance would not do. Everything about me advertised recent trouble in the forbidden heights. I needed to get into the house unnoticed. Once there, I should seem to have been there for several days if I needed to make a wan, washed social appearance.

Tobo and I retreated quietly, turned off the meadow through the corner of a thick stretch of conifers, and then —with me on foot and ducking my head—came up toward the stable under the thick cover of the clipped and bushed orchard trees. From the other side of the house, softened and distorted somewhat, came the unmistakable, well-enunciated, woodwind sound of formal conviviality. Tobo nosed his way gently into the stable. Before he stopped, I had the pack off his rump and the saddle girth unbuckled.

Behind me there was a sound, a darkening of the light from the door. I leaned deeper into the shadow until I could see who it was. Then, against the light, I recognized the shape of Atta, my younger brother, and heard him say, "It's Atta, Jonno. It's all right."

We grasped each other by the shoulders and he stood me off to look. "You did that well, Jonno," he said. "Nobody saw you. I was looking for you, and I didn't know you were here until the ponies began to move in the paddock." He gave me another, closer look. "It was something serious, wasn't it? How much hurt are you? How sick?"

"I'm not sick now," I said, "and I don't hurt too much. I'm tired, but that can wait. Later I've a lot to tell. Who are the visitors?"

"We began to look for you two days ago," Atta said. "You must have . . . You're right. Later. The guests are the American Consul General and a mixed following. You know most of them. The Consul is giving a speech tonight at the University of Reeves. I'll explain while you're cleaning up. You get inside. Rigg and I will take care of Tobo."

I did as Atta told me. He was two years younger than I, two inches shorter, a palm broader, and several shades darker. He resembled the Hyth men on our mother's side of the family. I was only slightly modified Lang. My father and my grandfather were both close to six feet, blond with blue eyes and fair skin, and in Islandian terms light for their inches. I was not quite as tall as they, a little heavier set, somewhat darker, but their image as compared with my brother. Between Atta and me there had always been affection and trust. They lay deep and solid enough to make firm ground for the competition of our different abilities and for the confrontation of our unmeeting wishes.

In the last year or so there had been several confrontations of wishes between us, and this was undoubtedly another. At least it was a large fraction of one. If I knew my brother at all, he felt he was better qualified than I for the job I'd just done. For some parts of it he certainly was, and maybe even overall. He would have been quicker there and back. He wouldn't have had mountain sickness and he wouldn't have been two days late on a schedule he considered slow to begin with. He might have done well in the north, too, although that was a different matter. It was different enough so that they gave me the assignment even though I didn't much want it. One way of putting it is that Atta finds it difficult not to make immediate decisions, whereas there is some Hamlet in me.

Atta came in while I was shaving. After bathing hot and cold and eating a bowl of thick soup, I was feeling much improved. He watched the final strokes of my razor with a smile and said, "That's good. There's nothing like having a month of beard to cut off when a healthy man needs to look like a convalescent for a few hours. What happened, Jonno?"

"Too much mountain for too long coming back. I was sick and took a fall. That's what held me up."

"You're all right?"

"I've told you. Yes. I'm tired and I've got bruises, but I'm well. Food tastes fine." I made a gesture back over my shoulder with my thumb. "What about the visitation?"

"You should appear. The way you look, it's a risk. But staying away would be worse. Talk as though you'd been here all along. There's no one who could contradict that, is there?"

"No one who would," I said, and then, "Sometimes, Atta, you let me read your mind. You think someone in this party is dangerous."

"Morana is dangerous."

There was no need to comment. Morana was the Islandian observer at the United Nations. I hadn't known she was home. She was dangerous without any doubt. Atta distrusted her, disliked her, and was afraid of her. I didn't understand her, was afraid of her, and liked her. The question about her was, dangerous to whom? She would strongly disapprove of my journey. There was no knowing what she would do if she guessed it.

Atta said, "And Dorna is here, also riding herd on the Consul."

"And on Morana?"

"Probably."

"And who else?"

"A young American, a student and a teacher at the University. Then there is Hanno—Civil Service. I think he knows. And there are two excuses for security guards. They might protect a man from a rabbit, if it was not asleep."

"All right," I said, "I agree I should appear. You go on now. I'll follow you in about five minutes."

"What happened to the back of your hand and your face?"

"If anyone asks, I had a fall when I was trying to climb up to a hawk's nest in the rocks above the northeast meadow."

✠

The angles of the doorway afforded a protected look at the alignment of forces in the main room. Down the kitchen hallway from behind came the faint smell of the hotbreads and meat stew that would be ready soon. Now people were having tea, cider, or brandy, along with flat-cakes. Islandian social gatherings are usually quiet. Here the sound of the talk was like the run of a brook around rocks. Except when someone made the Consul laugh, and then his bass resonance filled the place.

His name was William Commiter, and he was a big man even by the standards of Dorn men, six and a half feet at least, with a weathered face and spikes of white hair above a tremendous assembly of shoulders and chest and a flat, tapering body. He was standing beside my father in the curve of the treble side of the piano for which my grandmother had waited so eagerly when she first came to Islandia. Talking with them were Dorna and Morana. Across the room my brother Atta, the government escort Hanno, and the young American student and teacher surrounded my mother at the teapot. One of the security guards was near the door. Presumably the other was somewhere outside.

Crossing the room to pay my respects to the Consul, I nodded in passing to Dorna, whom I had seen recently, and spoke more formally to Morana, whom I had not—not for more than a year. She had always been slender and dark as many Islandians are, but now, even though she was wearing Islandian dress, I had the impression that in New York she had adopted a way of doing her hair and touching up her eyes that made her look more Indian than even a Mora normally does.

I offered my hand to the Consul in American style, and he shook it firmly once, answering my English greeting in good Islandian. "This is a pleasure, Islata Lang. I've wanted the opportunity to tell you how much we feel in your debt in my country for your fine translations." He was referring to two books, one of Islandian poems and one of fables which had been published recently in America. "Since your grandfather's book nothing from here has given us so much enjoyment and enlightenment." His gray eyes considered me for a moment, and he then added, "You have corrected an impression John Lang left with some people—I suspect that what he needed to say left him little choice—that Islandians are a pretty sober-sided lot."

"Thank you, sir." This perceptive, honest compliment pleased me greatly. "That is one of the main reasons I tried the job."

"I'm not a scholar of Islandian or English," he said, "and in my work I don't often run into literary problems. But I do have to translate a large number of unusual notions back and forth. Your language isn't like English/French, or English/German, or even English/Russian. With them you have sets of locutions on either side into which you can force almost anything. But I find the Islandian/English intersection very risky. What you've done is much more difficult than that. I admire your precision."

"It's kind of you to say that. Actually it's much easier going from Islandian to English than the other way. English is a much richer language, of course. It will reproduce alien subtleties in a way that Islandian cannot. With us, you know, meaning so often depends on context and pitch, and time relationships are so vague that a language like English suffers badly turned into Islandian."

I stepped back and there was Dorna looking like a cat with a mouse under its paw. "That was so beautiful, Jonno. So true, and not the least little bit sobersided. And you must have made it all up as you went along. I don't know how. You should be a diplomat yourself. Morana thinks so," and she turned to Morana. "She's been telling me all about the United Nations and how, if we refuse to join, we should at least have an observer from the Dorn party there to take the blame off the Moras." Then, seeing that I was looking full at Morana, Dorna said, "If you're wondering what happened to Morana's caste mark, Jonno, she left it in New York."

All this was delivered as lightly and inconsequentially as is possible with such heavy weapons, but the shots went home, particularly the last. Morana and Dorna are both twenty-eight, about a year and a half younger than I. In their very individual ways, they carry on the Mora and Dorn contrasts. Both are tall women and, like most Islandians, are nicely formed and stand and move well, but the resemblance ends there. Dorna's dark hair has glints of red in it beneath the surface, her gray eyes sparkle when she is interested, and there is a soft russet tone to the smooth skin of her face. Morana is somewhat light-boned, her face a longer oval, her hair jet black. She is usually slow-spoken, and her fine, wide-set, almost black eyes are so striking that one can miss the fact that her flexible mouth controls her expression. Morana is also an imperious, strong-minded woman. She doesn't suffer fools gladly or otherwise except, as some contend, on those occasions when she should include herself in the category. Now, surprisingly, she seemed to offer the other cheek.

"You're right, Dorna. I like Indians and Indian ways, but my hair is modestly American. In New York it's hard to keep a hairdresser from ironing you flat. But there's still some snake in my locks," and with the back of one hand she lifted the fall of hair from between her shoulders. "Not quite enough to let me turn you to stone." She spoke in a quiet, almost forgiving tone, and then said to me, "But there should be one of the Dorn faction in New York with me. It's wrong to ask a Mora, who thinks we should belong, to explain to the world why the Dorns keep us out. And more than that, it's risky to let people think that a Mora alone, or a Dorn, can speak now for Islandia."

Morana was talking hard sense. She was alluding to a situation that few Dorns or Moras would admit—that there was no Islandian government. There was only Lord Farrant's caretaker establishment that collected taxes, maintained civil order and services, and manned the armed forces. Each of the great political factions, the Dorns and the Moras and their adherents, claimed that with their support Lord Farrant could make decisions and initiate and carry out policies. In fact, Lord Farrant could do nothing except sit between them. Some Islandians, very quietly, compared the state of affairs to the ancient days of The League, long years of domestic conniving and antagonism that resolved themselves in multiple dishonor, murder, and civil war.

"You should speak to Lord Farrant," I said.

"I have," was her answer, "and he likes the idea, particularly coming from me. I suggested that he name you."

"Why me? I'm not a Dorn."

"Not a Dorn, Jon? I wish you'd find me as good a Mora by another name." Her swathed body was supple and poised as a ballerina's, she turned halfway toward the Consul and back. "And just now Mr. Commiter told us all why it has to be you."

"You mean he told us why it couldn't be me," I said. "Translators of fables and poems aren't diplomats."

"Perhaps," she said, and rested her hand on my arm. "But, Jon," and her voice was much lower, "they don't usually turn their ponies off through the woods and come in through the back way when they've been at home sick. Don't worry. Even Atta didn't see that. I was the only one."

She had the last word. I walked across to the tea table
where Atta, the Civil Service man Hanno, and Henry Ross,
the young American, were talking with my mother. She
was enjoying herself and looked very young. Her aunt
was Hytha Nattana, one of the half-dozen or so most important people in my grandfather's life. I never knew my
great-aunt Nattana, but my grandfather wrote about her
and also talked about her. I would like to have known
her, and oftentimes I think I do when I see a gesture or an
expression, or hear an intonation of my mother's that is
exactly what John Lang described. The style is comeliness
and vigor not beauty, and the qualities that go with it
are affection, patience, and a surprising capacity for self-
derision.

Hytha said, "Jon, you look as though you've been
worsted by Morana. This tea is very good."

✠

After the meal, I took Henry Ross, the young American, for a walk over the meadows to the edge of the drop.
The whole party was leaving at four o'clock for the Fraysedge elevator down to the monorail and the trip to Reeves
for the Consul's address at the University. The overcast
was thickening and the characteristic wet, chill wind of
early fall was coming off the mountains, but there were
still two hours before the rain would begin. We walked
through the orchard, the loaded trees about two weeks
away from picking, and on down along the dark green
edge of the fir woods.

Ross was a man of a kind I'd never seen before and
knew nothing about. I hadn't read anything or been told
anything to prepare me for him. Medium height and solid,
with his short dark hair going evenly thin across his head,
he spoke with a fine verve in what seemed to be a mixture of learned jargon, current slang, and clear English.
He spoke English to me because he said his Islandian was
still no better than adequate. My grandfather's generation
at Harvard, I suppose, would have called such a person a
grind, and he would have been a member of the brown-
paper-bag club. But Ross was much too worldly, aware,
and poised to fit in that category now, if it still existed.

Before we left the house he told me, "Your grandfather
saved me from becoming a neo-Keynesian economist, one

of the input-output, feedback, public sector-private sector, countervailing force, industrial state boys. I read *Islandia* the summer after my sophomore year and had the sense to see I wasn't for economics."

Now, with the thick grass underfoot and the mist a few hundred feet above, I said, "You haven't told me, Mr. Ross, what you are in your reformed state, after your escape from economics."

"I'm not sure I know," he said cheerfully. "Maybe I'm a social anthropologist. At any rate I'm a professional scholar. In my case that means I'm a semi-respectable, friendly snoop." After another score of paces he added, "That's not to say I'm here to study your country in aspic. I try to teach as much as I learn. I admit it's an uneven exchange because I'm not that good a teacher, but damn few are. Also I sense some limitations on what I may say. Reeves is a good school. It's not like one of ours, but it's alive and solid. I just wish you had more schools. And I wish your curriculum wasn't so relentlessly provincial. That isn't good. Look at Spain after six centuries of it. About half of you seem to want Islandia to stay exclusive, and I think maybe I agree. The trouble is you can't do it well this way. What's more important you probably can't do it at all unless a lot of you know more than you do about the other ninety-nine and forty-four one-hundredths percent of the world."

He was shrewd. I knew the Ivory soap slogan. There had never been any Ivory soap in Islandia, but it was sold in St. Anthony and Sulliaba now, still advertised as "99 and 44/100% pure."

At the end of the meadow we clambored over a rough stretch of bare granite. This was the lip of the Frays at a point about midway in the long sweep of south-facing ledges. Ross stepped up with me, looked down, took an involuntary step backward, and then came back again. "That was sudden," he said. "I don't get vertigo—I think —but I'm not easy with heights. What a sight that is."

Actually today the prospect was poor, cut off by clouds and mist, the colors dull. The one dramatic view we did have was down fifteen hundred feet to the beginning of the Islandia plain. From where we stood the drop seemed vertical. But in fact the grade along here wasn't much more than seventy-five degrees in most places and climbable up or down without too much difficulty. At Frays-edge, though, two or three miles to the west where the elevator was, the height was only about 800 feet but the drop was plumb.

From where we stood, on a bright day you could see hundreds of square miles of country rolling out below, the crystal and silver and glittering black of streams and rivers, the yellows, browns, and light greens of planted fields, and the darker greens of spreads and tongues of forest. Moving across all of it would be cloud shadows, and standing on some of it would be hill shadows. It is one of the finest overlooks in Islandia and, so travelers tell me, in all the world. Now it was soft and muted.

After Ross' initial reaction to the height, he fully recovered himself and ranged up and down the edge of the rock scree, finding vantage points from which he could see different parts of the slope and the terrain just underneath us. We were there for perhaps half an hour. As we turned away at last, he said, "Thanks for bringing me here. In a way this is better than fine weather. You have to look harder." And then, "You know there's nothing to see at Fraysedge"—he meant the screen of planting around the upper landing—"and the elevator was curtained coming up."

In a friendly silence we covered two-thirds of the distance back across the meadow. Then Ross stopped suddenly and faced me. He was pale and there was sweat on his forehead. I thought he was ill and reached toward him, but he stepped back from me. "No," he said, "I'm not sick. I have to say something impertinent. Something not my business. I have to risk saying it to somebody, and you're the first person who might understand. I'm scared for all of you. Doesn't it ever frighten you to have your country in the hands of a bunch of powerless incompetents? You're a national receivership in bankruptcy. The Dorns and the Moras are still able, but each faction just sits there sucking its pride, saying *we* can't do anything because *they* would stop it. It's too late here for that kind of stubbornness.

"There hasn't been a constructive political idea here—and I mean political—in fifty years, and that's a long time by any standard, even Islandian. You're in trouble. Can't you feel it? One of your holier-than-thous had better go to the other and say, 'Make a government for all our sakes and we'll give you silent support until we have an issue we can beat you with.' This is ancient wisdom, Islata Lang. You had it here once."

He shook his head, turned, and walked away, obviously

feeling he had offended me. He had, but not as much as he might think. Actually it's been a lot more than fifty years since Islandia has had a new political idea, but that's not the difficulty. Through the country there seems to be a growing, exasperating sense of being inadequate in the face of our own problems. The new position of Sulliaba is a harsh illustration.

After the Americans refused Egypt money for the completion of the Aswan Dam, Russian influence began to increase all through the Arab world. In Sulliaba, working from the Consulate and a trade mission, Russian technicians, advisers, and attachés encouraged the local nationalist faction and supported it with credit and equipment. Several years ago, during Dorn's last regime, Sulliaba abruptly seceded from Karain, declaring itself a sovereign state. North of Islandia nothing existed to prevent this.

Islandia did not have the will. Dorn wanted to intervene in force at once. He said to the Council, "Foreign manipulation of native ambition. We've always fought this. It's why we survive. In Sulliaba this is still a baby monster. We must scotch it now while it's still half in its shell. If not, we'll be hatching one of our own." The Council listened, divided evenly on the vote, and Dorn's government fell.

Mora was against intervention. He wanted to recognize Sulliaba, to offer cooperation and friendship. Although the Council voted three to two against Mora, it gave him a negative victory and the country a government on sufference under Lord Farrant.

I overtook Ross at the beginning of the orchard and touched his shoulder. "Tell me," I said, "what particular kind of trouble do you think we're in?"

Ross had his color back by now, but he wasn't rid of his embarrassment. "For a man who likes your hospitality," he said, "I've talked a great deal too much already. Let me change the subject a little. In the last few months have you been to a House of Quiet?"

Ross was referring to places of reflection and meditation within the spirit of Om, of Him who Is. Om is the major deity of Islandia, but he is not obligatory. He may be ignored or investigated. He easily subsumes Bos and Cam—the gods of home and field, the spirits of rocks, trees, and animals—whom Islandians treat with irreverence but love for the comfort they bring.

Om is something quite other. Christians, particularly Protestants, find Him difficult. He is not a god of love nor vengeance. He has nothing to do with perfection. There is no redemption in Him. He may neither be prayed to nor invoked. He is not the craftsman god, nor is He null. His only quality is that He Is.

Om allows a person to look at himself and the world in the silence of Om's house and make what he can of them, knowing that all he feels and thinks Is. Not many people do this. It is a demanding discipline and often dangerous. To some it's a purge, to some an ironic revelation, and to others it's an experience of terror.

One foreigner has said that Voltaire's famous epigram about the necessity of God was based on a knowledge of Om. Another Western philosopher said that "Om is the principle beyond good and evil." In any case, many come to Om's house to escape heat, cold, rain, or snow. A few come to assess themselves in terms of the powerful conjugation: I am; You are; He, She, It is.

Whatever their purpose all come into Om's house bound by silence, except for those who have something to say that must out. For such people there are alcoves and small doorless rooms where a person may, if his face is hidden, unburden himself to empty space, or to any who may care to listen.

To Ross I said, "A House of Quiet? I haven't been in one in two or three years. I remember going as a child. I think that was educational and not religious. My grandfather—well, he was my grandfather and he was the first of us. I loved him. He used to tell me stories of America, and of Islandia when he came here. You receive these things and ask for them. They're hard to estimate. I think my grandfather was agnostic but that there were generations of Congregationalism back of him. I've never wanted to know Om. Maybe I'm afraid to. Why do you ask?"

"Because I've become symbiotic with Om, or at least His Houses. I've been here about a year and I've been in every House of Quiet I could find. In Reeves I keep going back to the major one. There, in the big public room, there are always six to eight people enjoying or suffering different kinds of silence. This doesn't change. But a year ago the alcoves were empty. Now they are being used all the time."

"How?"

"I'm not sure. My speaking knowledge of Islandian now is barely good enough to get by with in class where the advantages are all with me. When it comes to a man speaking fast through a shawl, I'm lost. But I'll bet that everyone I heard was talking about the political meaning of one or another of Bodwin's fables. I'd love to know if this is going on all over the country. This is one way change comes when it's radical."

✠

When Ross and I came back to the house I managed a word in private with my father while the Consul was talking with my mother. We agreed that I would report to him on my journey to the north after the Consul and his party had left. In answer to his only question I said, "Yes, I have important things to tell you, but they're not so urgent that we have to let people know we're going into conference about them."

My father nodded. "In that case," he said, "I think it would be right for you to guide the members of the party to Fraysedge. They came in the livery carriage. After that experience they decided to walk back. And it's getting on for dark and rain." Putting his hand on my shoulder, he steered us on a publicly visible course toward the Consul.

To Islandians, whether town or country bred, difficult walking in poor light is no problem. I didn't know what to expect of my two Americans. They surprised me. They were as good on the broken ground as the best of us and much better than most of us.

In our latitude during fall and winter, night comes very early, even in good weather, on the lower southern slopes of the great mountains. On this day we came down onto Fraysedge fifteen minutes before four,* and the place was the next thing to dark. The misty underedges of the clouds were down close to our heads now and, from higher up, rain was beginning to fall through. From a distance of about a hundred paces we began to see the diffused glow of the single electric light bulb over the door into the elevator housing. This small beacon was the signal for talk to start again, with a laugh or two thinning the deep silence that had settled over us all about a mile back. Before there was any light or fire, the night world must have been a fearsome place.

We trooped across the level ground in front of the ele-

* See Appendix III: Time, p. 219.

vator shaft, grouped closely but not in any order. Ross stepped out ahead to open the door onto the platform by the car that would take the Consul and his party down to the monorail.

But the door opened before he touched it. A bulky figure in a gray, hooded cape filled the dark aperture. Ross stepped back, and we all stopped, milling around against each other. In his quiet, carrying baritone Mr. Commiter said to Ross, over the heads of the others, "Henry, ask the guard to let us go right down. We should be on our way to Reeves."

Ross merely stood still. I think he and I and perhaps Hanno were the only ones instantly alarmed—he because he had come up against the man in the doorway and sensed danger, and I because I knew there were no guards on the elevator. Even before the Consul spoke to Ross, I began to look around and saw figures moving toward us, three from one side of the palisade and three from the other. Then, as I turned back, another three, whom we must have passed, closed in behind us. Each wore the long parka, the hooded cape with sleeves. I couldn't see any weapons in the uncertain, swirling light, but there was something in the way the men moved and kept station on each other that said they were armed.

The man in the elevator doorway stepped forward and brushed Ross back in among the rest of us. Then through the door, in the same conical uniform, there came a short figure, brisk and bustling, and behind him a taller figure doing the same things with less motion. They looked to be Boss and Assistant, Adjutant and Captain.

Mr. Commiter had the same impression. He stepped toward the Captain and spoke down from his great height in Islandian. "Whoever you are and whatever you may be doing, I am the representative in Islandia of the Government of the United States of America. Everyone with me belongs to my party. We are here under the auspices of the Islandian Government. You may have known this, but I urge you to consider it now."

While this was going on, and the Captain was ignoring the Consul, I felt a nudge at my side and found Ross there. He had a pack of cigarettes in his hand and was trying to shake one out. He dropped the cigarette and then the pack with it. I bent down with him to pick them up. When both our heads were a few inches off the dirt, he said, "Have they guns?"

"Yes, I think."

"A little diversion by me, and you could get out."

"Yes, but don't," I said.

The Adjutant was now replying to Mr. Commiter as spokesman for the Captain. He was using border pidgin, the lingua franca made of elements of Islandian, Karain, and Bant—in proportions of the speaker's choice—but with a simple dynamics of its own.

Morana translated into Islandian, standing at the Consul's shoulder. "We know you, Mister American. We know others along you. We no scare. You foreigner. You American foreigner. You bad foreigner. Maybe you good man. Still bad foreigner. Some good foreigners bad men. Good foreigners good. Bad foreigners bad. No matter. We got bad government. Your government not like things we do now here. It hurt our government. Good!"

Our pidgin is no more obscure than any other. Each one encodes complicated notions in an almost binary system of slightly modified "yeas" and "nays." Another common thing is that it's easier, if you're familiar with one, to operate inside it than to translate it into a real language.

Morana did a good, rough, even-handed job, sticking exactly to all the bristling opposites that came from the Adjutant. He was clearly an Islandian. The choice and weight of his words showed it, along with his inability to avoid grammar altogether. For him pidgin had become more a form of elocution than a means of speaking to someone with a different language.

They gave the Consul no chance to speak again. At a signal from the Adjutant, the men in the cordon behind us stepped back three paces, took intervals from their opposite numbers, and produced weapons. I saw one submachine gun, a couple of automatic rifles, what looked like a Colt .38, and some billy clubs. Beyond that I don't know what they had.

Human encounters are never quite like Acts of God, even if they're equally sudden and no matter how many victims they claim. Vesuvius over Pompeii doesn't make an equation with *Enola Gay* over Hiroshima. Big or little, the human versions of these things have the greater validity. Deep in men and women, beyond the reach even of an arbitrary God, is an awareness that is not surprised by anything men may do. Whatever it is, if men have done it, the deed is naturalized by the recognition of other men that they, too, have it in them. Om, of course, includes all this. I now wonder at myself for once considering that

Roman a gentle fool who said, *"Nihil humani mihi al-
ienum puto."*

Things happened very rapidly and with no sense. At a
sign from the Adjutant, our two security guards were
seized and relieved of the knives which were their only
weapons. They were made to stand with their faces
against the wall of the elevator shed. Next they marched
Hanno up to face the Adjutant. "Farrant's man," he said,
and made a gesture with his thumb. They prodded him
through the door and into the elevator shed.

One by one we were brought to face the Adjutant,
identified, and pushed into the shed. To Mr. Commiter he
said, "American Consul? American Proconsul." To Ross,
"American student? American spy." To Dorna, "A Dorn.
In bad company." To me, "Lang. American blood. He'd
bleed treason." I was shoved after the others.

From inside when I turned to look back across the
muzzles of the guns covering our doorway, a new scene
was beginning in the dim light and the mist. Three men
were holding Morana. As I watched they threw her to the
ground on her back and spread her out, one man to each
ankle and one on her wrists above her head. The Adjutant
moved aside and the Captain took his place with Morana
at his feet. He looked down at her for a long twenty or
thirty seconds. Finally he turned his back and walked off
in a manner that said plainly he didn't mean to soil himself on her.

They lifted Morana and stood her in front of the Adjutant, a man still holding her from either side. To her he
said harshly, "Mora," and struck her hard back and forth
across the face with his open gloved hand. Then they bun-
dled her through the door and in with the rest of us.

Now, except for the man covering the two security
guards against the outside wall, the entire force was
formed in a half circle around our door. The Captain
moved a pace in front of his Adjutant and spoke for the
first time. He used Islandian, not pidgin. He spoke well
and slowly, forming his words with care as though he
wanted to avoid any regional idiom.

"You will take the elevator down to the monorail and
go to Reeves. You have been delayed six minutes only.
Your schedule is not disarranged. Lang, you will accom-
pany the party to Reeves. You will not return to the
Frays tonight. In any case the elevator will be discon-
nected when it has brought you down. Arrangements will
be made for your security guards to follow you."

The Frays elevator, aside from canals and locks, is the first and oldest major machine built in Islandia for public use. It was engineered, constructed, and put into service during the First World War, and was designed to run on a complicated system of counterweights. The capacity of the elevator then was ten tons through a vertical distance of 744 feet. To allow for uncertainties in loading and counterweighting, as well as weather across the open face of the cliff, stations were built at the 250- and 500-foot marks where either the weights or the carriage could be stopped to modify the loading. Brakemen manned the cables at the top and bottom, and pumps resembling hand car mechanisms were geared to the cable drums to assist the carriage to any landing stage if necessary. There are scale models of this first elevator in the National Islandia Museum in The City and in the British Museum in London. The thing scared people to hysterics, but it worked. It was one of the mechanical wonders of the world.

In 1940 as hydroelectric power began to be developed in Islandia, and when the Second World War suggested that more capacity was needed, the elevator was rebuilt. Load was increased to twenty-five tons and vertical travel was reduced to 723 feet by the construction of efficient inclined planes at the bottom. New, solid housing at right angles to the cliff protected the vehicle from the worst effects of weather. The basic principle of counterweighting was maintained, but an electrically driven motor then removed the need for hand braking, pumping, or for changing weights as on a balance scale.

This was the thing in which we all went down. It was very slow, partly because it was made that way and partly because the motor had to labor in low gear against our lack of weight. I don't remember any word being spoken during the long cold descent. In the top of the carriage was another faint electric light bulb. At first the mist curled in through the open grillwork at the front and then, as we dropped below cloud level, there were spatters of rain.

The two women stood together in the center of the car. Dorna put her arm around Morana as the elevator door was shut and we were started down. Soon, she withdrew the protective gesture and simply stayed at Morana's side, one hand lightly on her shoulder. At one point I took a step in their direction. Dorna saw my motion, shook her head, and I went no nearer. The feeble light showed Morana to be very pale except for the darkening red blooms

on her face where the Adjutant's hand had passed, but she
didn't seem to be in shock or suffering from outrage. Instead her eyes suggested she was carrying on some kind of
intense internal activity.

At last the elevator nudged and bumped its way into the
grip of the holding locks at the bottom. We opened the
door and stepped out into full night and a steady light
rain. Fifty yards away along the rock causeway, its
smooth, wet metal skin glistening from its own lights, the
car of the monorail waited in its dock. I led the party
toward it single file. Ross brought up the rear.

I don't know whether it is possible to hear the sound of
an object falling. In any case we all sensed something
that halted us twenty-five yards from the monorail. On
the instant, with a force we could feel in our feet and so
close together that one was a continuation of the other,
came two loud reports. The noise was like the bursting of
a waterskin dropped from a height. None of us had a
moment's doubt what it was.

Ross was nearest the place of impact. He climbed down
off the causeway and made his way slowly through bushes
and over rocks toward the cliff. At last he stopped,
dropped to his haunches, and remained there looking
down for a number of seconds. Then he rose, took a few
paces to his right, and repeated the procedure except that
this time he did not rise to his feet.

I was starting to climb down from the causeway after
him when he did stand up, turned, and raised both hands
palm out to stop me. "No need," he called in a loud, uncertain voice. "No need. The arrangements . . . for sending
them after us . . . were perfect."

✠

Our council meeting in the car of the monorail was
brief. By agreement among the Islandians, and at the suggestion of Hanno—I was placed in charge. "I am here as
an escort," Hanno said. "I have neither the authority nor
the local knowledge to take responsibility Lang has both."

"Very well," I said. "First I want your advice. Hanno,
what do you suggest we do?"

"We should go straight to The City."

"Dorna?"

"We should keep our engagement at Reeves and start now."

"Morana?"

"We should think hard before we do anything. This isn't just mindless brutality. It was intended—all of it. I can't guess what for, but something. And you can see that we're the ones to carry it from here. We must be very careful what we say and do."

When we organized ourselves as Islandians with me as the officer in formal control, the two Americans had courteously separated themselves from us by moving several seats down the car. Now Ross rose and asked my permission to speak. He obviously still felt most unwell, but he had himself under good control.

"I have two points," he said. "Only for the record because I'm sure you're aware of them. First, you have a major obligation for the safety of the Consul and a lesser one—but still important—to his commitment to speak at the University tonight. If you think what Morana said is as shrewd as I do, you will see how much easier it will be for us to be noncommittal about all this if the Consul can complete his routine. The other thing is that if you decide to go on to a full discussion here, as Morana wants, I suggest we do it in motion."

I turned back to Morana, who was sitting with her fingertips just touching her bruised cheeks. "That's the kind of thought I hoped for," she said. "What Mr. Ross says is unanswerable. Let us go to Reeves."

"Mr. Commiter," I said, "do you really feel equal to going through with your lecture?"

"My dear Lang, all Foreign Service officers are expected to be able to talk under almost any circumstances to almost anybody. Witness Robert Murphy. Of course I'll speak."

"Then," I said, "the sooner we go our ways the better."

Dorna nodded, saying, "You'll go back up to the Frays then. But not from here?"

"No. From where the cliffs are higher and easier. I should make it in less than two hours. The Isla needs to know about this more than anyone else." Then I satisfied myself about Hanno's authority to use the telephone in Reeves—in Islandia the only telephones are official, there are few of them, and these carefully restricted. I instructed him to call The City and what to report.

Finally, I asked Ross, "Why didn't we hear screams?"

"That's why I spent so long with them. Maybe an autopsy would tell you—if you could get one. I think they were hit on the head first. There were plenty of clubs up there."

Before leaving, I went into the front compartment for a word with the operator, and said goodbye to the others, telling them I expected to be in The City within a few days. Then I stepped out of the car onto the dock and scrambled down the rough, slippery side of the causeway. The engines in the monorail hummed, and there was a flash of blue light as the current burned through some moisture. The car moved away from the dock, its lights at first glittering individually and then all becoming suffused by the rain and mist.

After the lights and the vibrations went away, I slowly began to hear the small sounds of the ground; the drip here, the plop over there, the quick swash of some small animal's short trip through the brush. My ears could read what was going on. It was all familiar and should have calmed me. But I was expecting a different noise from larger animals. I leaned against the causeway. It stood between me and the remains of murdered men, the first new evidence of an old, unpeopled nightmare, the towering track of fire, the moving cloud of smoke from a valley beyond a ridge.

As a child I read many of my grandfather's books. I remember what an Englishman named Traherne wrote 300 years ago—"Place yourself therefore in the middle of the world as if you were alone, and meditate upon all the services which it doth unto you. Suppose the Sun were absent, and conceive the world to be a dungeon of darkness and death about you . . ."

At the moment that was much the way I felt, and Traherne's happy conclusion by way of the bright beams of God was no help to me because I had never understood the meaning or the syntax. As I pushed myself off the causeway wall it seemed that it must be the middle of the night. But, in fact, the ambush, the murders, the conference, and my self-indulgence together had not taken half an hour.

✠

On that forced march up to the Frays nothing attacked me except rain, and seemingly mobile companies of rocks and roots. Squirrels and jays, and the rest of the day animals and birds were asleep and took no offense. But I caused some disturbance on the night side. While I was still skirting the base of the cliff I interrupted a fox and saw him bound away. Partway up the slope I hooked my arm around a tree for support and looked over a branch into a pair of knotholes which stared back at me from the face of a great owl. Twice I thought I saw the toothy, gliding shadow of a ferret. Now and then lesser creatures, heard but not seen, would dash away on all sides of me. They weren't running from me. They were using my smell and my tramping to shake off the hunter who had found them that night. Some of them would make it.

I came onto the Frays not far from where I had talked with Ross. This was the place I had meant to rest after the climb, but the rain here in the open was such a steady punishment on my head and shoulders that I didn't stop. Over the rough grasslands the footing wasn't bad, but I did a lot of squelching, sliding, and falling in the orchard. I went into the house through the stables to the kitchen.

There, drenched both ways, with sweat and rain, I began to steam and smell like a sheep. The heaviest, wettest pieces of wool were off me and on the floor when Hytha came in to find out what was slopping in her kitchen. Mother looked preoccupied and worried. Then she saw me and the mess I was making. She looked, sniffed, and seemed to reduce the pitch of her worry.

"Jonno," she said, and put her hand to my forehead and face. Always Islandians have been afraid of fever, and with reason. "You seem all right. I'll tell your father and Atta. Come when you're dry. And have some soup from the stove, but don't drip into it. It's beef." She turned as she was leaving and added, "It must have been a hard trip." That was all she said.*

From his own people, my father had already learned almost as much about the incident at the elevator as I was able to tell him. He also knew, which I did not, that the raiding party had headed toward the northwest, but he did not conclude from this that it was making for the Lor and Mora passes. While I was still climbing up from Fraysbottom, a firsthand report came in from the chief of my father's irregular scouts. Hilko, also a senior member of the Frays' trapping and hunting syndicate, was a quick, dark, hard little man. Whatever he said about the Frays

* See Appendix II: The Frays, pp. 215–19.

you could take for truth, provided you understood the sim-
ile or the indirection he invented for the occasion.

My father said, "Hilko told me, I think, that these
people are not known to his people, and they are not
mountaineers. He says they won't attempt the passes—
they will come south off the Frays and go west toward
Dole."

We were all gathered around the fire in the central
room, Atta and I on either side of the hearth close to
the chimney, my mother in a low chair somewhat away
from the direct throw of the heat, my father pacing the
center of the room. Outside there was very little wind.
The cold rain, falling straight and hard, was heavy enough
to travel down the heat of the chimney and hiss in the
flame.

"Hilko is right," Atta said. "This rain will be heavy
snow higher up. The first big snow of the season. That
means avalanches in the passes. And most of the border
runners go in and out of Dole." This was true. The spread
of the Sulliaban oil fields west and south out of the delta
of the Karain River and the increase in sea traffic to the
port of Sulliaba in recent years made the northwest coast
of Islandia the favored region for illegal entries and de-
partures. "We should warn Dole and Farrant."

My father nodded, saying, "That's been done. By radio.
Our telephone has been cut. And word has gone to The
City and Reeves. Hanno won't have to argue to use the
phone at Reeves. It will be open for him when he gets
there. Jonno, you did well with your share of this. What's
your opinion?"

This was my father's way. He would canvass us all
once, consider what we offered, question us if necessary,
and then make his decision as Isla. After all the available
facts were in he used us as an advisory committee but
never as a sounding board to test his own ideas.

"I haven't given you any report on my trip to the
north," I said. "I don't mean to do it now. I made full
notes which you can read when you have time. But there
are two things I should tell you. The first is that I saw
travelers on Lang's Ladder." Then I described how the
two men had passed below me. "It would be foolish not
to assume they had something to do with what just happened here. So Hilko's reading of things needs to be modified. These men were mountaineers. They were sent north
at least two days ago which probably means that the
marauding party was on the Frays for the same length of

time. These people didn't find the pass by accident. They knew it was there. The only place they could have learned about it is The City, unless there was treachery in Hilko's department. It's possible to see the pass on an aerial photograph—one taken intentionally at the right hour of the right day of the right month and so forth. But even so, you have to know about it first or the picture doesn't tell you anything. As Hilko says, the party is most likely dispersing in the direction of Dole. They've plenty of their own kind there if they don't leave the country. But the two leaders—no. They will be going back to Reeves or The City."

It took my father four crossings of the room to reduce my mixture of fact and conjecture to the minimum degree of order he could tolerate. Finally he came to a stop and said, "Yes, Jonno, yes. No doubt. And likewise twice on preceding Thursdays. Bah! I don't know what we would do without your ability to encounter bad news. Yes, I do know. We'd die for lack of warning. Do you attract these things? Or are you able to survive seeing what would be death for another witness?" He shook himself from head to foot and I understood the reason for his excitement. The same notion had just begun to cross my own mind. Calm again, he said, "That was the most fortunate case of mountain sickness I know about. If you live long enough, you can come to be a very unpopular man. You had two things to tell us. Drop the other shoe."

"Yes," I said, "I hadn't forgotten. The rest is less dramatic and more serious. There is no possibility—almost none—that Sulliaba and Mobono will mount a joint operation against us. We can forget that nightmare—or that hope." They all looked at me with surprised, wary recognition as though a forbidden word had been said aloud for the first time. And it had. "But something else is going on. There are rumors and reports about Islandia. As of now they're all just subsurface. Nothing official, nothing on the radio, nothing in the press. But they're all over the north. In Sulliaba, in Mobono, in all the Bant tribes on the Steppes and farther down Karain, even in St. Anthony. And they're all the same. There is civil disorder in Islandia. There is rebellion in Islandia. Law and order have broken down in Islandia."

In the silence that fell on us the shifting and spitting of the fire grew louder. I fed it two more split pieces. Meanwhile my father did not pace the floor. The first one to speak was Atta, who said, "Then the two men you saw got out of the country with a real story before it happened. And this one will break the surface because it can be verified."

My father turned to my mother now. "Hytha, please help us."

"You won't approve of my help, John. It's not to the point."

"You mean I may not understand you right away," he said gravely. "That's different."

"Then I'll try," she said. "You know I'm a country woman. The gods I'm familiar with are Cam and Bos, indoors and outdoors, the what and the when that goes on every day. I'm glad that Om *is* and I'm happy just to have Him *be*. But, John, you're an Om person. You want to know all about His *isness*. You worry about the *should* and the *ought* of things, and I honor you for it."

"Yes?" my father said, and my mother laughed, saying, "And you're patient, John. You support Dorn policies because you are loyal to the family that befriended your father. Sometimes you forget that the Dorns were also in debt to him. You like the Dorns and admire them because they are able and honorable and courageous. So do I. Privately you think they're stupid, and I agree with you. You're closer to the Mora party than the Dorns on any issue, and you think like a Mora. But you suspect the Mora people are slippery, and I'm certain of it."

"I understand you Hytha," he said. "I don't know the answer."

"There's only one answer," my mother said, "and any Dorn would know it if he weren't a Dorn ahead of anything else."

✠

The daytime monorail trip to The City remains unbelievably beautiful and dramatic even to someone who has been familiar with it all his life. The line runs along river valleys, among mountains, and over long stretches of green rolling country. Great vistas open up on either side, are cut off by the shoulders of hills, and then are replaced by different ones. The long, aspiring view is reduced over and over to the immediacy of rocks, trees, and narrow gorges.

On this bright, windy morning it was impossible not to

be more cheerful than I had been in the rain and stress the night before. Just the same, I found myself noticing for the first time how vulnerable the monorail was to any kind of sabotage. One grows apprehensive quickly.

The notes I left with my father told why there is still no danger of a joint war on us by Sulliaba and Mobono. In the past each of them has attacked us, and each has had the assistance of allies from a common pool of Bant and Karain tribes. When we have warred on either of them, each one has called on the same help. But never in all the wars have we confronted a transmontane continent united against us.

Historically Sulliaba is a Saracen colony, and it is still strongly Muslim and Pan-Arab in its attitudes and policies. The Russians have made sure the Sulliabans don't lack for guns and aircraft, while the Anglo-American oil companies keep the important people so rich that even the poor ones rarely starve in public anymore.

Mobono is on the east coast and different. It is also originally Saracen, but more densely populated, less prosperous, less well organized, and more democratic in its hospitality to adventurers. Long centuries ago Portuguese came into Mobono and, during the last hundred years, Indians and migrant Chinese. The buildings of the port city, the laws and overt customs of the country show some Portuguese inheritance. More obvious are the overlays left by the British protectorate which was given up early in the dissolution of empire over which Churchill said he would not preside. There are fishing grounds off the coast, a good harbor, and some natural products in the form of timber, herbs, nuts, and fibers. But what gives Mobono its modern importance are the recently discovered goldfields on Mobono territory in the northern spur of the Islandian mountain range.

The cultural apparatus of the Peoples Middle Kingdom of China is well represented throughout Mobono. Chinese geologists and engineers are all over the place. Their opinion is that much richer gold veins lie south across the border in Islandia and possibly diamond deposits as well.

Once in The City I went straight to Lang House, a very small place for all its imposing name. It's in the delta and island section of The City at the mouth of the Islandia River where the streets for the most part run from roof to roof. The area is threaded with small waterways, natural canals running among stony islets. It is said that when the early Islandians who descended from the Frays seized the mouth of the great river, they found there a fishing village whose huts were often connected overhead across the smaller inlets by wood and fiber walkways. The device seemed to have been intended for structural solidity as well as access, but the Islandians liked it for its appearance and its convenience. They adapted it to their own permanent buildings and, as The City grew, even extended it some distance onto the mainland.

Our place sits on a rock hummock separated by a rivulet from the Dorn establishment on its own sizable island. Our house once belonged to the Dorn family who had used it to house caretakers, retainers, young relatives, and long-staying guests. My grandfather acquired it by some intricate and courteous form of purchase when he became Isla of the Frays and had to satisfy the requirement that provincial lords reside in The City during the months when the Council was in session.

I first sent off to Lord Farrant by hand a note I wrote on the trip south, and then bathed, dressed, and ate. His reply arrived within the hour. If it suited me, I was to call on him forthwith. As presiding officer of the Council and the country's chief executive officer, Lord Farrant had chambers in the old Council Hall in the mainland part of The City. Virtually all Islandian construction is of stone, and our public buildings particularly are heavy, massive, and dark. On the first few days of my return to town after months on the Frays I'm usually depressed by The City's concentration of these great piles, but not that afternoon with the rooftop gardens bright with our varieties of zinnias and asters and the trees in the mainland streets showing the beginning of fall color.

Lord Farrant was a vigorous man of about sixty who visibly detested his job as national caretaker. The last regular party government, that of the present Lord Dorn, collapsed in 1959. Since then a group of nonpolitical administrators has had the critical and unenthusiastic support of the evenly divided parties.

The task of presiding over the "dynamics of inanition," as the English Consul General has called it, has been enough to exhaust the resilience of a yoga or a fatalist, and Lord Farrant is neither. He has borne it by saying that he will be glad to be the "stone from which Islandia steps" onto firm ground.

The official secretary took down my statement, bowed, and left us sitting in the pleasant sunlight of a northwest window. We continued to exchange cordial but more or less formal courtesies until Lord Farrant got to his feet. He was a short man, square all over, with a light mahogany skin, pale eyes, and black hair with some white in it. He stumped back and forth across the room, his hands hooked behind him by a thumb and forefinger because his arms weren't quite long enough for four fingers to reach comfortably.

"The telephone," he said, "it was put back together this morning. I talked to your father. Talked? I can't use the thing. Neither can he. I shout. He shouts. Nobody knows how to listen to it except the foreigners and Morana." He allowed me a crossing of the room and return to fall into one jaw or another of his trap, but I managed to keep still.

He came to a stop in front of me. "I have the facts. You've reported them promptly and completely. But facts are everything and nothing. My job is to see that they stay nothing. It isn't easy to castrate one set of facts and spay another unless you *know* one from the other. I would be grateful for your opinion, Lang. It will be private, and I will not assume you are speaking for Lord Lang. What do you think was the cause of this brutal nonsense?"

He could infer, guess, extrapolate as well as I. Probably a lot better. I thought he wanted what I would have wanted in his position—a commitment from somebody, a tie of some sort to the emotional and moral strength of partisanship. He didn't want to be left alone as the caretaker of whatever portended now. I admired him and felt for him. But in my state, and in the state of our country, he would have to stay by himself. I couldn't give myself to him.

I pushed myself up out of the deep chair and said, "Lord Farrant, there are dozens of people in the country who can answer your question better than I. Some of them are on your staff. Hanno is one. But you asked for my opinion. I think this thing has no *causes* worth looking for. Analogies maybe. It was done to provoke something. That it will do. The question is what."

Farrant stepped back and looked at me steadily out of his pale eyes. "Thank you," he said. "The regular session of the Council begins in ten days. Your father said this morning he felt he should stay in the Frays for the time being. I agree with him. May I count on you to be present when I report to the Council on the happenings in Lang's

Ladder and on Fraysedge? Members will be curious about details."

"Yes, sir," I said. "You may depend on it."

✠

At Lang House there was a note from Dorna asking me to join her next door for dinner if I had no other plans. Not to reply. Just come if I felt like it. I told our caretaker, Hettin, to tell his wife she needn't worry about food for me, and then I put in an hour writing my father about the events of the day. This proved to be more difficult than it should have been.

I found myself unwilling, actually unable, to state directly what I had done, seen, said, and heard. I wasn't feeling evasive. The trouble was I couldn't stop with facts and was unwilling to give speculation the force of written words. Finally I tore up and burned several pages of ambiguities. In their place, in a note which I sealed and posted, I set down three statements. I had seen Lord Farrant; I had agreed to be present when the Council convened; I would keep them informed.

The way to Dorn House from our place is not from one roof to another but down through the rough rock garden and across the narrow footbridge over the stream. There is no overhead link at all between Dorn House and The City. Except in recent years for Langs, the only way to get to Dorn House is by boat. Long ago, in the times of the disturbances and disaffections of The League, the house of every provincial Isla in The City was raided and ransacked at least once—save one. The Dorns remembered how seventy yards of open water had helped them manhandle their attackers. After that, first as a policy and then as a tradition, the family declined to connect Dorn House with the aerial street system. For some years it had been mostly a matter of style. When our place was conveyed to my grandfather no condition was put on the overhead rights.

When I left the house everything on the ground was two or three minutes at most away from full night. In the far northwest a school of high cirrus clouds still showed a dull trace of crimson underneath the dark sky. From the southwest across Islandia Bay the light, chilly breeze smelled of low tide. Beneath the footbridge the water looked like black glass.

In Dorn House I found Mr. Commiter and Mr. Ross talking to Dorna in mixed Islandian and English. They were all standing, the two men apparently engaged in the American ritual of slowly diminishing recapitulation which ultimately terminates in departure. I didn't want to interrupt or prolong the ceremony, and so I nodded, spoke generally to everyone in greeting, and crossed the big room to the south windows overlooking the bay.

By now some stars were in their early autumn positions in a momentarily clear sky. They were all quite high so that the blackness of the water and the darkness of the lower edge of the sky made no sure horizon. As I shifted my gaze, not scanning so much as glancing, I seemed to see in the middle distance a patch of something blacker then the water. I turned my head and came back to it with the edge of my sight. Glancingly and irrecoverably I had a faint signal that I saw a shape as well as a shadow.

Sensing someone at my shoulder, knowing it must be Dorna, I said, "If I didn't love the hills so much, I'd never leave The City. But it's curious. I thought I knew this part of the bay very well. I've never seen a night fisherman out there."

"Where?" she asked.

"That darker spot," I said, and pointed.

"I don't see it." That was a man's voice. It was Commiter.

"I think I do." That was Ross. "Would you point again?"

Unpleasantly startled and uneasy, I did. "Yes," he said, "I do see it. But I don't think it's a fishing boat. If you look fifteen degrees to your right, you can see another one." And then he pointed. "Or way off to the left there." He pointed again. "The wind is freshening some and there's more starlight than we think. Unless there's a fleet of fishing boats, those must be patches of roughening water."

Mr. Commiter said, "We didn't stay on to give you instruction in meteorology, Islata Lang, just to say good evening. I hope you will call on me soon."

"Yes, we must go now," Ross said. "I must catch the monorail tonight. I have a class just after breakfast. I hope you can find time to come to Reeves while you're in the south."

✠

During the evening I discovered that Dorna was very much taken with Ross. Telling me what happened the night before at Reeves, she spoke more often of Commiter, but when she did mention Ross there was something hesitant and questioning in her manner. And she would speak of both of them when she wanted to ask a question, as when she said, "You know more about America than any of us, even Morana." This wasn't true, but I didn't contradict her. "All my life I've been told Americans were loud and snatching and horrible. I've known Commiter for years and I've always just thought he was a friend. But of course he's an American first and a friend second. The things I've been taught about Americans don't fit him, even take away the friend. I know that's not a great discovery, but I didn't make it until I saw that all those things don't . . . don't fit Ross either. Do you suppose there are lots of Americans like them?"

"Yes," I said, "I think so. But how many . . . well, Morana says that just in New York City there are twice as many people as in all Islandia. So what are lots of Americans? Most of them never heard of us. Most of us never heard of them. Anyway, now, the Americans who come here like us. What did Commiter say at Reeves?"

"The old man was marvelous." The old man, I guess, being about sixty. "In the hall we sat on the platform on either side of him. It was cold. Morana and I were beginning to shake again. Commiter began to talk and we stopped. We forgot. He made us laugh first. He spoke for an hour. Things nobody had ever said. He talked about the idea of Islandia in America and what it had done. What it meant to have an Islandia to imagine for people who lived and worked in New York or Chicago or Kansas City or . . . Kalamazoo, could he have said that? Some of it was silly—a man in California started a society of upside-down map readers because Islandians put South at the top of their maps.

"At the end he said the real Islandia of course was different in fact and detail from other people's dreams of it, but that the imaginings weren't far from what Islandians have wanted their country to be. We owe the rest of the world an obligation even if it doesn't seem like one.

Part of it is to stay real in our own terms. Whole and coherent was what he said. And part of it is to stay ideal to foreigners. The second depends on the first. The world needs an independent and admired Islandia as much as we want it, and these are the conditions. I—well—the Consul had me close to tears, and I wasn't alone."

I said, "After what happened at Fraysedge he was able to make a talk like that?"

She nodded. "Yes. Last night somehow it reassured me. Now it doesn't at all. He sees something plain. Do you?"

✠

Later at home I took out the charts of Islandia Bay and studied them for water depths and channel markings. Beginning way up south in the open water between Windsea and Stormsea, I followed down through the narrow gut of the entrance into the bay proper where an unobstructed line of deep water, off-centered markedly to the east, seemed to run north from the entrance to a point well beyond Dorn House. Surrounding this deep, there appeared to be a rough fan pattern of fingerlike channels reaching out toward the shores. Here the charts showed a ridged and dangerous bottom but plenty of water in most places even for large vessels except on the far side to the west and northwest. There the cartographers were vague, indicating indeterminate areas of silt and sand and giving no good location for the shelf to deep water.

Except in a very general way these charts were now useless. The date of issue was 1916, and there was no information about when or how the survey itself had been made. You wondered about the certainty with which the underwater hills and valleys were rendered. Artistically they were most convincing, but the data were gathered from a boat on the surface by means of pitch or tallow stuck to the bottom of a lead weight on the end of a more or less plumb line marked off in fathoms. In the unlikely case that nothing down below had changed in the meantime, the underwater contours were still guesswork at best, even simple things like maximum and minimum depth. You couldn't heave the lead often enough in enough places for that.

What the charts did say, probably as correctly now as in 1916, was where in Islandia Bay it was safe to take oceangoing ships. And what I wanted to know beyond this, I then realized, would not be on any later charts either, if there were any. Just the same, my 1916 antiques told me that whatever I saw, or thought I saw, from the windows of Dorn House was near the middle of the deepwater aisle.

Early next morning I took our boat out and spent several hours on the water. The day was bright and cool with a moderate, crisp wind from the west. The boat behaved like an eager, well-trained dog enjoying himself. Everything I asked it to do it did on the run, stylishly. I hadn't been in a boat for more than a year. The old familiar pleasure in the thoughtless concentration of sailing took me wonderfully by surprise.

We, the boat and I, sported around like a porpoise. It wasn't in character, but it was a great deal of fun. For years now our boat had been a familiar curiosity in the bay. No one had ever duplicated or adapted it, but watermen and sailors spoke seriously of its virtues. The reason for the boat, as I'd assembled the story, was my father's annoyance as a youth at the tendency of the family then to be somewhat more Islandian than the Dorns about almost everything.

First he acquired a sound, solid twenty-two-foot boat and unstepped the two-legged mast. Then, relying for instruction on an illustrated book of small craft he found in the Islandia Museum, he squared off one end to give it a stern, set in an inboard tiller and a centerboard, and decked it over except for an oval cockpit. A few inches from the bow he stepped a single mast that carried one huge, gaff-rigged, fore-and-aft sail. When the marine carpenter who had done the skilled work finally asked what kind of a boat it was, my father told him it was a Barnegat Catboat. It probably wasn't, but it certainly was more American than Islandian and, when properly ballasted, it became a fine craft, staunch, handy, and seaworthy. Of course it was no longer reversible and it wouldn't point very high, but on certain points of sailing, particularly a broad reach, it was remarkably fast. One man could handle it easily in almost any weather.

All that morning, after I indulged some exuberance, I sailed a search pattern over the stretch of water where I thought I had sighted something. Vessels do leave traces behind—a patch of oil, bilge, garbage, or non-Islandian things, an empty cigarette pack or food container, an opened tin can. On open water your chances of encountering a possible object that may be as small as a playing card aren't too good, particularly when you're on the surface yourself. I had a fine sail, and came in with an appetite and a windburn and that was all. I'd seen nothing but clean, green-blue water. My exercise didn't convince me that I hadn't seen a large boat the night before; only that if I had seen one then its housekeeping and/or its discipline was good.

That afternoon I paid a call on the American Consul. Mr. Commiter welcomed me cordially and with amusement. He said, "I hear you spent the morning on the bay. It's wonderful weather. I wish you'd asked me along. Did you find what you were looking for?"

"I didn't find anything, if that's what you mean. I wasn't looking for anything in particular."

"Yes, I know that," he said. "Last night you were sure you saw a ship from Dorn House. Are you still?"

"No less," I said. "I was certain then that I thought I saw something on the water. There is a difference."

"So there is."

He led the way then out of the big general room in which we were standing, with its tables covered with American periodicals and the shelves on its walls filled with American books, into a place I guessed to be his own study and not his office. I hadn't been in the American Consulate before.

Pointing me to a chair with a view of the river and the hills to the northwest, he said, "I'm going to have a beer at this point, a Dutch beer. What would you like? Tea, coffee, whiskey, brandy?"

"I'd like a Dutch beer."

This room was best in the afternoon and was arranged to take advantage of it. I left my chair and looked around while Commiter was away seeing to the drinks. This was indeed a private place, not a business office. The length of it ran from northeast to southwest so that the wide windows on the northwest caught the best light in all seasons, although not a painter's light. A big fireplace was in the center of the inside wall with open bookshelves on either side. I couldn't do more than glance at the books, but they were obviously not a display of recent American creativity. On each of the end walls, well away from any direct sun, was a painting. One showed a vast landscape of semi-desert bounded by great harsh, gullied mountains. The other, about the same size, showed grass, rocks, sticks, the surface of the clear water of a stream, and the brownish-yellow sand slightly displaced underneath the water. From where I stood I couldn't tell whether they were originals or reproductions, but I had never seen anything like them. In Islandia we revere the European Renaissance masters and some of the Impressionists, and we continue to cultivate our own tradition of amateur talent. No amateur had done either of these things. The lighting achieved was unbelievable. And in each one the intensity and precision of the chosen details combined to take you through the magnificent physical scene to a vivid, momentary, and unsettling sensation that you were somehow right in the middle of essence.

A few minutes later, sitting by the window and sipping the fine cold brew, I repeated what Dorna had said about Commiter's talk at Reeves and said I wished I had heard it. Then I told him that the Council would take up the Fraysedge affair as soon as it met and asked if he planned to attend.

"If the session is open to the Diplomatic Corps, certainly."

"Will you have a statement to make?"

"Not unless Washington instructs me to, and in that case of course I would make a representation directly to Lord Farrant. If members of the Council should wish me to answer questions, naturally I would."

"I'll be representing my father," I said, "and I'll have to make the initial report to the Council. Will you respond if I need to call on you?"

"Yes, within limits."

I nodded and thanked him and then asked, "Privately, have you any idea what could be behind this thing?"

"No," he said shortly. "Hardly even guesses. Nothing I could say even privately." After a moment he went on without the edge on his voice. "But there is something else I can say privately. It's what I was really talking about—improperly—at Reeves. You have a wonderfully apt phrase in Islandian that translates into *unmeeting wishes*. I think it usually describes a very recognizable and highly painful unspoken hiatus in a love affair. Well, perhaps it can describe Islandia's political situation, too. Unmeeting wishes hurt a great deal when two people have them. When they turn up in a nation's affairs for a long time then they're—well, dangerous."

"I know," I said, abrupt this time myself. "We all know." I had to change that. "Some of us know. We all feel it. The basic division—the one between belong-to-

the-world and don't-belong—is part of us. It's a way of
life. It's our history. But it's only in my time, and yours
here, that we've been paralyzed by it. You're right about
unmeeting wishes. They fester when they're unspoken. But
that's never been true, and isn't now, between the Dorn
party and the Mora party."

Open ranks of clouds were spreading across the northern sky. A fine sunset was in the making. I finished the
beer I had, declined a second, and was about to take my
leave when Commiter said, "Before you go, there is one
uneasy thing I should say. I am hesitant about this. I
hope I am wrong. I have the impression you wanted very
much to prove that you did see a vessel in the bay last
night."

"I certainly was curious," I said. "I still am. Why do
you apologize for noticing that?"

"Because of the direction of your interest," Commiter
said quietly. "I'm not accusing you of being a fool. Far
from it. But I think you have a wish that is unlikely to
have a meeting with anything. There is a notion in the
back of your mind that the United States will intervene
here if things become as bad as you're afraid they will.
Last night you were sure you saw a preliminary sign of
this help—the superstructure of an American submarine
come to consult with me. There wasn't one last night.
There won't be one. And in my opinion—for good reasons of history and politics which you know as well as
I—my government will not take a hand in your business."

✠

Islandia does have a career Civil Service, and has had
for a long time. Historians say that the notion began in
the seventeenth century after King Tor XI was killed for
treasonous dealings with the Spanish and the Council for
the first time chose a Head of State responsible to a vote of
its own majority. Council members then found themselves
part of government in addition to being regional Lords.
They needed continuing sources of information, ways to im-
plement authority, and cross bearings on how things were
going in other Islandian provinces. The Lords brought
staffs into The City made up of collateral relatives and
faithful retainers. Over the years these people and their
offspring, for the most part, became residents of The City

and kept on working for their respective provincial Lords in their generations. A kind of hereditary professionalism grew up and, by the time the Public Service was institutionalized and nationalized early in the nineteenth century, there was ready to hand a sizable caste, or guild, of trained government workers. By this time there was little provincial bias left in any of them and there was already the beginning of a strong sense of possession and exclusiveness, which in its turn became hereditary.

The Public Service occupied three massive, interconnected, two-story stone buildings facing the Islandia River a quarter of a mile upstream from its juncture with the bay. This was where I went to see Hanno. The Service deals with everything, military matters, from potato bugs to postage stamps to national security. The Service is, no doubt, departmentalized and organized into interrelated hierarchies. None of this, however, is published. You can't just ask to see somebody in Agriculture or Commerce or Public Works. You have to describe what you want to talk about and then someone will come and listen to you.

I didn't quite have to do that. I asked for Hanno by name. The young man I spoke to was friendly. "Hanno was here a few minutes ago."

"Where can I reach him?"

"He'll be back through here sometime. He usually is. He moves around."

"Where can I find him now?"

"Upstairs perhaps. Maybe in one of the other buildings. He's always somewhere."

"He's fortunate. May I send a message to his office?"

"Office?"

"I see. Then I'll wait for him here. If someone sees him somewhere please tell him I'd like to talk with him for a minute."

"Usually if he comes here in the morning he doesn't come back until afternoon sometime. I'm not likely to run across him, but if I do—or one of us does—who wanted to see him?"

"The want is in the future," I said. "I am here until I talk with Hanno. For the rest of it, just tell him I'm the person who's waiting for him. That should do it."

Three minutes later a plain, courteous young woman took me in tow through several corridors and up a flight of stairs. There she knocked on a door, opened it, and motioned me in. I was confronting Hanno in a large, well-appointed, very real office. He looked at me straight-faced until the door closed and then began to laugh. He was much more impressive in this setting than he had been on the Frays, and I also began to suspect that he was considerably more important than I had then thought.

"Islata Lang," he said, "never has an outsider bested the Public Service so neatly. Your method is inspired. What can I do for you?"

"I am to report to the Council on the incident at the Frays," I said. "If I need your testimony, may I call on you?"

"Certainly," Hanno said, "if Lord Farrant agrees. He would need to approve." He picked up a folder from one side of his desk, took out a large photograph, and handed it to me. "This should interest you."

It was an aerial photograph taken from medium range. The black-and-white print was beautifully clear. In the upper right it showed one face of a mountain peak with two large fields of old snow almost joined at the top but separated at the bottom by what seemed at least a quarter of a mile. The nearer snowfield tapered down smoothly to a narrow ice tail at the bottom. The other had its own ice tail but two wide, jagged gullies ran up on either side for a third of its length.

At the bottom center of the print a black hairline began a graphlike passage across the gray side of the mountain. Its course was plain to a point somewhat beyond the center of the print. Then it became indistinct, fuzzy, invisible, fuzzy again, and finally clear once more.

What the picture said was easy to read, but I couldn't tell whether it meant anything. Here was Lang's Ladder early on a bright morning in late summer or the beginning of autumn not very long after a big snowslide. Still holding the splendid print, I looked from it toward Hanno in a way I hoped was respectful without being idiotic, and said, "Naturally I've wondered what your function was. Your concern here then is mostly—security?"

This seemed to please him because for a moment, in return for I have no idea how many professionally incurred condescensions, he allowed himself to patronize me. "We don't use the term," he said, "even inside the Service. We've had no need to, and then we don't departmentalize anyway except for mail service and things the Agency does for us. We all work at what needs to be done. In a week or so I'll probably be in Shores and Niven checking potato deliveries to make sure that the harvest hasn't dangerously depleted the soil of small, brown stones."

I smiled and nodded. "I understand, I think, and I'm sorry about calling you a security officer. When was this picture taken?"

"The morning after you came back through the pass. You were still recovering from mountain sickness." He picked up another picture and gave it to me. "This was taken about sixteen hours earlier. You may have been in the pass at the time."

This one, evidently taken from beneath an overcast, had no shadows and consequently showed no trace of the track of the pass. But here both snowfields were undisturbed. "No," Hanno said anticipating my question, "that's as close as we can come to the time of the slide. Perhaps the two men you saw got through, but perhaps not. By your description you were already south of the slide when you saw them. They still had to pass under it."

"This seems like a great deal of effort," I said holding up the pictures and then giving them back to him.

"These two men of yours have confused things," he said. "You forget we never heard of them until you got back. We've been monitoring Karain radio and doing routine camera flights over the mountain border ever since the passes were closed. But your trip wasn't routine and your route worried us."

"It worried me, too," I said. "Lots."

"I'm glad to hear it. Anyway the best we could do was keep a close watch on that mountain. I had word of the second picture, the one after the slide, about three hours after it was taken. I telephoned your father. He said he was worried but not as much as he would be if it were someone else. Technically, it seems, you are not a first-class mountaineer, and you don't bear up well at high altitudes, but you are canny and resourceful.

"Lord Lang told us how to find the shelter south of the pass where you would go to sleep and eat. We couldn't land there, but if we saw your pony in the small paddock by the shelter then you were certainly all right. If the pony was still loose in the big meadow that wasn't so good —you'd probably had trouble. Well, the pony almost had his head in the shelter, but I was still very relieved to see you that noon."

There was something strangely embarrassing in learning now about all that effort and attention. I even felt resentful at having been watched while I slept off the sickness, but I tried not to let any of this show as I thanked

Hanno warmly for his care and asked, "How many know about the snowslide?"

"The fliers, your father, Lord Farrant, me, and now you," he said.

"And you think the men I saw did not get through?"

"I would have thought not, but someone did."

"By boat?"

"Possible, just barely. We're running very tight inshore patrols and we've closed the northern ports on both coasts. A boat always has a chance. The thing is, there hasn't been time."

"Radio then?" I asked doubtfully, not sure what he was getting at.

"No. Not out of Islandia. You know that. All the transmitters belong to the army. Diplomats have to send their codes over our transmitters. Ships and aircraft are allowed a wavelength for routine operational messages in the clear. Their sets are sealed on landing. Any ship or plane that sends nonoperational messages in our airspace and within one hundred miles of our coast is not permitted to return. We can police this, or rather it's self-policing because only two airlines and four shipping companies are licensed here. They behave well. Even Lord Farrant has to go to the army," he said with some pleasure, "before he can make a broadcast."

I knew some of this. For instance, the ingenious little transmitter at the Frays—low powered, one wavelength only, and highly directional—belonged to the military half of the Isla's job. The rest was news to me. "You mean, Hanno, that there couldn't be a secret transmitter somewhere?"

He looked around the room as if to say that there might be several of his own right here and who knew how many planted by the American Consul. He ended his joke there, however, and answered without condescension. "I'd be surprised if there weren't fifteen or twenty clandestine transmitters in the country. I don't care much so long as they don't send, and so far none has. That's all right. The longer an undeclared truce lasts the more binding it gets."

Hanno obviously thought he had made a clear statement of a simple situation. No doubt he had if you knew the facts. Clearly he was saying that if the army owned the transmitters, the Public Service really controlled their use. But beyond that he gave me only the glimmer of a notion. I said, "I'm sorry but you've lost me, except for what you said about there not being enough time. You're ruling out radio now. You've excluded boats. You think the men I saw died in the avalanche. And something has happened you can't account for. Would you tell me what it is?"

"Yes," he said, "it's the Karain radio. Not the big stations at Sulliaba and Mobono. You've just been in the interior. You know what I'm talking about. Hundreds of intertribal and then intervillage walkie-talkie say-sos. Electronic drum signals. And then, after that, word of mouth. Well, our listening gear is very good. From the frontier we can pick up two and sometimes three tiers of this chatter. You reported on the nonradio phase of it. Our monitored record shows that the Karain was full of the news of a civil battle in northern Islandia six hours before we were attacked at Fraysedge. How did the word get there? That's my time problem. Since then the Karain has informed us—and I say it that way because someone must know just about how much we can pick up from our mountain stations—of two, or maybe four additional disturbances in Islandia.

"The trouble is we don't know of any outbreaks. Either they haven't happened yet, or they've been concealed. Or possibly it's a suggestion."

"There is no counter to this?"

"Not directly," Hanno said, beginning to walk. "We haven't any psychological dragons we can stick in their ears. Once we could threaten people with the anger of an Alwin or a Dorn. Not now. It's the other way around. Someone knows us very well. He's as harsh as one of the first Dorns. What happened to my two men was a demonstration and meant as such. He has the imagination to turn The Descent from the Frays against us. The message is that we're to go the way we first did, down from the Frays.

"And there's something else in it. Why was Morana singled out to be humiliated? You know more history than I, Islata Lang, but you may agree with me that in the past Islandia's only real defense against danger was resourcefulness. It came from tolerance, trust, and a good deal of mutual watchfulness. In my father's time the job I have now wasn't important."

When I did say goodbye a quarter of an hour later, better informed than I expected but less well than I would have liked, Hanno showed me one more picture. At first I didn't know what it was. It had no depth, just white against dark. Then I recognized the shape of the mountain, a snow mountain here with no rock anywhere. From top to bottom the center of the print covering the track of Lang's Ladder showed an unbroken snowfield.

"Taken yesterday morning," Hanno said. "It's like that along the whole range almost to the coasts. Nobody is likely to cross the mountains on foot for a while."

✠

When I reached home I saw a line of boats moving between Dorn House and the mainland. Lord Dorn was taking up residence. There was no firm protocol for this occasion. Probably my father would have waited until next day and then paid an informal visit. In this there would have been a great deal of civilized affection, and some hierarchical obligation. But for me, veritably *in loco parentis,* things were different. In the first place I wasn't going to be here next day, and secondly no call of mine on Lord Dorn could be informal. The towering, formidable old man didn't intimidate me exactly, but social words had never moved easily between us.

I wrote a note of greeting and explanation which I asked Hettin to carry to Dorn House, and then sat down to the necessary long letter to the Frays. There was much to say and this time no reluctance about saying it. By now I had no doubt that Lord Lang should change his mind as to where his duty lay. It was here. For some time to come his major responsibility would be in The City and the Council. He should charge me and Atta with the safety of the Frays. I ended my letter saying I was going to Reeves the next day and would come on to the Frays from there. Next morning a letter arrived while I was eating breakfast. It was a note from my father asking if I could arrange a brief trip to the Frays before the opening of the Council. He gave no reason.

✠

The monorail stops outside Reeves, leaving a twelve-to-fifteen-minute walk to the University. The morning was soft and cool, without rain, but with streamers of mist depending from the low clouds. With the smoke from stoves and fireplaces held close to the ground, I walked occasionally through swirls of faint cooking odors and the smells of burning wood and peet. Ross' rooms had a fine northern exposure facing one of the main entrances to the University grounds.

Ross was still in his bathrobe when I arrived, with notes and papers spread out on a table among the remains of his breakfast. He wasn't expecting me. He was surprised when he opened his door. And he was pleased. Annoyance or boredom can be disguised, but there is something instantaneous that happens around the eyes and mouth when a person takes pleasure in the sudden appearance of a guest. It can't be counterfeited.

He welcomed me in, gave me a hot cup of American coffee black, and instantly confirmed his readiness to appear before the Council if I needed him. Then he said, "This is a good day for you to come. Morana is here for a day or so. She visited my English class yesterday and is coming to my American history class this morning. You will, too, I hope."

"I want to," I said.

"Good. You and Morana can be an informal committee to investigate what that Foreigner is teaching Islandian youth."

When I laughed, he joined me but added, "I wasn't really joking. You should. Somebody should. For me this is wonderful, all of it. I'm in a state of professional euphoria. And the kids are interested in what I'm teaching them. They want more than I can give. I love that part of it, too. Just the same, maybe you should send me home."

Even in his bathrobe, still unshaved, standing by the papers and the dirty dishes, Ross didn't look like someone who should be deported, but I had a far-off premonition of what he was talking about. I took the direct, hearty approach and said, "I know our students aren't as far along, or as well informed as the ones you're used to. But I've taught them myself. I know they want to learn. I don't believe you're telling me that you're corrupting them."

"You know what I'm talking about," he said, looking down at his notes, rubbing the dark line of his jaw. "Corrupting isn't quite the right word. I'm not doing it to them. I'm offering them the American experience in terms that are supposed to have some meaning for them. Comparable historical situations and the American response. That kind of thing. This is what I was asked to do in return for being allowed to study here. But the kids are getting drunk on the stuff. There's no corruption. There is a rapid recomposing of matter going on, a little of it intellectual and most of it emotional."

Leaving Ross to shave and dress in private, I went out to stroll through the University grounds. Many people think highly of the buildings that form and surround the long central court, saying that they are the finest examples anywhere of pre-Toran architecture. No doubt this is so, but until today I'd always found them monotonous and oppressive. Now, with the mist to soften the corners and to suggest the height and lightness they didn't have, they took on a semblance of ancient grace and charm.

Leaving the University in the direction away from the Islandia River, I walked on for some distance into the town, drawn on by the activity in the streets and markets, both of which seemed busier than I remembered. Suddenly, with nothing gradual about it at all, hard rain began to come down through the mist. I didn't want to sit through Ross' class sopping and steaming. I remembered passing a House of Quiet a little way back. Turning, I ran for it.

The swoosh and rattle of the rain stopped totally as the second of the two heavy doors closed behind me. I stepped into a domed, circular room about forty feet in diameter and thirty feet high. There were no windows or visible apertures, and here no tapestries or hangings. The room was faintly but evenly lit by lamps set at intervals around the wall. Masked from the front, these shone back against the soft yellowish-red stone facing. The effect was clear and ambient.

Across the room one other person sat motionless on a bench. I walked to another bench nearby, my steps soundless on the rush matting. I sat and was motionless.

At first there was silence. Then I can say only that this thickened into quiet. I was aware of an almost tangible noiselessness moving past me. It was remotely like the flow of very deep water. I found myself thinking that my own awareness might somehow be touching that of this room in which no word had ever been spoken. For a moment I felt I knew the unnamed questions of fifty generations through a thousand years. The sensation was not unpleasant but intolerable, like recognition to the tenth power. Then it was gone, and this room was once more a shelter from the rain which I was sharing with one other person.

Outside the room of Quiet as I left I noticed a narrow

corridor I had not seen when I came in. I thought I knew
what it was and followed it through two opposite ninety-
degree turns whose only purpose could be to cut off sound.
Beyond the second corner three alcoves, small rooms without doors, opened off the right-hand wall. These were
for the use of anyone, alone or in the presence of others,
who felt moved to preach, comment, read aloud, or con-
fess. In the farthest alcove someone was speaking, a man
by the sound, although the tone and timbre of the voice
were muffled. Continuing on, I came upon a ceremony I
had heard and read about, but never seen.

On benches around two walls eight people were sitting.
I stepped inside and took a vacant place at the end of the
bench nearest me. The speaker, head and face completely
covered as custom required, stood by the far wall quietly
reciting a fable. My entrance had no effect on him or anyone else there. The fable, more or less in the manner of
Bodwin, concerned a fruit tree of one variety carrying a
grafted branch from another.

I didn't know the fable. It seemed quite good, but it
differed from the Bodwin model in one obvious way. For
each genuine Bodwin fable there is an accepted written
text. A person telling one of Bodwin's tales from memory
is allowed considerable freedom with the wording, but
there is one liberty that is not taken. Characteristically
and consistently Bodwin used only indirect discourse, and
this element of his style is always observed. This narra-
tor, though, in his own Bodwinian fable attributed words
several times directly to his figures, as though the branch
and the tree could speak to each other and their human
owner through the voices of the field god Cam. In an Islandian fable this was startling, but I had to admit that
once or twice it was effective and dramatic.

There wasn't time for me to hear the story to its end. I
slipped out as I had come in, apparently completely unnoticed. Outdoors the downpour had slacked off to a drizzle.

✛

Ross' small class was just getting under way when I
reached the right room at the University. A dozen young
people, eight boys and four girls, sat along either side of
an oblong table. Ross was at one end and Morana at the

other. As I came in she smiled across the room at me and touched a vacant seat kept for me beside her.

Ross was talking informally. He had told me he first wanted to conduct the course as a seminar but had to give up the idea because there was nothing on the subject written in Islandian and he couldn't teach his students English fast enough to be able to assign American books. His command of Islandian was improving, but that day he called often on me and Morana for help.

He was still dealing with the American Colonial period. I gathered from the side remarks to and from members of the class—mostly with a boy named Banch and a girl he called Sarkana—that there had been no trouble with geography, terrain, or climate and that there was a natural understanding for the secular and political figures. The students spoke confidently of men like Miles Standish and Governor Winthrop and their successors down to John Adams and Franklin.

Today, though, Ross was beginning on the early theologians and their part in politics. This was harder going. He started with word sketches of several ministers. Some were men whose names even I had never heard—John Cotton, Thomas Hooker, Increase Mather, Roger Williams, Jonathan Edwards. They made a striking gallery there in the stone-walled room in Reeves. The students listened to the short biographies in fascination but not, to judge from their expressions, with much liking.

Next Ross set out what he said were the three most powerful concepts in American history. The Calvinist idea of a God who specifically ordained every event everywhere from the number and size of hailstones in a storm, the strength of a gust of wind, the arrival of a ship in port, to the number of ears on a stalk of corn and the appetite of caterpillars. Then there was the idea that an individual, if a participant in God's grace, could make a covenant with God for rewards in a future life in return for actively promoting God's designs on earth. Finally there was the original American notion that a community as a whole, made up of individual covenanters, could negotiate a group contract with God for rewards here and now in return for implementing His will on earth.

"This arrangement," Ross said, "created a formidable partnership."

The students had been listening with obviously growing unease and incredulity. One or two of them began to laugh in an embarrassed way when Ross stopped. Then the whole class joined them in whoops and rolls of energetic laughter. Ross let them work it off, smiling with them and at them while they did. After a minute or so, as the noise reduced itself to coughs and isolated cackles, Sarkana tried to speak. Then Ross spread his hands for quiet.

"Surely," the girl said, "no one in your country believes such things now?"

"No," Ross said, "no one does, not in that way." He took a book from among his papers and held it so that we could all clearly see the name Perry Miller on the front. Then he put the book down. "I didn't invent anything I've said. I didn't rediscover it. Professor Miller did, buried under layers of myths and facts. All I've done so far is paraphrase."

He sat silent for some seconds, and then, "Islandians have always been taught that they are members of a native white race that arose spontaneously here in the southern Karain." With the opening of this subject, tension of a new kind came into the room. Morana put her hand on my arm and held on. "I don't know how many Islandians actively believe this now. I guess that a large number of you accept it as a datum and don't think much about it. That doesn't matter. What does matter is that you all behave as though it were literally true. You owe nothing real, you seem to say, to Europe, to Africa, to South America, to India. You are originals.

"I'm not saying this to pay you back for laughing. I want to be sure you know the kind of thing you're laughing at. These things are very silly and very serious. Your traditional belief that your people is aboriginal is probably the most important fact in Islandian history. It's telling you how to respond to what I'm saying now.

"My country is more complicated than yours, but it didn't start out that way. The three notions of ours, and the one of yours, have to be called overriding ideas. I made ours as simple and harsh as I could so that you would have no trouble recognizing them when they turn up later looking different. It's true no one in America believes these things now. Our time distributes God's functions downward. But we did believe them, and they've left tracks in our minds we use for other freight."

There was a silence after that until Sarkana said, "I try to understand this, but I'm not sure. Why should a man today be bothered by this? If what he is doing is not customary and causes him difficulty, then surely all he needs is to do something customary."

"It's not that, Sarkana," said the boy Banch in the voice of one discovering something important. "It's doing something you know you must do. You can't do something else. That would be impossible. In Islandia we don't do . . ."

Before Banch could commit himself in some way to the responsibility he was recognizing and trying to describe, Morana interrupted him. She spoke in English. "Mr. Ross, I'm sorry Lord Lang and I must leave this session. It's been delightful. We'll expect you later for dinner."

And then to the class she said in Islandian, "Your professor is aware of fables. There is one that may not be familiar to you. It concerns two familes of foxes who were very fond of rabbits in different ways. One family loved to hunt and eat rabbits, thereby keeping down the population and improving the breed until the rabbits became big and powerful as great hares. The other foxes preferred fowl and geese for food and ate rabbits only when very hungry, but they enjoyed playing with rabbits and learning rabbit things and teaching them fox things. In doing so they made the rabbits every bit as smart as foxes, which was something although not a great deal. In the end the strong rabbits put muzzles and harnesses on all the foxes and set them to plowing plots for lettuces and carrots. Soon after that the rabbits who had learned fox things were governing the strong rabbits and the foxes, too.

"I've never been certain what this fable means. But it is about the power of knowledge. Thank you for letting us visit you."

Outside, the rain had stopped and the clouds showed signs of lifting and breaking. Out the gate we went, across the narrow quadrangle, and into a curving street. There we stopped and Morana began to laugh, not loudly but with every bit of her. She put her hands on my left shoulder with her head back, and then finished with her head on her hands on my shoulder.

"Oh, Jon, oh my," she said at last. "Poor Ross. I think I saved him from Sarkana this time. And Banch, too."

"Morana," I said, "what about those foxes?"

"The fable comes from the south, from Winder. It's from a fragment I have of a manuscript by Altain. You'd have no way of knowing it."

"I'm sure of that," I said. "The fable is by Morana, and it was told for the first time ten minutes ago."

She said, "Jon, I didn't expect to fool you. And I hope not Ross. The fable isn't really Islandian. It's too easy. There's too much Aesop. But those children don't know that. And Sarkana doesn't know it. It should keep them busy for a while."

We were walking again now and I asked, "Where are we going?"

"The inn."

"What?"

"It's a good one. I'm staying there."

"You, Morana? An inn?"

"Yes, me," she said, "at an inn. I do have three establishments of direct relatives in Reeves and about six others not quite so close. Of course it would be customary for me to stay with one of them. You don't have my embarrassment of families, Jon, but I can think of two of yours here. Do you want a room at the inn?"

"No," I said, "I'm staying with Ross. Abiding by custom. A friend can take precedence over family."

She took my arm. "It's going to rain again," she said, urging us on. There was a heavy half-minute shower and then another letup. "You should visit your ancestral country, Jon. There are things I like about the northern world. They have ways of personal privacy and independence. They have separate families and not tribes. They use apartments and hotels, and they build new houses for new families. This isn't all bad. We could use some of it. But the Mora clans think it's vulgar, and say there's too much of it now in the industrial parks like Suburra. Any Dorn will say 'unnecessary and unwise' and then just stand there looking handsome, and stubborn."

At the Reeves Inn, Morana had open, colorful rooms on the second floor looking out over an inner court. Her quarters and her argument strongly supported each other. Everything in the rooms was Islandian—tapestries, chairs, tables, rugs, fittings—and the effect was light, spacious, stimulating and at the same time quiet. I'd had the same feeling about Commiter's house I now remembered, but that was American. Morana watched me take it in and made no comment.

"Is the whole inn as good as this?" I asked.

"No. But it's all good enough so that you'd ask the same question if you saw any other part of it first."

"It's good," I said. "I didn't know there was such a place in Islandia."

"You sound doubtful, Jon."

"Yes. In America, or Europe, I suppose I could go to a hotel easily enough. Most Islandians could."

"Customary?"

"Customary. But not here. I wouldn't know how to think to behave to use this place. It's wonderful, but it must be an expensive venture."

"You're right. The inn loses. But the proprietor tells me the loss is decreasing. He thinks he could turn a profit if Islandia radio would allow him a minute between the news of the produce market and the University program. I hope he gets it. I would miss the Reeves Inn."

✠

By the time Ross arrived we had covered a remarkable amount of ground, personal and other. She was in the direct line of one of Islandia's two greatest families. I was the grandson of immigrants who were the hangers-on of the other preeminent family. Morana's unusual beauty, her dark slenderness, and her capacity for intensity all alarmed me. I thought of her as brilliant, sharp, unaccountable, and dangerous. Probably the most important part of my attitude was the feeling that her informal, slightly ironic manner contained a thoroughgoing contempt for me.

I'd known for some time that this wasn't sensible, but emotional sets of this kind persist against reason. It needed her behavior all through the episode at the Frays elevator to show me that something was wrong with my collection of assumptions about her. Now, after the first few minutes of conversation, I knew my picture of her was wholly false even though some of the elements in it were not. What notion would take its place wasn't yet clear. Morana simply was not the person I'd constructed.

About our country and its troubles we were in closer agreement than either of us thought. She was no more committed to the letter of the Mora internationalism than I was to the Dorn insistence on tradition and the exclusion of foreign influence. We both were certain that the danger to the nation was close and critical. We felt that the threats were domestic as well as foreign and that they were connected. But where I thought of the two as different ends of the same thing, she disagreed.

To Morana the danger at home was the more important or, if not that, it was what would determine the form of foreign action against us. When I asked her about the United Nations she said flatly, "There's no help for us there."

We were not a member and not likely to be one. Even if we were, the outlook would be no better. The U.N. didn't interest itself in civil wars. If Sulliaba, or even Mobono, should intervene in a disturbance of ours the Russians would veto any proposal in the Security Council for a peace-keeping force. And it was a certain bet that the Assembly would not override the Council in our behalf.

"Jon, you have to spend some time in the outside world before you understand how much we don't matter. People know little about us, but what they do know they don't much like. We aren't racist like South Africa and Rhodesia. We haven't had any reason to be for seven hundred years. But we are exclusionists in every possible way. For most of the world, that's a distinction with very little difference, even if we exclude everybody equally."

"Would the Americans help us?"

"They're certainly the only people we could ask. But if I were the Americans, I'd decline."

"We've been too rude to them too often?"

"We have, but that's not the reason. I used to think things like that mattered. Now I don't believe they do much. Not with great nations."

This was along my own line of thought. I'd never been out of Islandia, but the immense reality of the United States had overhung my whole life. Strange as it would be to me, I knew that I knew the country in my bones. As Morana gave me her up-to-date foreigner's knowledge— the very good reasons why the Americans would like not to get involved in one more confrontation of great powers on one more continent—I felt myself completely American for a second or so. But then she said, "The Americans and the Russians have the unlovely job of not blowing up the world while they keep it from falling apart," and I was an Islandian once more.

"Then we're on our own," I said. "That's it?"

"I think so. Unless we can show we're worth saving. In this world we've no complaints. We said we were too good for it. We wouldn't join it. We chose to stay pure. We wouldn't pay the premium when it was low. Even in America it's hard to get life insurance in the middle of a heart attack. But if we can prevent a civil war, and if the Dorn military geniuses can hold enough of the country long enough, then maybe the Mora traitors can do something."

When I asked her if she had any idea now who had been behind the outrage at the elevator, she replied by asking me, "Did you know that Lord Dorn and his party were attacked on their way to The City day before yesterday, and Lord Dorn was humiliated in somewhat the way I was?" All I could do was sit looking at her. "This time nobody was killed. The suspicion was left that it was done by Mora people. At the Frays, you remember, it was made to seem like Dorn work."

"How did you hear of this?" I asked her, thinking of what Hanno told me.

"From Dorna yesterday. She sent a letter by messenger when you were out and she couldn't reach you. She said her uncle was in such pain and fury it was the most she could do."

"I suppose Hanno knows?"

"I'm certain he does, but I'm not sure how much help that is."

She didn't elaborate, and I didn't ask her to. Hanno's job was to know about political events, not to take part in them or bring them about.

On impulse I said, "I'm going on to the Frays from here tomorrow. It's not just a family visit. Morana, would you come with me?"

She didn't answer right away. I went to the window and saw a pale sliver of blue sky above the rooflines of the inn. The tiles of one high gable sparkled in the setting sun. On the grass of the darkening court below three ground-feeding birds still pecked for worms. As I watched, they observed the onset of night, lifted their beaks, and flew away.

Morana was standing beside me now. "I know you want me to come, but you don't say why. You give me the impression you want me to intrude. If custom were everything, I should say no. But I've lived some time in the north. You still have some of the North in you. Is there anything you can tell me, Jon?"

"Not much, Morana." I kept looking down at the grass where the birds had been. "I don't know what's going to happen. I'd like to have you with me. That's a personal thing. Beyond that, for everyone's sake, I have a feeling you should be a witness."

There was a sound of voices in the corridor outside Morana's rooms, a distinguishable word of thanks, and then a knock on the door. "Good, that's Ross," she said, without moving. Then she touched my arm, saying, "I'll come with you tomorrow, Jon, if you ask me again after dinner."

Ross came in and apologized for being late. "I was delayed downstairs listening to Islandia radio. It was going in the lounge, or whatever you call the public room, and someone was reading a fable. It's the second new Islandian fable I've heard today. I thought I knew all of them from your book, Jon. This was about the troubles you get into when you graft fruit trees. It was almost as good as yours, Morana, but this one had some direct discourse in it. Isn't that a fault?"

A girl came in with a tray and three glasses of Islandian Camar. It looked like sweet vermouth and tasted much like Dubonnet. Morana said to the girl, "Thank you. Please wait five minutes and serve us then."

She tasted the wine and said to Ross, "Your question about direct speech in fables. It's not exactly a fault. It's different. It changes the classical form and the attitude. Maybe it's Romantic in your sense. Incidentally, Jon, you were right. I did make up that fable."

"You did?" Ross said. "I knew you wanted to stop the discussion. Why?"

"To have the chance to tell you I think that bright girl Sarkana is Hanno's creature. She's his way of keeping track of you."

Ross obviously didn't like this, but he asked quietly, "You heard all that was said. Was there anything objectionable in it?"

"Probably not. But that isn't the point. Hanno doesn't approve of things or object to them. He tries to make sure he knows them." She set down her glass. "I think dinner is ready."

✠

When we left I repeated my invitation to Morana, and she accepted as she had promised. Ross and I stepped out into a moonless night, brilliant overhead with stars. The air was cool, almost cold when the southeast breeze dipped down from the rooftops or swept around a corner. The streets were empty and silent except for us. We walked at a good pace our heels ringing on the cobbles.

As we approached the broad paved road that runs beside the University, I was suddenly peripherally aware that we weren't alone any longer. A silent shadow or two were moving some yards behind us. There might be another that had slipped around the corner ahead. We spoke to each other in the same instant.

"We're being followed," I said.

He said, "We're surrounded."

Without breaking his stride or turning his head, he spoke conversationally, "I don't want to be manhandled again, do you?"

"No."

"Then listen. They're not ready to attack us yet. When we get to the big road we're only about a block from my place. Keep on out into the open road, but not too far. When I stop, stand shoulder to shoulder with me. They'll stop, too. Make a business of looking through them and over them but not at them. Raise your arm straight over your head so it looks like a signal to people behind them. When I start to move, charge straight for my place."

We came to our halt in the wide road. The shadows surrounding us stopped, too, momentarily, five to ten yards away. I thought I could make out six of them. They didn't seem to have firearms, but I could see clubs that looked like nightsticks. I raised my arm slowly with one finger pointed, making the motion as semaphoric as I could. I saw two heads turn away from us.

Ross waited for a count of three. They were beginning to edge toward us. Ross deliberately took his hand from his pocket, placed two fingers to his mouth, and blew out two shattering whistles. I whipped my arm down to my side.

"Now!"

Ross shouted this in Islandian. We put our shoulders down and ran. I passed one man and then felt a hard blow from a club glance off my right upper arm. I could see the club rise again and start for my head. I strained away from it. The blow did not fall. I heard a gasp for breath and then a confused sound of falling, sliding, and rattling. For a moment or so I was running alone, and then Ross was beside me again.

As Ross opened the street door of his house, I looked back. Some windows and a few doors were opening along the wide road. Here and there lights were coming on. Our attackers had disappeared into the darkness, but two or three men from neighboring houses were gathering around a shape that still lay in the roadway.

Upstairs Ross had me push up the loose sleeve of my tunic to look at my shoulder. Then he inspected the scratches and abrasions on his forearm and thigh. "We're all right," he said. "You got hit pretty good. But you're in good training, and the thick meat up there cushioned it. You'll have a stiff arm for a day or so. I'll just have a couple of patches of scabs."

He poured us each a portion of whiskey and sipped his own. "Drink it slowly," he said, "but don't dilute it."

I tried it. He was right. My breathing grew easier and my heart began to slow down. "Just now," I said, "you haven't been behaving like my idea of a scholar. Does a social anthropolgist act differently?"

"Differently from what? Evidently not from a quiet folklorist like you, Jon." He laughed and said, "No, we were both sociologizing and anthropologizing very professionally. We were just performing the process instead of observing it." He sipped his drink, adding dryly, "In this form it's a surprisingly Christian discipline. I hadn't known how much more blessed it could be to give than receive . . . Bad joke. It's about time to quit."

"Did you kill the man, Ross?"

"No. Not unless he had very bad luck. I think he got a dislocated knee, the breath knocked out of him, and some bad bruises."

I was beginning to feel sleepy and tired, but I was still alert enough to be curious. "How did you do it?"

He looked at me appraisingly and said, "I was never heavy enough for college football, but I was a good running guard in high school. In American football there is a very useful and sometimes unavoidable foul. Blocking from behind. Done with discretion on grass it's not too dangerous. Done with malice and skill it can maim. I clipped him, but good."

He was standing now and I was swimming in drowsiness again. I made one more effort. "I know you saved my life tonight. Thank you."

Ross smiled and said, "Accepted. I did my best. You may need to repay me in kind. I'm not a fatalist, but I believe in process. This is some process you've got going here." He began to point around the apartment. "There's your bed. The john's over there. It's still early. Sleep well. Good night."

✠

Morana and I reached my home in the Frays about midafternoon. We could have been there much earlier, but the weather was fine, and this in itself delays people.

The interest Islandians take in the weather was one of the things that deeply impressed my grandfather about his country-to-be. He said they paid even more attention to it than the early American colonists, and without the necessity. We still do. No Islandian daybook, journal, or letter is quite respectable unless it contains a passage about the current state of the weather along with comparative treatments of other relevant weathers.

We also modify our ordinary behavior to match the weather in ways that other peoples would think frivolous or idiotic. There is an Islandian saying that goes, "Guests arrive on ill winds." This gains something in translation. What it refers to is the age-old habit of Islandians—barring emergency or a precise commitment—to go on foot and roundabout to their destinations on a fair day and to slog directly to them on a foul one.

In this case the fine day led Morana and me to ignore the Frays elevator when we left the monorail and walk up the cliff by my old route. By the time we crossed the meadow beyond the ledge and went into the orchard we were hot and well covered with burdocks. Ross had been right about my arm. It was stiff and very sore when I got out of bed and almost useless at the beginning of the climb. Now I felt it might belong to me again.

Our welcome—except from my brother Atta who wasn't there—was as warm as usual, but somehow not as casual. There was a gentleness in it I wasn't prepared for.

The explanation came soon after we had cleaned up from the climb. It shocked me more profoundly than anything that had ever happened to me. We gathered in the main room—my father and mother, Morana and I—for refreshments, light cakes and white wine. I asked where Atta was, and my father answered almost absently, "He's at the base questioning two men who were brought in yesterday. We think they were in the raiding party at the elevator."

While I wondered at his lack of interest in this, my father sipped a little wine, set down his glass, and looked directly at me. I thought he seemed tired and I noticed how much white there actually was now in his blond hair. He said, "I have something very serious to tell you, Jon. I am resigning as Isla of the Frays."

"Oh, no!" I said, "You can't mean—" But he held up

his hand saying, "Please, let me say what I need to say, Jon. My usefulness as Isla is over. I'm not ill. Perhaps I'm not as strong as I was fifteen years ago, but that has nothing to do with it.

"Personally and officially I'm very pleased to have Morana hear this. It will be good to have this news carried firsthand by a Mora. You will see why in a moment. As things are now, I can no longer be the Isla I should be or would like to be. Some might say I never was, but until now I have been able to satisfy myself and the few people of the Frays."

He looked at us, observing my incomprehension and Morana's disbelief. My mother, who must already have known this, sat expressionless, but I had an intuitive feeling that she wasn't displeased. "You find this difficult?" my father said gently. "Or improper? An Isla should not step down voluntarily? He should stay until he is carried out? You really shouldn't feel that way. To the contrary. More Islar should do this. The compelling reason for me"—and he sipped again from the chilled wine—"is the rational conclusion that Islandia must do things I do not want her to do. She must enter the world immediately while she can still control some of the terms. You, Jon, and you, Morana, represent her chance of doing this."

Morana walked to my father and stood in front of him. "My dear Lord Lang," she said, "you are wise and courageous, and you must not do this. I know now that the most serious part of our trouble comes from members of my party who would not listen when you said we were asking for disaster if we kept a government without purpose or discipline or responsibility. More Mora people are aware of this than have been willing to admit it. Now the people of my party must come as far toward you as you have to them. They must meet your positions on things at home if Islandia is not to go down. They have always trusted you in disagreement. You are the one man with a chance of unifying the Council. Lord Dorn can't. Lord Mora can't. Lord Farrant can't. You, sir, are the only one. If you state your conviction and your reasons, men on both sides will try to move toward you. If they aren't frightened yet, they will be the day after the Council opens when they know what's happened. Please stay on, Lord Lang. We all need you."

My father was visibly affected by this. He took Morana's hands, pressed them quickly, and said, "Morana, I thank you. There is truth in what you say, I know. Men

of my party and maybe of yours might listen to me and
even trust me. But you overlook the important thing. I
wouldn't trust myself. I'm too compromised. Not by emi-
nence or by historical attitudes in the ways of Mora and
Dorn. And not by the suspicion of complaisance and ve-
nality in the way of Farrant. I'm compromised by human
nature. In matters of this kind you cannot set the mind to
control an unwilling heart. Sooner or later the heart will
have its way."

In the next few minutes we learned how far things had
already gone. My father's decision was virtually irrevers-
ible. Two days ago he had explained his intentions to the
heads of communities and of multiple families. These men
had now consulted their responsible voting members. They
were meeting this afternoon to put together the tally.
Tonight they would report the result to the outgoing Isla.

As the recital of events went on I found myself feeling
tired, dispirited, and finally resentful. I tried, not too well,
to hide these disaffections. At last I brought myself to ask
the only sensible, constructive question left. It was also
the most difficult one, and it was up to me to put it. Who
was to be the next Isla for the Frays? I knew who it had to
be; he was a man of about forty, of good family, intelligent, devoted to his country and the Frays, and with a
long record of leadership locally. A good man. A good
man in the Frays, but not good in the Council. Not now.

Looking first at my father and then at my mother, I
said, "Things seem to have gone beyond discussion," and
then with a deep breath, "I can't help it. I'm shocked. Father, I can't believe your heart did not take the same journey your mind did. There must be something else . . .
Let it be. I'm sorry. Who is the principal candidate for
Isla? Mangolan Mar?"

There was a long silence, and it was not my father who
broke it but my mother. She said, "No, not Mangolan. I
expect that the next Isla of the Frays will be you, Lang
Jon."

To avoid looking at anyone right away I stared down
through my hands at the floor. I'd lost all sense of what
was going on. My father said he was well, and yet he
must be suddenly and seriously ill. My mother lived by
intuition and feeling and was often difficult to read, but
she always held hard to her own. She never intrigued or
showed preference, and yet here she seemed to be schem-
ing. I must be the one who had lost touch somehow. I
raised my head, met their eyes in turn briefly, and said,

"Let's wait on what happens. Father, I'm sorry to have spoken as I did. I haven't quite caught up with things." This didn't sound well, but it was the best I could do. I stood up, rubbing my sore arm. "I know you told me Atta is away somewhere. Will he be back today?"

"Perhaps I should have begun with that," my father said. "Yesterday we picked up two men between the approaches to the Mora Pass and the headwaters of the Doring River. They were in the raid on the Frays elevator. They tried to reach the Karain through the passes and couldn't. Then they looked for the western valley to the sea. They were glad to be taken."

"So would I," I said. The source of the Doring River is a small, high bog. All around, but particularly to the north and east, lie ugly stretches of great boulders, gullies that dead-end against steep, scrubby ridges, and countless stony holes and pockets. It seems to be a place where the earth once broke a small bone and here are the shardish lumps of the knitting. The whole area is tumbled and directionless. It is bad country in decent weather even for a man who knows it well. In snow, for tired strangers, it would be the end of the journey. "And Atta is with them now?"

"He's been questioning them all day."

✠

Atta was at the desk in the main room transcribing notes when I walked into the administration building. He looked up, dropped his pen on the papers, and said, "Greetings, Lord Lang."

"Shut up," I said. "I'm not Isla yet."

"And don't intend to be from the way you sound. Is that it?"

"Maybe. I don't understand it."

"Well, I'm glad it's you and not me."

"Why not you?"

"Out of the question. You have the seniority, the experience, and the reputation."

"Stop it," I said. "Why either one of us? I can't believe what father says about the mind not being able to govern the heart. Do you?"

"Yes, I think I do. But then I have a notion of what he means by it. He told me, and I don't suppose he's had a chance to do that for you."

"No," I said. "What does he mean?"

"You know the history of the time of The League. Betrayals, kidnappings, murders, ugly sexual bargains. Treachery among old friends. He's afraid we're heading for that again. It would be his own good friends with whom he would have to trade stratagems and treasons. They aren't our friends—yours and mine—in anything like the same way. He's afraid he just couldn't do what has to be done."

"The League was a long time ago," I said. "Do you think he's right? I mean about what we're coming to."

"What I think doesn't matter," Atta said. "Do you want to talk to these two people?"

"No, just look at them. What have they told you?"

"What they know, and that's not much. They're not too bright. One comes from the industrial village outside Doring and the other is from Farrant way. The one from Doringata is the better, but they're both just hired hands. They don't know the name of the leader of the raiding party. They think he's important in a countrywide movement of some kind.

"The business at Fraysedge seems to have had two purposes. The second was what we guessed. To make a seriously disturbing incident. To show that the Farrant government hasn't enough civil authority to protect an important foreign diplomat. To humiliate a Mora in the presence of a Dorn and of foreigners. To suggest that there was Dorn influence in it. And I think it was also meant as cover for another piece of work which began several days earlier. This was to get something out of the country across the mountains into the north.

"The separate stories of these two don't amount to much, but they agree at important places. And they support something we know—the men you saw on the Ladder. I'll give you my composite. Two men arrived here on the Frays at about the same time, one from Suburra and the other from The City. One probably had an engraver's proof of a map or chart he'd lifted out of the government printing office, and the other had a typescript of the text explaining the map. The materials were examined by the chief of the raiding party and his aide. They were then given to two experienced mountaineers who were sent north over Lang's Ladder. The band then waited for the arrival of the Consul to make an incident and a diversion."

Atta's general outline seemed reasonable. "I suppose," I said, "that one of your prisoners saw the shape of one of the documents from a distance and his description led you to deduce a map. Could be. What would it be a map of, Atta?"

"No clue. But you shouldn't have too much trouble getting wind of it in The City. Something's missing there."

"Perhaps so," I said. "Tell me, why were the two guards killed?"

"That's not clear. The prisoners tell different stories. One says it was because the guards recognized one or both of the leaders. The other says the leader ordered it to make the incident really important and to insure loyalty, or at least silence, by implicating everyone in murder. I think they may both be right. But it seems to have been a mistake. The prisoners agree that there was a bitter row between the leader and his aide right afterward, and that the band broke up within an hour. They say some struck out for Doring and others for Farrant. These two were the only ones to try it to the north. Do you want to look at them now?"

Atta crossed the room, unlocked the door, and showed me what I had expected and did not really wish to see— two frightened, battered men, each with a scraggle of beard, and each with the unfocused, unmistakable glow of stupidity in his eyes.

✠

The heads of communities and families began arriving at eight o'clock. My mother, Atta, and Morana were there to welcome them and show them places in the main room. My father and I, presumably the principals, waited together in his small library. A procedure of this sort is customary in a small province like the Frays where there is no need for the formalities necessary in the large ones.

At word from Atta that the gathering was complete, my father led the way to the meeting. He stood by the fireplace, greeted the twenty men present, and thanked them for consulting their constituencies so promptly. He said he had explained his desire to step down as Isla and had given his reasons for proposing me to succeed him. He would not repeat them.

"It is usual at this time," he said, "to determine whether there is more than one candidate. Are there others?" The silence indicated there were none. "It is also usual at this time for any candidate to state his position to you. Do you wish to hear him?" At the quiet chorus of "yes," my father stepped aside and I took his place.

"I have no ambition to become Isla," I said. "If any of you doubts my capacity for the job, I doubt it with him. Because I sympathize with Lord Lang's personal and ethical reasons for wanting to retire, and because I agree with him in part about the advantages a change may offer, I will accept and will give my whole effort if you name me.

"In that case, I will try to give Islandia a government once again by urging agreements between the Dorn and Mora factions. I will work for our entrance into the United Nations and for an arrangement of friendship and exchange with the only power that can support us against those who support our hostile northern neighbors, if that is possible at this late hour. I will try to broaden our educational system so that our students learn something of the great realities of the outside world—ugly as they may be.

"These policies may sound extreme and unpalatable. But I believe that we are in the opening phase of civil war at home and that this is directly connected with the daily increasing danger of invasion from outside. Here we live on the frontier. We know what is preparing in the north. And we've just had a foretaste of what can happen at home. I can't tell you how any of these aims can be accomplished because I don't know. It may be too late for any effort of any kind. I will do my best if you tell me to."

The four of us and Morana then withdrew to the library where we waited in silence. The twenty would discuss and decide the issue. They all knew the wishes of the men and women they represented, but each would have discretion at this point to vote in whatever way he felt might accomplish what his people wanted. They took their time as we expected them to.

When the knock finally came at one side of the doorway, we filed back and took seats as a group facing the twenty. Momnath, the senior member of the body, rose and said: "We regret the Isla's decision, but we respect and accept it. In his place as Isla we name his son, Lang III, known to us as Jon." Here his gentle, old-man's voice faltered and he paused for a moment. "We regret the need for the policies decribed by Lang III, but we are sharply aware of the conditions calling for them. We know these

would have been the policies of Lang II if he had remained as Isla. We endorse them—unhappily and of necessity. We request that with the help of his younger son, Atta,
Lang II continue as magistrate and resident governor of
the Frays and that he give assistance and counsel in all
matters to the new Isla."

Momnath lowered his head, pressed the back of his
sleeve against his eyes, and then came to my father, my
mother, and to me. The other men stood, said goodbye to
us one by one, and went out into the chilly, starlit night. I
felt undone inside me, and as lonely as though death suddenly stood between me and my family.

✠

In the morning Morana and I walked back across the
meadow to the ledge and climbed down the steep slope
toward the monorail. We stopped at the spot where just
the day before we had become lovers. I took her hand as
we stood side by side looking and remembering.

There was a small, shaded hollow a few paces back
from the edge. I had carried her there, knelt with her in
my arms, and laid her down softly on the ground. The
low, sweet-smelling ferns and the short grass still showed
the outline of her body. Alongside were the deeper im-
prints of my foot, my knee, my elbow, and my hand.
Fewer than twenty hours had passed and they might almost as well have been a year. We kept looking down at
the bruised ferns, and our fingers intertwined.

There had been nothing coy or even accidental about it.
She had not slipped for me to catch her. I had not
stopped short so that she stepped up against me.

The next small ledge below this one is about 300 yards
obliquely down, a steady, unbroken climb. Yesterday we
came up the stretch without stopping and paused here to
look out over the Islandia plain, which at this point first
begins to open out in splendid dimensions. In some ways
the view from here is better than at the top because, although the visible distances are not as great, you feel still
that you are part of what you are seeing.

I stood close behind Morana and to her right. In the
dry, light breeze that touched us from the south, I caught
the fresh smell of her skin, warm from walking. Her lips

were moist and parted. Under her dress her breasts rose and fell with her still quickened breathing. As I watched her she turned her head and our eyes met.

She obviously meant to ask me something or tell me something. Whatever it was her eyes were sharp and alert with it. But as she looked at me the intention and the self-awareness softened and disappeared, leaving her eyes clear, deep, and totally unguarded. I found myself looking through them down into what I knew was her suddenly open self.

There rose through me an unbearably powerful emotion that came as tenderness rather than desire. I reached out my arms for her and drew her toward me. She came to me with her arms open for me. We stood embraced, hearing each other breathe and our own hearts beat, feeling along the length of our bodies each small motion of the other's different one. I bent down and kissed her mouth for a long moment. Then I picked her up.

On the ferns in the hollow as I bent above her Morana untied the sash of her dress and then in a series of movements bared to me the front of her smooth, slender body. From where I knelt I opened my angular, white self to her. Without playing we caressed gently, firmly, intimately. Finally Morana took me by the hips and guided me down to her. We began a slow, sweet exchange of motion.

Now, as we turned away from our fern bed, she lifted my hand and kissed it. I took her face between my hands, with her one hand still in mine, and kissed her mouth. Freeing her hand, she came to my side and put one arm around my waist while I put both of mine lightly around her shoulders.

"What was it—is it, Jonno dear?"

I said, "It isn't *apia*, or a silly *apiata*. It can be *ania*—if we want it."

"It could be—maybe—sometime."

Through her dress I touched her left breast, stroking, lifting, holding, feeling it grow and become firmer. Morana accepted this but made no voluntary response. Looking down, I saw her face wet with tears and more swelling out from under her now closed eyelids.

Shocked and frightened, I stepped back and held her by the shoulders. "Morana—dear Morana—what's wrong? What have I done?"

She opened her eyes, touched my face with her hand,

blinked at the tears, and then shook her head. "It's not you, Jon. Not me. It's things. It's last night."

"What do you mean?" I said, although I knew and didn't want to.

"You are Isla now, Jon. It will be a long time before you can have a Mora for a mistress or a wife. It would ruin everything. When we were coming down I tried to think it would do no harm if we allowed ourselves a second time. But when you touched me I knew I couldn't bear it. If we don't make love again, I can stand living with the once. I can be your colleague and your friendly enemy, and I can work with you. But if we lie down together now, it will be too much. I'll betray you, and you'll betray yourself and me. We'll lose our country and be left looking at each other and hating ourselves."

We stepped away from each other and looked away, trying to tamp down our individual turmoils in what ways we could. In general I knew what she said was true. A liaison, or marriage, would be political disaster for everything we hoped for together or separately. But today, and for me, with time between us and the schedule of the monorail, it seemed that one more total indulgence in each other might make the long months ahead easier and not more difficult. They might not be so long at that. If we won out, the decision would come before too long and then there would be no problem. If we lost honorably and still lived, we would have only each other to make the world tolerable.

For a time I could not stop these self-serving thoughts. I wanted Morana—now—with an urgency that compressed judgment, generosity, and even love into the tiny, black compartments of the mind where lunatics imprison these things. I knew, too, that I had thought—or seen in my mind's eye—that there were other places where a second encounter here might safely become a third and a fourth. I wanted Morana, and suddenly I wanted to be sick, and I still wanted her.

And then it was all gone, or most of it.

I loved her. It was *ania,* not *apia.* If she felt it mattered for her, then it mattered for me. If she could foresee what something clandestine could do to us, I had just lived through it in a few seconds.

In the best voice I could manage I said the only thing that came to me as words. "I don't know how to be a political figure—a man of party. If you say I must be, I will. Until Farrant is out. That's as far as I can think."

✠

Things began well, or at least easily. In behalf of the Council Lord Farrant accepted my credentials with a proper mixture of regret and congratulation, and made no comment of his own. On the way to present myself to Farrant I had left a note at Dorn House asking Lord Dorn if I might call on him at his convenience. When I came back I found his reply suggesting four o'clock that afternoon.

I was shown into the big room overlooking the bay where Dorna, Ross, and I had talked. The towering, white-haired man met me at the entrance and walked with me to chairs by the window. He used a stick to ease the weight on his injured leg.

He listened without interruption to my account of how I had become what I was now supposed to be. At the end he said, "Thank you. I believe I understand why your father moved in this way. He is the only one who could. He is the linchpin here. He may have been wise. I hope so. And now, before I say anything for myself, may I ask you some questions, Isla Lang?"

I've been questioned before by skillful people on a range of subjects, but this decent, relentlessly resourceful interrogation was like nothing I had imagined. Very soon I privately recanted all the slurs I had heard or made on the perceptivity of Dorns. After a while I began to think I was being taken seriously. Lord Dorn took a long time, and I did the best I could.

At the end he said, "I can't apologize for putting you through this, but I do thank you for your patience." He then suggested that we have a drink, and opened and poured the wine. "Now," he said, "I should do some explaining. I hope you will question me as you wish.

"I imagine your father thought Mora and I might agree generally with what you and he have in mind, but I don't believe he expected us to follow his example. I think I do agree to a considerable extent. But if Mora or I were to resign in favor of a younger man, it would be impossible to accomplish anything. Each of us still has some control over his so-called party, not a great deal but some. New men in our places would have none, and your father knows this.

"I won't make any private commitment to you now as to

the position I will take when you present your plea in the Council for a new government. That will depend on events. So far you've done well. Morana is the right person to talk to her uncle. But you should have no direct word with Lord Mora before the Council hearings, and on no account should anyone try to arrange a meeting between Mora and me. There must be no collusion or suspicion of it. You are right to have all the participants in the Fraysedge affair on hand, and you should be prepared to call each of them if you need to. But remember that witnesses become public property when you've finished with them. As a diplomat, Commiter's testimony is voluntary and he can decline any questions he doesn't like. Besides he's an old hand and formidable, and nobody is likely to take liberties with him. But young Ross is a different matter. He's an inviting target to some people. He could have a rough time and do you some harm. If you call him, I'd be careful about the range of questions you open up."

This was all very sensible, though Lord Dorn now seemed to be walking around the issue. Still, I had come a much longer way than I expected and I had to admit that in his place I would have been far more cautious. I said, "What do you think about Hanno?"

"Yes, there is Hanno." Lord Dorn looked out at the bay for a long stretch of moments and then went at my question indirectly. "Let me go back a little. You said earlier that there is no race problem inside Islandia, but that there is a huge and growing one pushing down on us from outside and compounded by other things. I agree with that. You said you thought there is good material for insurrection in our government manufactories in all the industrial villages like Suburra and Doringata. You estimate that this population has grown at a rate about ten times that of the country overall.

"You describe these people as *unfamilied* in our traditional sense. Their *alia* is split. They have no connection anymore with locality, or land, or particular customs, no down-coming sense of belonging. They do have a love of country that becomes more and more like the nationalisms of the other small states of the world. They no longer have the satisfactions Islandia has always offered its people, so now they want what Islandia hasn't given them— things, machines, innovations, comforts, and an attitude of arrogance. If that's a fair summary of what you told me, then I agree with that, too, for the most part.

"And so again to Hanno. Civil Service. Chief of Security. In the last sixty years the Civil Service also has grown much faster than the population. And the people in it are mostly *unfamilied* within your meaning. This is true of Hanno himself. What is left of his *alia* is bound up in his service and his profession. Under a weak government like this one, he is an extremely powerful person."

I said, "But there is one more question. We think a map has been stolen. Is that likely?"

This time there was no delay whatever. "You have a sense for real issues. To answer your question, I think it is highly likely. My own last government began the preparation of a chart of Islandia Bay based on a thorough geological and oceanographic survey. The work went on, in a way, under Farrant. The whole thing was slow because of the difficulty of finding competent people for the different parts of the job without telling the world what we were doing. Farrant received the final report and the drawings six months ago.

"The findings gave him a week of sleepless nights. Then he made the mistake of calling me, Mora, and Hanno to a private conference. He told us the survey showed the virtual certainty of large sources of natural gas, oil, and sulphur, as well as the probability of other things none of us knew much about. Altogether it looked richer than the recent developments in the North Sea or the possibilities in the gulf of Maine. Farrant wanted us to tell him what to do about it.

"Well, just by asking us, he'd done it. Mora would have handled it one way. I'd have done it another. Neither of us would have let Hanno into it at that point. The policy Farrant finally accepted sounds more sensible than it is. He decided to classify the drawings and the written survey as Full Reserved and to reproduce six copies of each. These were for consideration by a special committee of the Council. In addition, a good navigation chart would be adapted from the drawings and released for general use."

Several questions were running through my mind, all concerned somehow with why Lord Dorn had begun the survey in the first place. But this was not the time to go into the details, and in an overall way I was sure I knew the answer already. He had wanted to know—as I would have in his place—what the real situation was so that he could estimate the possible threats and pressures.

"So then," I said, "what Atta's prisoners saw was one of the classified sets."

"There's not much doubt of that. What's very uncertain is where it is now. It would be nice to think they were underneath that convenient avalanche, but you have only Hanno's word for the time sequence, and he doesn't claim to be sure. The sound thing to do now is to publish a summary of the survey. If one enemy has secret knowledge of it, then the best thing is to tell everyone. But Farrant won't see it that way. You haven't told him your information?"

"No, not yet."

"I think you should. Hanno will have told him something. Much what he told you, plus a little. Farrant will want to assume that the snowslide did the job and secrecy is still the wisest course. But, as Isla, you should give him what you know. Is Morana informing her uncle about this?"

"She can't. She doesn't know it."

"I see. Of course. But Mora should know it, too. He was one of the four. And Hanno hasn't been to see me, so he probably hasn't talked to Mora." Lord Dorn looked out again at the bay—now newly unfamiliar to me—and then went on carefully and tentatively. "If you are as able as I think, you will know that my inclination now is to force your hand. I offer you advice, but the difference between that and pressure is hard to distinguish. It is true you did seek me out, but you are also now Isla and came as my peer. This is your affair, but only up to a point. Let me put it this way. If you agree with me that Mora should know, and if, as I suspect, it could make dangerous misunderstandings for you to tell him, I can do it in this case. It would not compromise anyone and wouldn't enlarge the circle. We wouldn't meet, but Mora and I have sometimes exchanged private letters on important matters."

"I would be grateful," I said. "A moment ago you asked me whether I had told Lord Farrant and I said not yet. The same is true of Hanno. One thing he does not know is the prisoner interrogation. What I did first as Isla, Lord Dorn, was to instruct my brother to prepare a report on it. Two copies. One is for me. The other I will give to Lord Farrant. I think he should decide about showing it to Hanno."

Lord Dorn listened to this noncommittally, seeming to consider its possible consequences. At last he smiled, slapped his injured leg by mistake, and then, grimacing and laughing at the same time, said, "Splendid! You discharge your responsibility and make them both very unhappy, whatever Farrant does."

✠

The Fraysedge matter was scheduled for the second day of the new session of the Council. The first day was brief and formal, presided over by Tor XXI, now an amiable, portly man in his middle sixties. Tor had two married daughters with children of their own, and a much younger son who arrived at almost the last possible moment, once more assuring the succession. Young Tor I had never seen, but he was said to be a handsome young man and much under the influence of his cousins, who in turn were reputed to be a wild lot by Islandian standards. I had never heard anyone say just what forms their wildness took.

The first Council business was the roll call of members, the presentation of new members—I was the only one—the interim report and partial agenda by the executive Isla, and then the ritual statement by Tor that as Regent he declared the Council "properly convened to consider and dispose of such matters as might be decided by the King."

This is one of Tor's few official duties. Another is to dissolve the Council at the end of its six-month sitting. The most important one is to ratify acts of the Council, styling himself "By courtesy King of Islandia." In earlier times the Regent exercised real power, and it was the job of the Council to keep him within bounds. But the weight of authority has steadily shifted. For more than three hundred years no Regent has initiated an act or a policy, and for a century and a half none has failed to ratify a bill of the Council. The function of the Regent is not arduous, but the fiction he embodies has tided the country over some rough spots and has been generally more useful than many Islandians admit. All our parliamentary procedures rest on this pretext.*

When I began my hearings on the second day of the session, Tor was in attendance. This was unusual, but I didn't realize it was shockingly extraordinary until I saw the astonishment among the senior Council members. Tor

* See Appendix V: The Regency, pp. 220–21.

was not a member of the Council, but he had the privilege of attending any of its meetings, open or closed. This one was open to the public. A scattering of people was in the galleries already, but within an hour, when the real nature of the hearings worked its way out to the streets, the benches up there would be jammed. I was nervous, in fact so frightened I didn't know whether my voice would work.

There had been some changes since I talked with Lord Dorn. Farrant suggested, inasmuch as there were three episodes to be investigated and I had personal knowledge of two, that it would save time and confusion if I conducted one consolidated hearing on all of them. I did not protest this, but I did stipulate that I would present the cases in my own order and would select the primary witnesses. My guess was that Farrant felt the impact of the events would be lessened if they weren't given independent status, that the assignment of the whole thing to a newcomer would downgrade it, and that the newcomer himself could be trusted to create the confusion that was supposed to be avoided.

This was very possible. But there were advantages to me, if I used my witnesses well. So, without warning anyone and still being sure that everyone would be on hand, I devised a procedure based on concentration. When Lord Farrant turned matters over to me, I made my duties to the dignitaries and the assembly and said:

"Lord Farrant has explained why three separate episodes of violence and intimidation are to be considered in conjunction today and why I, so newly accredited to this body as to belong only technically, have been charged with the conduct of the whole matter. To accomplish Lord Farrant's intention I intend to call one competent and principal witness for each case, and one or two special witnesses if necessary. I should also say that every participant in these events, on the receiving side, is in this building and may be called if members wish and Lord Farrant so rules. The folders now being distributed to members by the ushers contain copies of the statements of all the participants I do not plan to call. They include two by me.

"Now I would like to begin with Fraysedge. My witness is Morana. Will she please take the chair."

There was a stir and motion of bodies in chairs as an usher left the chamber. In a moment he returned followed by Morana. She walked down the sloping aisle to the flat pit of the hall and took her place on the square, uncushioned seat just below Lord Farrant and next to the table where the two recording secretaries worked.

"Morana," I said, "will you tell us, as you recall it, what happened from the time Consul Commiter's party left Isla Lang's house on the Frays until it was decided that the monorail should stop at Reeves?"

"Willingly," she said.

Her account was direct, complete, unembroidered, and dreadful. When she finished there wasn't a whisper, a rustle, or a cough for seconds.

"Thank you," I said at last. "Morana, did you recognize any of the attackers?"

"No. I felt then and have thought later that there was something familiar about one of them, but the answer is definitely no. I did not recognize anyone. But two of them I would certainly know again."

"Have you any idea why you were selected for humiliation?"

"Yes. There was no secret about the Consul's visit or who was in the party. It was all international relations of a sort. What was done was meant as a rebuke to the Mora policy, an insult to the Mora family in my person, and an embarrassment to Consul Commiter and his government. It was also intended that the Dorns be blamed for it."

"Do you feel that there was any Dorn involvement?"

"No. I'm sure there was not. It has never been a Dorn habit to degrade anyone nor to antagonize friendly foreign governments. In the Dorn and Mora families there have been many examples of strength, ability, and weakness, but no Dorn or Mora has ever behaved in this way, even in the time of The League."

I turned to the Council. "Are there any questions for Morana?" There were none. I thanked her and excused her. "Next on my schedule," I said, "is the episode at Reeves. My witness this time is Henry Ross, Visiting Professor of American Subjects at the University of Reeves. As your written statements will have shown you, he also went through the affair at Fraysedge. Will he take the chair, please?" At this signal an usher left the chamber and returned shortly with Ross.

When he had taken his uncomfortable place, I said, "Mr. Ross, I am going to ask you to tell the Council, as you remember it, what happened from the time we finished dinner until we reached your lodgings on the day Morana and I visited one of your classes at Reeves. If it would be easier for you to speak in English, I would be glad to call an interpreter."

"Thank you. I would rather speak in Islandian. If I have difficulty, I know there are many fine linguists within reach of my voice. Let me see. We came out onto the street into an improving night . . ."

His narrative was short, sometimes awkwardly put, but active and vivid, evocative of that strange, running, dodging encounter. It was also completely without personal animus. He ended by saying, "I remember telling you that you would have a very sore arm in the morning. You did, and that was all for either of us. We were fortunate."

I thanked him, and then began a line of questioning I knew would be very difficult for him. I did it without conditions or mitigations. There was only so much empathy for a man in his position. If I treated him too gently, the Council would behave as though I had burglarized its own store of mercy.

"Do you have any thoughts, Mr. Ross, as to why we were attacked that night?"

"It's true we were both at Fraysedge," he said, "and neither of us was molested." He considered my question for a moment or so more. "Naturally I have thought about why we were attacked, and why that particular night. The things I think are not easy to say because they are not my business as your guest. Facts are one sort of thing. But my opinion now is another. It seems to me both rude and irresponsible. However . . .

"I have assumed that the incidents are connected. They're different but they make related points. In Reeves I think the demonstration was anti-education and anti-foreign, at least anti-western. These people were telling you, and probably Morana, that interest in a wider, modern teaching program wasn't healthy. Particularly they wanted to get rid of me—the American, the foreigner, the corrupter. The leaders of that mob may not have had specific instructions to kill us, but I remember feeling at the time that they were doing the best they could with what they had."

"Mr. Ross, why do you suppose there was no attempt in Reeves to involve the Dorn family?"

"I've wondered about that. But you were one of the intended victims, Lord Lang, and your Dorn connections are known. It may be that they—whoever they are—thought, just for this reason, that suspicion would touch the Dorns sooner if their name wasn't spread all over the business. But I can't believe it was that subtle. I think there simply wasn't enough time to get that part of it organized."

"Can you tell us how any of it was organized?"

"I think so—now. I've had time to reconstruct. It has to have been two of my good students. Not my best but my most vocal ones. I think you heard them the day you visited, a young man and woman. They were able to foment a kind of dialectic out of any material that came up for discussion. The intention was to get me involved and provoke me into making unconsidered remarks. Sometimes it worked. At the first class after the attack the young man was there and the girl was not. The next time it was the other way around. Since then neither one has come. I've learned that they've withdrawn from the University and left the city of Reeves. But they didn't hurry. They didn't seem to be running away. They acted as though they'd finished one job and were moving on to another."

"Mr. Ross, did you tell your class in advance, or anyone else, that Morana and I would visit on that day?"

"That depends on what you mean by advance, Lord Lang. About two hours before the class met I put a notice on the bulletin board in the classroom."

"Then actually anyone in the University could have known an hour or so ahead of time, that we were coming."

Ross thought about this and said, "Theoretically, yes, but not actually. The classroom is public, of course, and anyone can go into it. But it's out of the way and no one does except to attend a class or to check posted information about a course that meets there. This term the only two courses that meet in that room are mine and more than half of my students are enrolled in both courses."

"Then you think your two students managed to get word outside the University in time to have you and me followed on leaving and to arrange a plan for an attack, a plan flexible enough to cover whatever we did."

"Yes, sir. I can't think anything else."

"You've been clear, Mr. Ross, in defining the time limit. It was very short. Without anyone knowing what our individual movements would be, at least a dozen men were recruited into different parties and given instructions good enough to make a concerted attack on us. How do these people communicate with each other? Do you have any guess about this?"

"None, I'm sorry to say."

"Thank you for your help, Mr. Ross. Are there any other questions for the witness?"

There were two, one from the Dorn side of the chamber and the other from the Mora side. They had to do with the number of students Ross had, the kinds of students, and the range of his courses. They were not hostile and there seemed to be no disposition anywhere to bait Ross. He had made a good impression on a Council that was obviously disturbed by what it was hearing. At this point Lord Farrant recessed the session until afternoon.

✠

At home, waiting for lunch to be ready, I stood looking out over the shining, imprecise, steellike surface of the bay. Part of my mind was on how to handle my part of the afternoon's Council session and another was wondering what really lay under that shimmering water. Glancing toward the south, I saw a sizable vessel approaching from the general direction of the sea gate to the bay. When I had binoculars focused on the ship, I could make out that she was a large ocean trawler of the sort the Russians are reported to use. I could see very little bow wave and the speed seemed to be very moderate for so powerful a ship.

To the north now, as I swung my glasses, there was activity offshore from the navy building and the docks of the Islandia Bay Patrol. Two armed cutters moved out into open water, turned south abreast, and put on speed. I saw the white water rise suddenly in slanting sheets on either side of them, and the twisting plumes behind from their propellers. After them came an unarmed launch, traveling fast but falling behind.

The confrontation occurred almost in front of me and less than half a mile out. When the cutters reached the trawler, they diverged and began to circle her at high speed from opposite directions, coming closer to her bow each time around. My glasses are good, strong enough to pull your eyes painfully if you focus too fast or inaccurately; and like all glasses of this strength they make it difficult to follow objects whose range keeps changing quickly and erratically.

I had trouble with the two cutters. I was sure that their guns were manned, and I had the impression that they were kept trained as the boats circled, the automatic cannon on the trawler's bridge and rudder, and the machine guns on the decks. The trawler reduced speed even more and finally appeared to stop engines entirely. By the time the launch reached the scene, the trawler was lying still in the water. I had no difficulty distinguishing the Russian colors at her stern or, at the bow, the Cyrillic letters of whatever her name was.

The launch took position between me and the trawler within hailing distance of the starboard wing of the bridge. The cutters decreased their speed and increased their radius, but kept on circling. In the forward cockpit of the launch a man who looked very much like Hanno rose to his feet and raised a megaphone. The ensuing scene, lasting several minutes and reaching me as dumb show, was too good to need any of the words I could see being shouted from one side to the other.

At this distance the launch and the trawler were close enough together so that I could move my glasses up and down without refocusing. On the bridge, in his master's cap and jacket, the captain of the trawler reached out his hands in entreaty, pointed sadly down through the stern of his ship, shrugged in resignation, put his hands to his head in dismay, and then shook his fists in protest—visibly shouting all the while. Down below, the hatless man with his legs braced in the rolling launch held out a hand in reasonable request, pointed to himself and the men with him, pointed to the trawler, shook his head, shrugged his shoulders in dismissal, made a negative sign with the flat of his hand, and then pointed south toward the sea gate.

With variations they went through this exchange several times. Finally the trawler captain said something over his shoulder to one of his crew, slapped the palm of his hand on the rail, and turned back to the center of the bridge. A second later the water under the stern began to roil, the ship gathered way, and then turned slowly to port through one hundred and eighty degrees. Escorted now by the cutters, the trawler headed back the way she had come. I was interested to see the cutters force the ship into the smallest possible turning circle and then herd her over to within a few yards of her northbound track.

✠

Lord Dorn opened the afternoon Council session as my witness. He walked carefully to the chair, carrying but not using a heavy, polished stick. Seated, and holding the stick across his knees, he said, "With your permission, Isla Lang, and subject if you wish to later questions from you and the Council, I would like to offer my account directly and without formal interlocution. It will save much valuable time. You may take it that I am on oath. May I do so?"

"Please do," I said, and sat down.

Without hurry he took account of his audience, the Council with no absentees, the crowded public galleries, and the special section of diplomats. "Most of you know the way I travel," he said. "So do many others. There's nothing secret about it, and nothing rational. It's preference.

"Each autumn when I come to The City from Dorn Island I send the heavy and bulky things like wheat and corn, and winter-keeping fruits and vegetables by boat around Winder and in through the bay. One can buy all these things here, of course, but we grow them on Dorn Island and I see no reason to raise prices in The City. Sometimes I send tools or furniture this way, and once or twice I have even sent myself.

"But almost always I come by land with ponies. This time we were a party of five with four additional pack ponies carrying clothes and light stuffs. Our route was south of Doring City through the widest of the grass valleys that open into northern Inerria. It was here we were waylaid.

"My wife and her sister along with Pleiko and Feyar, the men who keep me and my things in working order, were riding with the pack animals. I was two or three hundred yards behind them because, as usual, I had felt I must turn off the track to look at this, or see what was in back of that. Between me and the others at this point there was flat grassland and, off to the north, a set of grass-grown dunes that looked almost like *tumuli*. I thought I should go and see.

"Just then six horsemen appeared on the crest of the nearest dune, paused, and then rode fast down into the open space between me and my party. Three of them turned toward the big group ahead. The other three came at me. They were shouting. When they came closer I could hear, 'The Dorn! The Dorn! That's The Dorn! Get him! Get The Dorn!'

"One of them pulled up and kept himself between me

and whatever was happening ahead. Another rode across close in front of me and then back again. He had a cudgel." Lord Dorn raised his walking stick, holding it out. "It was about as long as this and half again as thick, and there was a metal cap on the heavy end. Each time he went in front of me he struck my pony full across the face with it, high on the nose and below the eyes. The other man went behind me. He had a blade of some kind in his hand. Probably a saber. I couldn't see what he did, but I felt it. He chopped through one of the pony's hamstring muscles.

"The pony was screaming, fighting, rearing, falling, all at the same time. I was trying to get clear of him and couldn't quite do it. He fell on his side with my leg under him. Under the grass there was light, deep soil. I worked my way loose, tested my leg as well as I could, and thought it wasn't broken. Then I looked up and around and saw my three assailants. At the points of a triangle, each about fifteen yards away from me, they were sitting their mounts and watching.

"My pony wasn't kicking now or screaming. He was trembling all over, pawing for purchase with one front foot, twisting his neck, raising his head, and snuffling. I had no firearm, but there was a knife in a sheath in the saddle. I spoke to Tog and put my arm around his neck. He knew me and trusted me, and relaxed long enough for me to stab him up through the larynx.

"My watchers, once they saw this done, turned and rode away.

"I learned a little later that nothing had happened to the main party except alarm, shouts, and a temporary dispersion of the pack ponies.

"I did not recognize any of the men who attacked me, but I would know them again."

Lord Dorn stopped speaking in the center of a tense, thick silence that reached down from the galleries and across the floor of the chamber. He sat erect and massive in the chair, waiting motionless for the moment to resume.

"As a member of the Council," he said in an almost informal manner, "I was privileged to hear the testimony of the two preceding-witnesses. They were not allowed to hear each other, but I hope they have been permitted to listen to me and are here now. They behaved admirably—this I say as a member of the Council. As a fellow witness, I cannot vouch for their facts because I wasn't with them. But I can support their conclusions, and I do.

"Specifically I agree with Morana that no Mora and no Dorn had a hand in any of the three episodes. I think that at Fraysedge, and in my case, it was planned that Dorn and Mora involvement should be suspected. This has happened. The plan was successful. This is what I am now coming to think of as the benign conspiracy. But what happened at Reeves may have been part of something else. I'll come back to it.

"Some of you may feel I was sentimental about the death of my pony. I could have said I dispatched him, and left it at that. That's what I would have said if it had been an accident of combat. But consider. Nothing happened to the rest of my party. It would have been easy to kill the two men and women and steal the pack ponies. It would have been even easier to kill me. Or, if that wasn't the object, I could have been unhorsed and left on foot. People would have been much more likely to credit Dorn and Mora involvement if this had been the whole style of things at Fraysedge and with me. Instead, three of them deliberately maimed my pony, forced me to kill a being I loved very much, and watched me while I did it. I wanted to be explicit about this.

"For if you think back over Morana's account of Fraysedge, you can't miss the similar split between a controlled demonstration in force and a contemptuous, self-gratifying exhibition of cruelty. It seems to me that everything that happened at Reeves was of the second kind, or would have been if it had succeeded.

"This witness has no more facts to present. I think we are engaged with two, or possibly more, intermingled conspiracies. The primary one appears to want to behave in a civilized way, and its aims, for all I know, may be what most of us here would consider constructive if they were pursued legitimately. But imbedded in this operation, and using it for cover, are people with other interests. I don't know what they want, or if they in turn are at odds with each other. One quality they have in common is malevolence.

"My direct evidence is this, and experience is not always a reliable guide. Just the same, applying one to the other, the opinion of this witness is that we are deep in troubles we know nothing about as well as the ones we have become familiar with."

He looked at me to tell me that was all he had to say.

"Lord Dorn," I said, "it would be unusual if you did not have your own shrewd idea of the reason for these outbreaks. Is there anything you can tell us?"

"Not from this seat, Isla Lang. Here I am a witness. It's been awkward going, but I've made that plain. Over there," and he pointed his cane toward the floor of the chamber, "my capacity for thinking and speaking is different. From there I will be extremely interested in what you develop after this."

"Are there other questions for Lord Dorn?" I asked in a public voice. It was clear at once there weren't but I waited a full half minute which I needed to settle my own plans. He had introduced a new dimension to events in his testimony—one he hadn't suggested to me—and at the end he had told me in effect, "Light the fuse, son, or blow out the match."

With more pleasure in my voice than in my heart, I said, "Thank you, Lord Dorn." He stood, touched my shoulder with his hand in passing, and went to take his seat in the Chamber.

✠

Lord Farrant opened a folder of papers in front of him, thumbed them, and said to me, "Isla Lang, I don't know what more you have to present to us. You have already opened several serious matters that require thought and time for consideration. Meanwhile," and he flicked his papers again, "there are urgent decisions the Council must make. May I ask you to postpone the rest of your inquiry until tomorrow afternoon when we should be up-to-date?"

There was a powerful part of me that wanted to accede to this, to agree that nothing real was happening. Instead I forced myself to say, "The Council itself scheduled this hearing, Lord Farrant, and no time limit was put on it. I think it is more urgent than anything else the Council may have to consider."

"By that, I take it, you mean you will not agree to a postponement?"

"No."

Farrant could now get his postponement—which I suspected was a euphemism for indefinite delay—only by a vote of the Council. Calling for a vote after Lord Dorn's testimony was a serious chance, and Farrant didn't contemplate it long.

"Very well," he said in an unfriendly voice, "please continue."

I called Hanno as a witness. This was a risk. I took it because I couldn't see any other way of provoking a public controversy over secret material. When he had arranged himself, I said, "I am sure there are many here, Hanno, including members of the Council, who do not know who you are or what you do. I would like to present you myself, but even after finding you in your office and having a long talk with you there I don't know the exact style of your position. Would you tell us?"

"Willingly," Hanno said, "except I have none. The Civil Service is famous for having jobs without definitions. I am in the Civil Service, and what I do mostly is to look after the nonmilitary aspects of the country's security."

"Thank you," I said. "Now. A few weeks ago, before the first heavy snow in the barrier range, I came south through a high, difficult, and almost unknown pass. Two men, who did not see me because it was foggy and I was up the slope resting, crossed me going north. I later told you of this event. You then showed me aerial photographs of an avalanche in the northern part of that pass and conjectured, by comparing times, that the men I saw were buried in it. Is that correct?"

"Yes."

"Have you since had any reason to change your opinion?"

"No. I was never positive about it. I couldn't be. But I think that's what happened."

"Good. So much for that. Shortly before the incident at Fraysedge was it reported to you that two men, one from the staff of this building and one from the government printing office in Suburra, disappeared from their jobs and were reported missing?"

"This may be so," Hanno said. "From time to time people just walk off the job at all the government shops. It happens often enough so that I can't identify these two from memory."

"Nor could I," I said. "However, at this same time, was it reported to you that a proof of a chart was missing along with a copy of its supporting text?"

I think Hanno might have evaded me, but Lord Farrant didn't give him the chance. He rapped with his gavel and said, "The witness will not answer the question. The subject is reserved. Isla Lang, you will please change your line of questioning."

With my mouth open I stood looking at him. Farrant took it for confusion, and in a sense it was. I had never expected such good luck. He said, "All right, Lang, get on with it."

Addressing myself again to Hanno, I saw I had gained no advantage there. His face and manner gave me nothing. But now he wasn't the one I was talking to. "When I went to the Frays a short time ago," I said at Hanno, "we had just picked up two men who were members of the raiding party at Fraysedge. They were questioned separately. Each of them said he had seen what he thought was a map and . . ."

The gavel again. "Isla Lang, you are returning to the same reserved subject. I instructed you to change your line of questions."

This time I replied, saying, "I'm sorry, Lord Farrant. It isn't easy to know what is reserved, or classified. To be precise, at the time you stopped me, I wasn't asking questions. I was making a statement from first hand. I gave you a report several days ago containing all the information we acquired from the prisoners. Until now I haven't been told this was secret."

"Well, it is," Farrant said, looking at me now with a kind of disgusted amusement, "and, even at your age, most people wouldn't need to be told. I don't actually think you do. There is a special committee looking into this matter, and that's where I'd like to have it stay. Have you any more questions for Hanno on a, well, different subject?"

"Yes, I have some more questions for Hanno." And now again they were for Hanno. "Can you tell us what that big trawler was doing in the bay this noon?"

At this there was laughter from the floor and the galleries. Lord Farrant came down once more with his gavel. "I didn't ask you to be frivolous, Isla Lang. Is this relevant?"

Thinking simultaneously that I might better be hanged for a horse than a sheep, and that Farrant had delivered himself to me, I said, "You instructed me to change the subject, Lord Farrant. I've done that." Again there was laughter, more of it this time, of a kind I didn't like. It was witless and self-generating. "If you feel it's not relevant, look at the witness. He isn't laughing. There was a midday dramatic comedy for those who had waterfront seats, but that's not all it was. I hope my new line of questioning won't become so pertinent that you feel compelled to stop me again. May I continue?"

"By all means."

I turned to Hanno and changed the question, not much but importantly. "Can you tell us why the trawler was here?"

The mood of the heterogeneous audience was now swinging from levity back to tension and quiet. Hanno said, "It's partly a matter of jurisdiction. The ship approached the sea gate about midnight or a little earlier. It opened radio communication with our navy people who have charge of the ocean approaches and the sea gate itself. The trawler said it had been in Antarctic waters, had encountered ice unexpectedly, and had damaged a propeller blade and thrown one of its shafts out of alignment. The ship requested permission to enter the bay, anchor in protected water, and make repairs. The navy passed the trawler into the bay, instructing the ship to establish radio communication at once with Bay Patrol, which ultimately is my office, to ask for final permission and instructions. The navy gave the trawler Bay Patrol's radio frequency, which is not the same as any the navy uses."

Hanno paused and, as much as his professionally schooled face could show such a thing, seemed to feel distaste for what he had to say next. I didn't prod him.

"The trawler didn't send a signal to Bay Patrol until she was almost recognizable by sight from our docks. Unfortunately, the navy didn't think it necessary to let us know. They have transmitters at the sea gate that can use our frequency."

"Then nobody knows where the trawler was in the bay during quite a long time?"

"No," Hanno said, shrugging, "that's not a problem. The ship spent more than two hours sitting still, talking to the navy, before she came into the bay. Then the navy sent a patrol boat in with her as a guide, until half an hour after sunrise. By the time things got started, of course, sunrise wasn't too far away, and the trawler was only willing to make four knots. But we know where she went. It was along the main shipping route."

"I suppose," I said, "the patrol boat didn't send you or the navy any signal because it didn't have the equipment to know that the trawler wasn't following orders?"

"That is correct."

"What about the navy itself? It didn't monitor the trawler from stations at the sea gate?"

"No."

"Why not? Did it think its job was done for the night?"

Hanno weighed that, wondering perhaps whether I would accept a simple agreement that the navy was asleep. He said, "The navy isn't like that. No. It goes back to what I said in the beginning about jurisdiction."

It was my turn to ponder. This had to be some kind of tangle in military, not political, security, and just now I didn't want to press him on it. But I needed to know what he meant. From what he said, and it would be characteristic of the way we do things in Islandia, it began to look as though each of our services could send a signal to another service on a designated frequency but agreed not to monitor any frequency not its own. If so, the systems for coded messages must be remarkable indeed. At any rate this could explain why the trawler, with the help of some luck, was able to remain silent for so long.

"Hanno," I said, "right now I would give odds that the two men I saw in the pass were not caught in the avalanche. Tell me, what did you and the trawler captain say to each other?"

"I asked to come aboard to verify the damage he described. He said it was contrary to standing orders for foreigners to be allowed aboard Russian ships and he had no authority to make an exception. I told him, in that case, I could not permit him to anchor."

"And over and over again, wasn't it?"

Hanno actually smiled in public. "Yes, over and over and over."

"Did you think he had other reasons for not allowing you aboard?"

"I'm not sure what you mean, Isla Lang. I know Russian Masters do take this position."

"Did you suspect that he didn't want you to see there was no damage at all, and that he didn't want you to find that he was equipped with underwater ranging and detection gear?"

"I did think of the first, but not of the second."

"Hanno, I have to doubt that. If you thought the Russian might be deceiving you about damage, you must have assumed a reason for the deception. I watched the whole encounter through glasses, including the trawler's turn-around and departure. You reached the same conclusion I did. You told your cutters to see that the trawler went out over the same bottom she covered coming in, didn't you?"

"I didn't put it that way but, yes, I did."

"To do this the cutters had to force the trawler a full half mile to port. Is that correct?"

"At least that. At four knots the Russian took a very wide turn."

"Why did you give this order if it wasn't to prevent the trawler from scanning more of the submarine landscape than she had done already?"

"Isla Lang," Hanno said, "I wasn't thinking about submarine landscape just then. If you were watching, you know I was furious. I told the boats to take the trawler out—now—the way she had come in. And the boat crews were angry. They chose to understand me literally. If they wanted to humor themselves by pushing the trawler around, I didn't feel like stopping them."

"Hanno," I said, knowing how much he had just hurt me, "you may have spared Lord Farrant any more wear on his gavel today. I can't compete with furious patriotism from a senior Civil Servant. Especially when the fury is so much in character. I have been silenced so often that I know I cannot expect now to establish the few connections among these events that are known so far both to you and to me.

"Just the same, it is known that Russian ships of this class can, and often do, carry effective, modern devices to look at the ground they're sailing over. No one pretends that this gear can produce a geological survey, but it can verify important features of something else that's supposed to be a survey." I was talking to Hanno, but to the side I could see Farrant fingering his gavel. He wanted to stop me. There was no doubt. But I hadn't made any identifications yet. His trouble was that if he graveled me down, he would establish my point before I got to it. Maybe, if I was careful of the order of things in my next two sentences, I could come in ahead of him.

"For this kind of verification, Hanno, two tracks by a ship would be better than one, and several better than two, wouldn't they?"

"Yes. No doubt."

"Without contradiction I asserted earlier that we were missing a map . . ."

Then the gavel did come down. I didn't mind. It was emphasis. I'd done as much as I could.

Lord Farrant said to me, "Your behavior is obsessive, Isla Lang. And irresponsible. I try to attribute it to your newness as Isla. Have you now completed your hearing?"

"No, Lord Farrant," I said, "but I accept the fact that it is ended. I wish events had forced someone else, not so guilty of newness, to present this unpalatable stuff. I thank you for your patience. Hanno, thank you."

Before Farrant could dismiss Hanno or release me, Lord Mora rose in his place on the chamber floor. Over medium height, lightly boned and slender, as awkward and as graceful as a larch tree in winter, he waited to be recognized. Mora was perhaps sixty-two, a year or so younger than Dorn, but there were only a few shots of white in his heavy and elegant dark hair. His face was long, the cheekbones and jawlines plain. His olive skin gave an impression of depth, lying smooth except for two heavy sickle lines down his cheeks almost to the corners of his mouth, wide, flat-lipped, and versatile.

Taking his time, Farrant said, "Isla Mora."

"Thank you, Lord Farrant. We have now, all of us in our ways, appeased and aroused Amenity. Very dangerous. She should have been one of the Fates, but she was too implacable even for the Greeks." It was an extraordinary voice. Completely audible when Mora spoke quietly, it had great power and range without becoming strident.

"Before Isla Lang returns to his place in the Council, I want to put on the record my regret and distress that his efforts to establish facts were met by obstruction and hostility. This was foolish. What he did convey was most important and entirely convincing."

Farrant replied, quite mildly, "I gave Isla Lang time and leeway. He kept returning to reserved subjects."

"True. But you were the one who classified them and, whatever the wisdom of that in the first place, you should see that they must be declassified now. Your security prevents me from presenting the case, just as it did Isla Lang. Surely, you can understand that our only course at this time is to make these matters public to all the world. Naturally, I have not consulted my colleague, Lord Dorn, but I would like to know his opinion."

Dorn stood and said, "I agree with you completely. Publicity is the best defense we have and maybe the only one."

Farrant looked from one to the other and smiled. "Surprising," he said. "But I'm not convinced, and I will not remove any of the security restrictions. I now declare the day's Council session ended."

"Not so," Lord Mora said, and remained standing. "As head of government you have the right to reserve from public knowledge any information you consider harmful to the interest of the country. You may do this by the authority of your office, but you may be challenged at any time. By custom you have the privilege of recessing a session of the Council at midday. You do not have the power to terminate a Council session. You know very well this requires a vote of the members. Because I am still speaking it will be a moment or so before you can ask for that vote.

"It is clear that the country is in danger from internal and external enemies. The government has shown that it will not respond to reasonable questions from responsible sources. My belief is that government is ignorant of the facts and the significance of most of the testimony offered here. Serious and frightening trouble is in the accounts of Morana, Mr. Ross, and Lord Dorn. But the only attention government has paid to this evidence was to get through it as fast as could be. It meant nothing until Lang began to make cross-references. Government then had an opportunity. It didn't take it. Instead it called on security to throw a fog around the visible part of the iceberg. At the least this is stupid.

"I move a vote of no confidence."

"And I second the motion," Lord Dorn said as in a continuation of the statement.

The shock spread with the speed of sound. Within a portion of a second the silence first magnified the sounds of human breathing, of our chairs, and of the building itself. Then its density overrode even these.

Farrant looked down at his desk and then across at Mora who was still on his feet. "In other circumstances," he said, "your motion would be open for discussion before being put to a vote. But in this case discussion would be out of order. It would necessarily violate the security regulations which, as I understand it, are the reason for your motion. I believe I am within my rights in ruling that there be no discussion. Do you concur?"

"You are within your rights," Mora said. "Please put the question."

Raising his eyes, but not his voice, Farrant spoke to the Council as a whole. "You have heard Isla Mora's motion, seconded by Isla Dorn, for a vote on the question of your confidence in this government. I now have the choice of designating a roll call, record vote or a simple standing one. On previous occasions like this my predecessors generally have used the standing vote. They have felt that issues of confidence in a small country like ours are very touchy but often temporary matters, and they have not wanted to turn them into irrevocable political and personal differences. I agree with them and will follow that precedent.

"The question you are to decide I put to you in the negative form in which Isla Mora stated it. Will those members who share his lack of confidence in this government please rise and be counted."

The silence returned. There was no jack-in-the-box jumping up out of seats. One by one, deliberately, almost as though the spring had left their legs, members began to stand. Leaving Hanno still in the witness seat, ignored and forgotten, I walked slowly onto the chamber floor and took my place among those standing.

After some two minutes, Farrant said, "That is enough. It is clear Lord Mora's motion has carried." He turned then to Tor. "I must inform you that your country now has no government. With your permission I will resume my membership in the Council."

As he walked away from the desk, Tor rose and said, "As is usual when governments change, I suspend further sessions of the Council until noon tomorrow. By that time, Lord Mora, I will expect you to have formed a new government that will command the support of the Council. Meanwhile, if necessary, I will act in place of government."

✠

When I arrived at Dorn House that night in response to the invitation brought verbally by a messenger, I found Dorn and Mora alone together in the large room overlooking the bay. Deep in the inner part, two low-burning lamps gave enough light to keep me from running into tables or falling over chairs, but not enough to reach as far as the windows which were flooded with brilliant white moonlight. There the two men were sitting.

Mora rose and greeted me cordially. From where he sat Dorn asked me to bring up a chair and join them. "Share the night with us a little longer," he said. "We met to arrange a government, but we haven't begun yet. You made it necessary, and we'll need your help." Then the three of us sat there quietly.

I couldn't know what kept them silent, what thoughts

they had, or what power this scene held for them. For me, looking through spaced conifers and over the rocks on the shore, the shining track of light across the huge inland water brought the suggestion of final things or, even less cheerful, of penultimate things. The sight was unbelievably calm and beautiful. The easy motion of the water, full of possibility, reached backward and forward in me. The times I had seen the bay this way weren't so many. Would I see it so again? If I did, what would other things be like?

At last Mora said, "This is fine moonshine, but I suppose it's enough. The two Americans will be along soon and, no doubt, Morana and Dorna. At least we must appear to have done something. Before coming here, I spoke to the Council members who share my views more or less. To be brief, I said it would be fatal to underestimate our danger and that I would be glad, under certain circumstances, to support a Dorn government. They agreed that would be their position, too."

"In my meeting," Dorn said, "I went further than that. I told my colleagues that a Mora government was our best chance, if a few conditions were met. They said they felt the same way."

Both men laughed, and then fell silent again until Mora said, "What should we do? Cut cards for it?"

"No. We've said what we mean. It should be a Mora government. In the outside world your credit is stronger than mine, and we will need to draw on it heavily. Even if you were willing to take over foreign affairs in a government of mine, that wouldn't be good enough. Our Head of State now has to do more than be responsible for foreign policy. He has to be it. And that is you, Mora. I'll take on some nasty jobs for you, but I don't see any other possibility."

Mora looked doubtful and turned to me. "Lang, you didn't commit yourself to either caucus today. And it's been many years since your father was a party man. What's your opinion here?"

"Lord Mora," I said, "I don't even know why I'm here. My opinion can't be of any use to you."

Dorn and Mora exchanged looks, and Dorn said, "Mora, I think the explanation would come better from you."

Mora nodded. "It's simple enough. Lang, you brought down the Farrant regime. I realize you had help and advice, but politically you did it. And if you hadn't been determined and skillful, it wouldn't have happened. You made a new government possible and you should have a voice in how it's set up. Also, the new government will need your support. You are the bridge between Dorn and me. We must have your opinion, whether or not we follow it. And from experience, I can tell you that it will be a disservice to all of us if you soften what you think by being modest."

"I'm not modest," I said. "On this question I'm incompetent. But I see your point, or I think I do. I agree with Lord Dorn, with a qualification. This should be a Mora government, and for the reasons Dorn has given. But there should be a Dorn part of it. He should be in charge of all domestic things that have to do with the Civil Service, the military, manufactories and agriculture, communications, and the obligations of the provincial Lords to each other and to the country as a whole."

Mora looked from me to Dorn and back again, not suspiciously, but without any pleasure. "You may both be right," he said. "Actually, I agree with you. I suppose I was hoping, Dorn, that you would want to take on this disaster in your own name. I see you are sensible."

"I know what you mean," Dorn said. "Nobody wants responsibility in this form. But it doesn't matter. If this doesn't work, then everything, and all of us, go down together. Just the same, I'll say what you're testing me for. I'll take the government in my name if you refuse. Our chances are better with you."

"Very well. I accept, provisionally. Lang has listed the powers I thought you would ask me to cede. I'm prepared to do this. In a general way he suggested police power, too, although he didn't name it. This should be included. Is there anything more?"

"No."

Mora stood and deliberately walked the length of the room and back along the line of the windows. He stopped between Dorn's chair and mine, behind us, and spoke over our shoulders. "The concessions I need aren't as easily recognized as the ones I gave you. But we have to do something about them. Dorn, would you start?"

"You'll want membership in the U.N. and a long-term recasting of our school system. You'll want to send more ambassadors abroad and receive more permanent diplomatic missions here. You'll want a member's seat, so to speak, in the international diplomatic stock exchange. You'll want to admit a comparatively large number of foreigners to the country for many different purposes.

These things cover quite a range, and I'll support them all. Is this what you want, so far?"

"Yes," Mora said. "Go on, please."

"I can anticipate certain kinds of problems," Dorn said, speaking slowly now. "For instance, the question of an alliance or a multination treaty. Or it might be a matter of inviting foreign investment and technical resources. In the past, of course, we've always refused these things because we wagered rightly that we could survive without them and felt we would be more our own masters if we did. You will say that in its extreme form this has been a Dorn attitude, but actually, when it mattered, the Mora positon hasn't been very far removed.

"The world is now quite different, and we are changing. But even so, if any of those questions arise for your government—and I expect all of them will—I don't know in advance whether I will say yes or no. What I can tell you is that I won't automatically say no as a matter of principle. Is that good enough?"

Mora nodded. "That's as much as either of us can say." He went around me to his chair and sat down. "That covers it. With your help, I'll do my best with the government. Now for an urgent matter. The U.N. Perhaps we can settle it here. I will request membership tomorrow as soon as my position is official. We also need an ambassador designate. Lang, would you consider taking the post?"

This had never occurred to me, although I had thought my father might be suggested. The reasons against both of us were the same and, to my mind, strong. I made no sense of the proposal, unless perhaps Mora wanted to get rid of me. "Lord Mora," I said, "if you and Lord Dorn feel I should take the ambassadorship, I'm willing to accept it. But I think I'm a poor choice."

"Why so?" It was Mora who spoke, but they both looked puzzled and interested.

"Because I belong to the only foreign family that has ever been given an official grant of Islandian citizenship."

"Of course. That's why you should be our first ambassador to the United Nations, our first permanent ambassador anywhere. For three generations, ever since it has been Islandian and even before that, your family has given distinguished service to the country. You know the outside world, and your name is recognized and respected there. Your ability and qualifications are without question. Does all this add up to a poor choice?"

Neither of them saw the trouble. For the first time in my life I felt foreign—not American because I knew I wasn't that, but alien. I didn't know the outside world. I'd never been there, nor had my father. The only Americans I'd ever met were Commiter and Ross. But some knowledge, intuitive, inherited, or both, told me Mora was plain wrong. I had no good way to explain it to him.

"Lord Mora," I said, "those were generous words and I thank you. I appreciate them too much to question them. But I'm sure the facts are a prescription for an unsuccessful and unhappy ambassador. Let me try to tell you why.

"I am a third-generation Islandian. My countrymen accept me as one of them whether they approve or don't approve of what I do, so long as I am in this country dealing with the domestic affairs of this country. But my family is unique. Islandians have long memories. Whoever goes to the United Nations, there will be no immediate successes for us. Compromises will have to be accepted. People here will recall that I still have many relatives in America, and it really hasn't been so long since all Langs were American. They will begin to wonder if I'm making the best possible bargains for Islandia. And some will have worse suspicions. On the other side, the American press will never refer to me except as an American gone native. This probably won't fool many Americans, but it will almost certainly reduce my credit with the representatives of other nations.

"I think the best appointment would be the most Islandian Islandian you can find. His position in the U.N. would be stronger than mine, and people here at home would have some sympathy with his trouble."

With no comment of his own, Mora said, "Dorn, what do you think?"

At first Dorn just laughed. Then he said, "I started out thinking you had had a stroke of genius, Mora. Lang was just the man. But he's right and no doubt about it."

"I'm afraid he is," Mora said. "Lang, have you a candidate?"

"Yes," I said. "I'm sure the best appointment would be Lord Farrant."

Dorn was clearly interested. Mora looked at me as though he suspected me of making a joke. There was no chance then to discuss the matter because Dorna brought in Commiter, Ross, and Morana.

Greetings were exchanged, chairs were brought, the

lights were turned up, and bottles of wine and glasses placed on the big table. The night was recognized and the moon excluded. A part of me was very grateful for this. Dorn and Mora were older and much more experienced than I—and maybe this was not happening to them—but I knew that without some chatter and some bright ordinariness it wouldn't be long before I was saying things that should never be uttered.

Dorn, the host, and Commiter, the envoy, almost the same age and almost of a size, stood facing each other, dwarfing the rest of us. When Dorn said that Mora and he had agreed to form a Mora government, Commiter raised his glass to the Islar Mora and Dorn, saying, "Strength and wisdom to you both. This is excellent news. After this afternoon I hoped something like this would happen. I've already cabled Washington that a coalition was likely. I'm sure the other ministers have done the same. But I am not a journalist looking for a scoop, and I won't send anything more until the official event tomorrow."

"It's perfectly true," Mora said, "we're very partial in our treatment of diplomats—the few we have here."

Commiter laughed, but when he spoke his tone carried no assumption of privilege. "I've no objection when it's to my advantage. Actually, I've no objection in principle. Governments have an obligation to handle their information in their best interest and that doesn't always mean share and share alike."

"Mr. Commiter, what would be the attitude of your government in the event that Islandia was . . . ?"

"Lord Mora, please don't ask me hypothetical questions. I can't answer them. All I can do is quote you the gibberish about our support of the territorial integrity of states and the right of a people to choose its government. But you know as well as I do that, just like beauty, virtue is in the eye of the beholder, and how easily circumstances can alter vision."

"Then I'll be specific," Mora said, and following Commiter's example began to talk less formally. "Dorn, you should listen to this. You may not agree with me entirely. Tomorrow we will publish the general results of a survey of the underwater resources of Islandia Bay and the adjacent territorial waters. This, of course, is what Lang was hammering at all day in the Council and what finally got us our vote of no confidence. Mr. Commiter, will you ask your government what its response would be if we requested American technical and financial help in developing a selected number of these resources? Dorn?"

"No objection so far."

Commiter said, "Your proposal would be for an agreement between governments?"

"Yes," Mora said. "On our side we are dealing with public, not private, resources. I realize that the technology and equipment would come from private concerns, and the funds probably from debentures they offered. In our proposal we would not ask your government to give us financial aid. We would not want the World Bank for this either. The contracting companies could satisfy themselves that the resources to be developed would be security for the investment. The project would be self-liquidating and would give a generous return to investors. What we will ask is that your government stand with ours as a guarantor of the terms and duration of the agreement."

When Mora stopped speaking there was nothing in anyone's behavior to indicate that we had just listened to the most radical official proposal in Islandian history. All of us heard what Mora said, and each of us doubtless made a different estimate of its importance. My knowledge of what was actually involved in the arrangement Mora outlined was so vague his proposal may have seemed more dangerous to me than to the others. I approved, but I was frightened. This was a road we had always avoided. Once taken, was there any way off it? My family, in the days when it knew something about such things, said it was a one-way journey to economic and mental peonage. This opinion still carried authority, although my brother and I, and even my father, had no experience to test it by. Also, this was a different world. Once again Islandia had to choose between going its own way and making some kind of common cause, and the price of the alternatives now seemed to be reversed.

Commiter took the offer with complete composure, exchanging some small talk with Dorna about Islandian wines as she refilled his glass. Then he turned to Mora. "Your idea sounds sensible and prudent to me, Lord Mora. I'll send it tonight if you like." Reaching into a pocket with his free hand, he drew out a newspaper clipping. "This may not be as much of a change of subject as it sounds, particularly when you remember that it's now spring in my country. It's from the *New York Times* of two days ago."

He put on his glasses and read,

"The new United States missile cruiser *Bangor* completed preliminary sea trials today and then put back into Boston for installation of final components of some of her complex electronic systems. A Navy spokesman described the two-day exercises as highly satisfactory. Official photographs of the *Bangor,* one of the few new surface vessels equipped with nuclear propulsion for greater seakeeping ability on detached missions, give the ship a surprising resemblance in silhouette to the older, conventional *Northampton.* The *Northampton,* which France ordered withdrawn from the traditional French Mediterranean harbor for British and American warships at Villefranche, is now attached to the Atlantic Fleet and also claims Boston as her home port.

"The *Bangor* is scheduled to undergo an exacting series of all-purpose trials late this summer. In the autumn the new ship will depart for a six-month cruise of the south Atlantic and south Pacific with ports of call, according to the Navy, welcome but not necessary."

At this point, Mora, taking Commiter and Dorn each by an elbow, moved away from us down the room. Walking between them, he looked as slender as the blade of grass you choose for a whistling reed when you place it between your thumbs. Dorna and Ross had moved to the dim inner reaches of the room for a discussion of their own. Watching these divisions with amusement, Morana raised her index finger to her chin in a gesture I remembered seeing her make as a child. "Secrets everywhere," she said, "but not the same ones. Come, let's have some of our own."

I followed her toward the moonlit windows at the end of the room nearest my own house. Her dress, crimson in the lamplight but black now under the moon, flowed around the supple motions of her waist and hips. This was the first time we had been alone, or almost alone, since the day we made love. Her nearness and the way she walked made it intolerable not to reach out for her. I was certain she was aware of this and took some pleasure from it.

When she turned and saw what must have been in my face, she winced and said, "Oh, I see. I did, didn't I? I'm sorry, Jonno. I shouldn't have done that to you. And I've done it to myself, too. I'm a fool. Let's go back."

"No," I said, "let's not. It will keep on happening until we can do something about it. We can stand it. Now, what was on your mind?"

She seemed very puzzled now, and hesitant. "Has my uncle . . . ?" she began, and then tried again. "Did Mora ask you to be ambassador to the United Nations?"

It was my turn to call myself a fool. This was an occurrence, not so much of unmeeting wishes right now, as of unmeeting thoughts which could produce a fine case of unmeeting wishes in another few minutes. She must have assumed that I had accepted the ambassadorship. She may even have urged Mora to offer it to me. She thought we would be in New York together soon and felt it was all right to tease me a little now.

"Yes, Mora offered me the post," I said, "and I was very proud that he did. But I said no to it, Morana. I'll try to tell you why."

When I had done my best, she said, "You're right, of course. You must be because you did it." She stood facing me, no longer pliant but upright and brittle. There was enough hurt and anger in her voice to tell me that my guess about her part in the thing wasn't far wrong. I had no answer to make. We confronted each other without speaking. A silence like this usually becomes more hostile as it goes on. But that didn't happen.

First her eyes softened and moved, in answer to some thought, and didn't look at me anymore with the cut-stone fixity of a statue. And then her body relaxed. She said, "I take it back, Jonno. That was cut-to-the-quick Morana talking. But you deserved it. You are still a righteous, moralizing Yankee. You think that hair shirt you're wearing is a toga. You think Islandia is really Rome when Horatius saved the Republic at the bridge. What do you know about America, or what would happen if you went to the United Nations? You've never been there. You're a pious fraud, Jonno." On top of this she smiled and put her hand in mine. "Even so, you probably *are* right. And your suggestion of Farrant is very good. I should have thought of him myself, but he's the kind of man I don't think of."

"So what will you do, Morana?"

"Go back to New York right away. The ground laying should start now. No matter who our ambassador is. And if it's Farrant, whether he wants me to or not, I'll have to stay with him for a while after he gets there."

"Morana, before you go to New York . . . ?"

"Yes?"

"We'll see each other?"

"Oh, yes," she said. "Right away isn't this minute. Yes."

✛

Something woke me out of solid sleep. When I raised myself on my elbows in bed, the house was quiet and no noise came in from outside. I didn't know what time it was, but the moon had set because my room was black and so, except for a star or two, was the sky beyond the window. Some internal clock told me it was near four in the morning.

Then I heard what had waked me, a brisk, echoing fusillade of blows on the main door downstairs. I felt I was on the inside of a drum. Some determined person was using the knob end of a stick. I climbed out of bed, put on a bathrobe and slippers more against the chill than for propriety, and felt my way down the stairwell. Then around the corner in the main hall I turned up the night lamp and swung the door open just as one more roll of timpani began.

With his stick raised to strike and his head covered by the hood of his parka, the burly man on my doorstep was a frightening thing to confront of a sudden. "Who are you and what do you want?" I asked in a voice I knew very well had alarm in it. He pushed back his hood, letting me recognize him as Lord Dorn's boatman.

"I'm sorry, Isla Lang," he said. "It's no time to rouse people. Isla Dorn sent me to ask you to join him and Isla Mora at the King's palace as quickly as you can."

I shut off all my questions, and said, "Lord Dorn is already there?"

"On his way, sir. With a cane and a man to help him. I think the man will get left behind. I put Isla Dorn ashore and then came here."

Within ten minutes I had dressed and was on my own way through the dark streets. Largely through the kind of choice imposed by accepted habit, there are no streetlights in The City and none in any other Islandian town except Nivenana, the newest industrial suburb, where aircraft are made. There is a growing feeling that The City should have a public light at difficult and important places, but this is years to come. An empty, lightless city on a black night is darker and more arbitrary than a rough field or even a thick woods. I walked as fast as I could, stubbing my feet on curbstones, sliding on the domes of over-height cobbles, and even taking wrong turnings.

"The King's palace," as Dorn's boatman called it, was a palace by the same kind of courtesy that made Tor a king. It was a substantial mansion and no more. Just the same, massive, dark, and forbidding, the house was formidable enough when I stood in front of it that night. There was no chink of light showing anywhere, and no sign of activity from inside the place or around it. I began to doubt the boatman's message. For several unpleasant seconds I hesitated before I raised the nerve to knock.

But with no delay the door opened inward onto a hall as dim as mine had been before I turned up the lamp, and at least six times the size of mine. The person admitting me was a vague shape beside the straight edge of the door, and not a big one. Family, or guest, or servitor, I couldn't tell, or even whether it was a man or woman. I had the one strong impression the person wasn't young, but until there is motion Islandian dress can disguise anything except height.

I said who I was and asked for Lord Dorn. I was led down the hall, around a corner to the right, then another to the left, and into a room in which there were lights and people talking. As my silent guide turned to leave, I could see now that he was a man, fragile and elderly. I wouldn't have known how to guess his position in the household.

In front of me were Dorn and Mora, looking as though they had merely been taken up from their conversation in Dorn's moonlit house six hours and more ago and set down here without any lapse of time. With them were two others; a friendly-looking, untidy, somewhat fleshy woman in her late thirties whom I took to be one of Tor's daughters, and a taut, short, sharp-faced man of about fifty.

Dorn saw me at once. Instead of beckoning to me, he left the others, crossed the room, and led me through the door a step or so down the hallway. "I'm very sorry to have routed you out at this hour," he said, "but we need your help. It was good of you to be so quick. I couldn't put the fact in writing. Tor died about three hours ago."

I made no response to this, and I don't think Dorn expected me to. Before he went on he gave me several moments, for which I was grateful, to accept the news and begin to consider the new situation.

"In there with Mora," he said, "are Tor's older daughter and his physician. Tor's wife is in bed under sedation."

I thought of Tor as I had seen him this afternoon—yesterday afternoon—and asked, "This was sudden. Was it unexpected?"

"The daughter says he was happy and well. The physician says he expected Tor to live for another fifteen years. What seems to have happened is an acute case of food poisoning."

Just then I knew there was something appallingly wrong. Dorn had been taking me over the jumps as gently as he could, letting me prepare each time for the next one. Now, though I couldn't see the rest of the course in detail, it began to look very rough.

I said, "All right, sir. I've begun to catch up with you. What really did happen?"

"We don't know yet. Hirk, the physician, thinks Tor was poisoned. That means an autopsy. In an hour or so, when Falda can be talked to, I hope she will consent to it. If she does, things will be much quicker and easier. But there must be an autopsy whatever she says." He paused, and then as though the words had a rotten taste, added, "To make things worse, young Tor isn't here and nobody knows where he is."

I thought about that for a moment and decided to leave it exactly as Lord Dorn had said it. "You spoke of needing my help. What can I do?"

He handed me a piece of paper with a list of eight names on it. They were all influential Council members, four with Mora and four with Dorn affiliations. "You know where these people live?" When I nodded, he said, "It's now a little after five. The doorman here has a pony ready for you. Please see these men now. Tell each of them that Tor died during the night. You don't know anything more than that. Ask them to come to Mora's house for breakfast and counsel at seven o'clock. And don't forget to come yourself."

✠

I'll not forget that ride through The City during the end of night and the coming of dawn. The interviews and encounters are not what I'll remember individually. They all become one. When you go in the small hours to the house of a distinguished man, hammer on his door, rouse him out of sleep, shock him senseless with a piece of unbelievable information, and then urgently charge him with a duty, he responds in the way the men before him on your list did and those after him will. He says, "I understand. Very well. I'll be there," or, "Thank you. You may count on me." That's all there is. You turn away, and he closes the door.

The things that will stay vivid and differentiated are the pony—a willing and friendly animal who thought this trip was a splendid improvement in his routine—The City itself as it began its daily metamorphosis from something only touched and felt into something also seen, and the changing weight in me of the word I was carrying.

Between the sorry laconic confrontations at one door after another, I began to consider myself as all manner of people, known and unknown, real and fictional, who had the job of telling other men what they didn't want to know. I was the messenger who reached the first Alwin with the news that the Bants had seized the Frays and raped his wife. I was Paul Revere pounding into Concord. I was Cassius stiffening the spines of the conspirators by warning them what would happen to them if they failed. I was Grimaud telling Athos, D'Artagnan, Aramis, and Porthos that Milady had a son who had just dispatched the Executioner of Bethune. I was one of those in Paris during the Terror who must have carried word of the latest arrests to the ones next in line. Before my last stop, there was a moment when I felt that maybe the best thing I could do would be to gallop through the streets shouting, "The King is dead! Where is the King?" My pony would have liked that.

And then, when the eighth door swung shut on one more man reduced to numbness, all my impersonations and fancies stopped. I relapsed into nonfeeling myself, rode home, made arrangements for the return of the pony, and then bathed and changed clothes.

The Council convened at ten o'clock as scheduled. Dorn and Mora sat side by side at the table where Farrant had been yesterday, and where each of them and many other Moras and Dorns had sat before. At the last stroke of the hour, Mora rose. The floor and the crowded galleries became silent within seconds.

"We will present the day's business in order of functional necessity," he said. "But last night there was a national and personal tragedy. All members of this Council should know of this before they are asked to act in any way. Tor Twenty-one died early this morning." There was a sigh all through the chamber, and then a taking of breath, as though the building itself were stirring. It was hard to tell what it meant, except that rumor had spread fast and wide. Otherwise there would have been a stillness and then . . . "O-O-oo-hh."

Mora listened to the response of his audience and then continued matter-of-factly, "An autopsy is being performed, and we expect the physician's report in another hour or so. Tor Twenty-two is away from The City and has not yet been reached. News of the King's death will be broadcast over Islandia radio at ten-thirty this morning and at intervals throughout the day."

He picked up a sheet of notes from the table. "One task of overriding importance is to establish a new government at once. Yesterday, after the vote of no confidence, Isla Dorn and I consulted with members of the Council. We are prepared to form a government that will handle the country's affairs with energy, discretion, and purpose. It will carry my name, but in fact it will be a Mora-Dorn regime, the first of its kind. In general, and insofar as these things can be separated—which is not very far—Isla Dorn will deal with our domestic life and I will devote myself to the problems and opportunities beyond our borders.

"In validating a new government, it is usual for the clerk to call the roll of Council members. But before he does, we would be glad to entertain any questions from members."

At once three men rose from their places. As Mora recognized their political spread—one Dorn man, one of his own, and the third uncommitted—he began to smile as he did when he was truly pleased. The smile gradually consumed his face—not like the Cheshire cat who vanished from behind it—until everything was relish and pleasure. He said, "I'm glad I remembered the procedure. It's been a long time. You may all be raising the same question. If so, there's hope for us. We'll see." He nodded toward the independent, saying, "Camia first. Isla Trine?"

Camia is a large province in extent and population, and it grows many of the seasonal fruits and vegetables The City eats, along with much of its milk and cheese. It must be on reasonably good terms with any government, but not deeply involved with one in particular. On their side, governments need to deal gently with Camia up to a point.

"My concern," Trine said, "is whether it is legally possible—constitutionally possible may be the better way to put it—to inspan a new government when we have no King, no formal Head of State, to sanction it."

Mora glanced at the other two members who had indicated they had questions. They both nodded and sat down. "I am glad this issue has been raised from the floor," Mora said, "and from all sections of the Council. It was on our agenda, but it is much better to have it put this way than for us gratuitously to justify something that wasn't challenged." He looked toward Dorn and said, "Your knowledge here is better founded than anyone's. Will you reply to Isla Trine?"

Dorn could have done it sitting down, but he rose to his feet, slowly and seemingly easily, summoning back momentarily a young athlete's ability to make one leg do the work of two. He stood towering in front of the Council. "There are two possible answers to questions of the kind raised by Isla Trine and other members. The first is that in unique and dangerous circumstances a state has a preconstitutional right and duty to maintain itself." Dorn's voice, quiet and restrained, flowed through the silent chamber like a deep tide. It suggested the recurrence of original things. When he said, "This is not such a case," there was no easing of the tension.

"The Islandian Constitution, I don't need to remind anyone, is not a written document. It is an accretion of customs and precedents, some of them ill at ease with each other if not mutually contradictory. The point here is that what are precedents for us were themselves, in their time, new things based on earlier customs or memories. Seen in this way, our Constitution is not a set of rules defining what we can do, nor a limitation upon action of any kind, but a guide for approaching and performing whatever needs to be done. Any action of the Council that has not run counter to the spirit of generally accepted custom has always been considered valid.

"In my opinion we don't need to look for specific authority to do what is proposed here. But we can find it if we want. The Council is historically senior and constitutionally superior to the present monarchy. After the mandate of the great Assembly, the Council appointed the first Tor and set the terms of tenure for him and his successors. It can also alter or abolish those terms, presumably after consulting the people. In other words, the Council is its own master and the King its creature.

"But if we don't want to invoke that ultimate sanction, we need to refer only to the duties the King now performs.

He convenes the Council. That has already been done.
He prorogues the Council session at the end of the term.
That is still several months away. In addition, as a lesser
formality, he usually, but by no means always, ratifies
acts of the Council. In times of illness, absence for other
reasons, or delayed succession—such as this—countless
perfectly legal acts of the Council have gone onto the
record without the King's seal. The act of choosing a new
government is no different in kind from all the others.
On any of these grounds we have more than adequate
authority or precedent for the business before us."

He sat down. Council members seemed surprised, relieved, and completely satisfied. They had had a severe
shock. There were still many uncertainties. They weren't
ready for a testing decision. They had wanted to deal with
the change of regime as a routine matter and were afraid
that it wasn't possible. Now they knew it could be done.
It suited their mood. It was obvious just the same to anyone who listened, and there were undoubtedly many, that
Dorn had used the occasion to provide justification for
genuinely radical moves if the need came. Later that day,
Commiter told me he had never encountered so masterly
and concise a presentation of any constitutional system.

Meanwhile, the clerk began to call the roll of members.
It seemed likely that the vote would be unanimous. Of
course, this did not mean that a vote in favor of the new
government was a promise to support its policies. While
the clerk was still in the first part of the roster, an attendant came down the center aisle and gave a paper to
Mora. I saw him read it and hand it to Dorn. Dorn read it
then, wrote something on a separate piece of paper, and
gave both back to Mora. He put some words on a third
piece of paper and handed all of them to the attendant
who went out the way he had come, and just as un-
obtrusively.

At the conclusion of the roll call, Mora stood and said,
"We are now a government. These are difficult and dangerous days. We thank you for your confidence and, in
our turn, are confident that, with your support, we will
find ways through the dangers, and answers to our problems. We don't expect this to be easy.

"As was indicated in yesterday's debate, we will at once
make public the general findings of the survey of Islandia
Bay. We will also make immediate application for membership in the United Nations.

"But we have much stranger and even more urgent

matters to deal with. While you were recording your votes with the Clerk, I received a message from the Porter's office. As you know, there is a radio there. The regular program of music that runs from ten to eleven was broken into twice, once at ten-twenty and again at ten-forty, with the request that all radios be kept turned on at two o'clock. Tor Twenty-two would make an important statement to the country."

Mora paused and let the implications of this sink in. Without official permission or connivance, there is no way to insert an announcement in a radio program, but an unauthorized transmitter could intrude. Also, at two o'clock Islandia radio goes off the air for two hours. The chamber and the galleries, which had begun to relax after the vote, now grew as stiff and brittle as uncut, frozen grass in the winter. The only sound was the squeak of a chair in one place and then another.

"I don't know what this means," Mora said, "if it means anything. But I think we should all find out. From the facts we have, this appears to be a message from an illicit transmitter. Isla Dorn has given orders that the two o'clock broadcast of Tor Twenty-two, or whoever he is, is not to be jammed, or interfered with by electrical stoppages. In another twenty minutes or so, Islandia radio will announce that it was intruded upon, that it knows nothing of any statement by Tor Twenty-two, but that at the request of the government it suggests that Islandians listen at two o'clock, radio time.

"A radio will be in operation in this chamber by then. It is now almost eleven-thirty. There is a great deal to be done in the next two hours. I would welcome a vote to recess until one-forty-five."

As the members and spectators gathered to talk in small, puzzled groups, or edged singly toward the doors, Dorn beckoned to me. As I moved against the stream of people, I passed Commiter making determinedly for the street. His expression was grim, and he didn't speak, but he put his hand on my shoulder as we went by each other. One's mind wanders oddly in a crisis. I found myself wondering how long it would take him to code the message he would request Islandia radio to send.

Dorn said to me, "We've heard nothing yet about the autopsy. A *no* or a *yes* will do for now, but we have to have that much. Please go to the hospital and get something out of that doctor."

Outdoors it was a fine day, bright, cold, and windy.

The walk cheered me. I'd never been in this, or any other hospital. The main part, for the living, seemed reasonably human from the little I saw of it, but where they sent me was something else. I went down a steep, narrow stair into a small, low anteroom some twenty feet below ground. The air was still, and heavy with a smell I'd never encountered, death mixed with preservative. The stone floors and walls looked damp and slippery. Actually they weren't; I felt them more than once in the endless hour and more I spent there. The place was dimly lit by two kerosene lamps with chimneys but no shades.

At a table at one end sat a gaunt elderly man in a gray cotton tunic. He was the only person there. I went up to him and told him who I was and what I had come for. He paid no attention. I told him again, slower and louder. This time he looked up at me, pushed himself erect, and shambled off down a dim corridor behind the table. When he came back, he muttered something that sounded like "A little while," and sat down again.

I tried sitting on a wooden bench along the wall. Then I tried pacing the floor. After twenty minutes I asked the old man to go again. He did, reluctantly, and returned with the same mumble. After another twenty-five minutes I urged him to go a third time, but he shrugged his shoulders and stayed where he was.

"Then I'll go myself," I said, starting around the table.

At this he actually spoke to me for the first time. "Go if you like. It won't do any good. And you won't like it there." There was something surprisingly like sympathy in his voice. I looked down at him, and I didn't go.

Eventually, slow, heavy footsteps sounded in the corridor and the doctor himself appeared, looking pale and very tired. He nodded to me in recognition but not with cordiality, and merely shook his head in response to my question. Waving the old man away from the table, he sat down and wrote several lines on a piece of paper. This he folded and addressed on its unbroken side. Next he held a stick of gray sealing wax in the column of heat over the lamp, daubed the soft end across the loose edge of the paper, and stamped the wax with a small seal. Finally he handed me the missive and turned away, still without speaking. By then I was so nearly sick I didn't think of being offended. I went up the stairs and out as fast as I could without really running. If the brisk, clean day had seemed fine before, it was glorious now.

It was after one o'clock when I got back to the Council

building. Workmen were busy in the Council chamber. I stepped my way across wires and cables there to get to the King's rooms which Mora and Dorn had taken over as temporary office quarters.

I gave the sealed paper to Mora, who glanced from it to me and back again before breaking it open. Then he read aloud, "Tor's death resulted from ingestion of an extraneous toxic agent, not from food poisoning or organic natural failure. Prolonged chemical analysis may identify the lethal agent."

He passed the note to Dorn, saying, "His chemistry will make gold before we get an answer." Then he looked more closely at me. "You must have had a trying time. There is lunch on the sideboard there. Help yourself, please. The excellent beer is from Mr. Commiter, whose generosity is equalled only by his intuition."

The beer was very good indeed. It and the food began to put some heart back into me. While I ate, Mora and Dorn sat opposite each other, writing and trading drafts of papers back and forth. Messengers came and went.

Dorn put his pen down, stretched, and looked across the room in my direction. I was finishing a second plate of meat and salad and a second bottle of beer. Also, having been away from it for an hour, I was going over my experience in the morgue underneath the hospital and was beginning to have second thoughts about the doctor. Some of this showed, because Dorn said sharply, "What is it, Lang? Something's just come on your mind."

I said, "I didn't like the doctor. I didn't like the place. I didn't like what happened. But the doctor had been there all night and all morning. He's supposed to be competent. He may have felt the way I did, only much worse. I think I'm doing him an injustice. We demand a report from him, of course. Perhaps it means civil war. On his authority. I wouldn't want to say even as much as that," and I pointed to the unsatisfactory document that was bothering us. "He's passed on all the responsibility he can. I can't blame him. He knows now everything he's going to know. That's why he behaved that way. He's never going to say anything more. It's up to the government to call it murder, or suicide, or inadvertence." It was time for me to get back to my seat in the chamber, but something else occurred to me. "I suppose Hanno's people will try to get a bearing on that transmitter. Are they any good at it?"

"I don't know," Dorn said. "Hanno will say they are."

✠

The galleries had looked full in the morning. Now they were jammed tight. People were standing two and three deep at the balustrades in back of the seats, and some were sitting on the risers in the aisles, their knees turned in against the person in the first seat in the row.

The Council chamber's new radio was turned on at ten minutes before two. For five minutes no bulletin of farm, fishing, and marketplace information ever had a more attentive, distinguished, and ignorant audience. At five minutes before the hour this program was unceremoniously stopped, and an older-sounding, more formal voice took over.

"We interrupt to bring you our latest information on the King's death and the attendant circumstances. A preliminary medical report to the government shows definitely that the death of Tor Twenty-one did not result from natural organic failure, or from food poisoning as that is generally understood. An unusual toxic substance, not yet identified chemically, was the lethal agent. Although accident and suicide have not been excluded as possibilities, neither of them now seems to be a reasonable explanation. In a separate and earlier statement the government disclosed that Tor Twenty-two was not at home at the time of his father's death, and has not been in touch with his family or the government since.

"Our scheduled four o'clock concert of woodwinds and continuo will be delayed this afternoon. Instead, at that time, the First Minister of the government, Isla Mora, will speak to you directly from the Council chamber over these facilities. Islandia radio now leaves the air. Good afternoon."

I knew now why I'd had to pick my way over cables coming in from the hospital, and why there had been so many workmen. I was giving the announcer good marks for not having described all this as unprecedented, when it crossed my mind that this would never have occurred to him. In a custom-built society like ours, the occasional, truly revolutionary thing gets done as a matter of course.

There was silence for about a minute, then a scratching from the radio, and finally a man's voice. "This is your King, Tor Twenty-two. It is gracious of Isla Mora and Isla

Dorn, instigators of my father's murder, not to interfere with this broadcast. They have not yet accused me of their own crime, but they will. As you have just heard, they have already implicated me. It is true that I was not at home when my father died. I fled The City to escape the death that was prepared for both of us, and which my father would not believe. I am alive to speak to you now because, for two days before my flight, I ate nothing.

"Centuries ago, after the disappearance of Alwin Seventeen, in their own interest and to the great hurt of the country, the Dorn and Mora families, along with lesser ones, began the systematic enfeebling of the monarchy. For most of the time since, the Dorn and Mora factions have ruled the country in alternation, disagreeing only to agree that power, wealth, position, education, and travel abroad were privileges restricted to them. To do this they have kept Islandia backward, undeveloped, primitive, ignorant, and completely out of touch with the great progressive forces transforming the rest of the world. Only in the last few years, through the neutrality of the Farrant regime and the active help of the monarchy, have a few fresh and vigorous ideas found their way into the country.

"These signals of progress and emancipation to come have been welcomed eagerly by the people. Mora and Dorn have met them with fear and hostility. You have seen how these men, with the help of a *ci-devant* American imperialist, accomplished Farrant's downfall. Now for the first time in history they have banded together formally. They wish to destroy the monarchy altogether and rivet their control upon the country unbreakably. You will see.

"For myself, I repudiate the fiction that makes the King and the country into the toys of the men who dominate the Council. Alwin Seventeen is not missing. He has been dead seven hundred years. I am his direct heir. I claim his authority until we have rid ourselves of Mora, Dorn, and their henchmen, and until Islandia is a full partner in the work of the great modern world. At that time I will return the kingship to the people, and Islandians will decide for themselves how they want to be governed and what associations the country should have in the outer world.

"For the time being, we should watch, work, and be quiet. Think of what I have said as the government makes its moves. I have many supporters, and their number is growing fast. Those who wish me well and want to join me will know how to find me. Those who wish me ill will find me invisible. But I will appear to them, with the power to destroy them, when they least expect it. Thank you."

The radio went silent and was turned off. The quiet in the chamber began to give way to excited talk. Before this could take on a life of its own, Mora cut it off with two hard raps of his gavel. "That was very interesting," he said in an informal, conversational tone. "I learned at least three useful things. Someone has declared a rebellion. He has a pretty taste in rhetoric. And what we heard was not a recording, as I thought it might be." This drew some uncertain laughter. "Now, we have serious decisions before us and a limited time to reach them before I follow our talented opponent on the air. Spectators are welcome to stay, but, please, no conversations among you or comments from you."

Mora and Dorn then began to present and develop their proposals. Obviously these had been carefully thought out. They needed no modification because of what we had just heard, although the discussion of them was much influenced by it. The arguments came down to a single issue, one drastic demand by Mora and Dorn—a new national mandate on the order of the one in the year 1280.*

The opposition was immediate and strong. It was based on two grounds, one actually only a milder version of the other. The extremists held that this was a time of civil crisis and rebellion, complicated by severe international dangers. The government should take a tough position. Without declaring martial law, it should bring the military into all the domestic affairs of the country. It was interesting that none of the military Council members spoke in support of this policy.

The other dissenters felt that it was unwise and risky to go to the people now. Why ask for more trouble than there is? The Council and the government had more than ample authority to deal with problems of this sort, or any other. Use the authority, get beyond these troubles, and then go to the people for a mandate of approval.

At this point Mora and Dorn set to work. They took the approach that this was not a poor or ill-advised time to go to the people. On the contrary, there could never be a better or more necessary one. In days of trouble the most valuable asset you could have was mutual confidence and

* See Appendix IV: National Referenda, pp. 219–20.

trust among the people themselves, and between the people and the government. Going to the voters now would create this. No enemy would expect it or be prepared for it. The country would gain a sense of common purpose, determination, and shared responsibility. But all this and much more could be forfeited—lost to the promoters of mistrust and resentment—if the government allowed itself to be frightened into military controls, or if it tried to impose its own solution for ratification later.

The two men, of course, were completely different in all the obvious ways of size, shape, manner, voice; and just as different in the not so obvious ones of assessing and dealing with difficulties. They shared tact, resourcefulness, and intellectual force; and each had an individual felicity of expression that became increasingly characteristic as it was stimulated by the other.

Now they took on all doubters and opponents, supplementing each other's arguments shrewdly and without hesitation, and making no fumbles in referring questions back and forth between them. It was an exciting, convincing performance with a style all its own. One surprising thing to me was that, working together, Dorn and Mora both displayed a wit and good humor I had never known them show when they were opposing each other.

Shortly before four o'clock the proposals were brought to a vote. They were passed, by no means unanimously, but by a remarkably strong majority. Then a most unusual thing happened. Applause, clearly intended for Mora and Dorn, began of itself in the Council, was taken up even by those members who had voted *no,* and spread resoundingly through the galleries. The two ministers looked startled, pleased and, for the first time in memory, embarrassed.

At four o'clock the radio was turned on. We listened to the studio announcer with his ritual words, and then we saw Mora turn to a microphone that was being put in front of him on the table. After that we watched him talk, but we heard him, like the rest of the country, through the radio speaker. Or at least some of us watched him. Many others stared at the radio, as though Mora was really in the box where the sound came from.

"On this unhappy day in our history," he began, "this is Mora speaking to you as chief minister of the new government. You will have no difficulty believing I am who I say I am since this *is* Islandia radio, the woodwind concert *has* been delayed, and because, so I've been informed, the provincial office of every Isla has by now verified this broadcast by telephone calls to The City.

"I make this point because the relative credence you give to the things you are hearing today will be of immeasurable importance to you and the country.

"There is no certainty that it was Tor Twenty-two who spoke to us all at two o'clock this afternoon over an illicit transmitter. This will have occurred to you. For my part I regret to say that I think it was Tor, and that he spoke of his own free will, although not necessarily on his own initiative. Believing this, I cannot ignore some of his assertions.

"Tor Twenty-two, or the man using his name, said that Dorn and I, the government, would accuse him of killing the King. There is no doubt in my mind, or Dorn's, that the King was murdered—poisoned. But we do not charge young Tor with regicide and patricide, and we will not unless and until there is a great deal more evidence incriminating him. Yet the speaker this afternoon was certainly correct in saying that young Tor was implicated in the assassination. He has implicated himself by his absence and by what he has said, or what I must assume he has allowed to be said in his name. There are other possible explanations, it is true, and we can hope that a favorable one is established.

"The two o'clock speaker said that Dorn and I instigated the King's murder. To this I say merely we did not. Here, you will have to choose whom to believe. In making your choice, however, there is one useful guide when there is little evidence. Consider the crime in terms of the question, *to what purpose?*"

Mora said very little here about himself and Dorn, except to point out that, even if Islandians considered them capable of murder, it would be hard to imagine any aim they might have that could not be better accomplished by supporting the late Tor's regime than by destroying it.

"But this is not true of the man who spoke to us earlier. He has a purpose. It is a clear, frightening, and visionary one that requires as a first step the end of the limited monarchy we have known for centuries. He offers us absolute rule, and a path of bloodshed, civil war, and invasion from abroad. He says, and he is right, that there are others, inside the country and out, who want what he wants. He may believe himself when he tells us that he will return his powers to the people in the end, but by that time he will no longer possess them. If he begins to succeed, the sad lessons of all history are that Islandians will not be masters of their own affairs again for a long, long time.

"There are other recent and related events that should be more generally known now." Mora then told the story of the Islandia Bay survey and the episode of the trawler. Next he described the series of incidents that seemed intended to divide the country along lines of Dorn versus Mora hostility, and to stir up anti-Western feeling. "We have determined reformers among us," he said, "and we are also surrounded by them. Some are clumsier than others.

"The attacks were all ugly. In time they might have worked. But as things stand, Mr. Ross is now much respected in Reeves. And no familied Islandian, no Dorn, or Mora, or Fanning, or Hyth, or Herso, or any other finds it easy to believe that a native enemy has hired an anonymous band to frighten and humiliate him. He wouldn't do it himself. Familied people amount to considerably more than three-quarters of us. It is this great majority that was supposed to be alarmed, splintered, and finally made fratricidal by these cruel little violences. But the plan was cut short by events."

Mora sipped from the water glass on the table, exchanged a penciled note and reply with Dorn, and continued, "When the Council rose yesterday afternoon, the coming of a Mora-Dorn government was certain. This marked the total failure of the stratagem that would have embroiled the country along old factional lines. And within a few hours the King was murdered. The sequence is not accidental. It would be dangerously childish to think so. This is another blow from the inside intended to break the country apart. It is a hard and hurtful blow. This tragedy can be fatally divisive if we permit it. With your help we will not permit it.

"In this government neither I nor Dorn takes precedence. The order of our names is a convenience for us. At an easier time we will be glad to explain why. But now there are things still to be said, and immediate things to be done. Dorn knows these better than I. Isla Dorn." He pushed the microphone gently down the table.

Dorn's voice, no louder than Mora's, seemed to fill the radio and overflow it. I've spoken before of his natural voice, and how at times it echoed the ocean. Now, with this quality somehow emphasized by the radio, we might have been listening to the tides of Winder suddenly given the ability to speak.

"The man who spoke in Tor's name," Dorn said, "told us the Dorn and Mora families, chiefly, shaped this country to their will and their advantage. I raise the point not to defend my own ancestors in particular, but to vindicate all our ancestors. Any reading of our history that is not intentionally slanted shows that the country was made and maintained by the Islandian people, all of them. Its virtues are their virtues, and its weaknesses are theirs."

He then gave much the same review of constitutional history that he made to the Council that morning. "We have discussed and debated our problems here today. We have come to the conclusion that this is the time, in spite of the risks, for the Islandian people to reaffirm, or redefine if they wish, the national society they created in twelve hundred eighty. We are several times more numerous than we were seven centuries ago, so it is fortunately impossible to think of assembling all eligible and interested voters on the plain between the Reeves River and the Aira, as was done then. We can vote better in our own provinces, following local procedures.

"We will ask you to vote on two questions. First, the present Council and this government want a mandate of approval from the country. To ascertain this, every Isla will stand for reelection. If you return the present Council intact, or with few changes, we will take this as the mandate we hope for. If you elect a substantially different Council that, naturally, will be a vote of no confidence, and a new government will be formed to satisfy the new majority.

"The second question on which we want your decision, as in twelve hundred eighty, concerns the monarchy. Do you want to continue the present form of limited kingship, or do you want to abolish the institution altogether?

"Parenthetically, if you want an absolute monarchy, an election is redundant, and no constitutional government would put the choice on a ballot.

"In case the country decides to continue the monarchy, there are two important procedural questions on which everyone should vote, no matter how he felt about the monarchy itself. Should the throne be left vacant until the fitness of Tor Twenty-two is determined? Or should the office be given now to Tora, our late King's eldest child, and in succession to the line of Bering, her husband? There is only one precedent for this, but it is strong and important.

"Voting information will be posted tomorrow in all provincial government offices. As usual, provinces may vote when they choose, but this time within a limit of ten days. A longer period of uncertainty would be most unwise. Good afternoon, my countrymen. Thank you, and think well."

Two days before the voting in the Frays, Morana left for New York to prepare the ground for Farrant's arrival two weeks later. She thought the job would take her six weeks to two months all told. I planned to go home for the election. My father and my brother both told me it wasn't necessary, but I wanted to be there to be seen and to answer questions if there were any.

After the epochal session of broadcasting from the chamber, the Council rose for the ten-day period in which the elections would be held and certified. The weather stayed fine for several of those days, and Morana and I spent most of them together. There was no longer any reason for us not to see each other.

In these new circumstances, it didn't take us long to think of how few the days were before what began to seem like an interminable time apart. We made bad jokes about it, calling it a case of separating wishes, and a crisis of unexpected expectations. Our very real regrets gave a sharp edge to pleasure, but except for moments of different and obscure foreboding, we took what we had in good spirit and recognized our self-pity for what it was.

Sometimes we took walks through The City, and on others we rode out through the tan and brown countryside of early winter. One wonderfully warm, soft, out-of-season afternoon we even took my boat out on the bay. That time Dorna and Ross were with us.

A light breeze out of the northwest moved us along at a gentle two or three knots. North and east of us, four or five miles away, The City rose up blurred and almost white in the haze along the horizon. "Just now it looks like San Francisco," Ross said. He trailed his hand over the side of the boat into the water, and took it out quickly. "Chilly," he said.

The water was cold, even on the surface. If the warm air had been brisk enough to throw spray on us, the pleasant sail would have become an ordeal. "I keep forgetting it's only Indian summer," Ross said, "not the real thing."

The phrase was new to me, and I liked it. I asked Ross

what it meant. "The term is used pretty loosely now," he said. "Most people will use it for a spell of fine, unseasonably warm weather like this any time from late September to almost Christmas. But the purists say that Indian summer can come only after the first solid freezes and before the first heavy snow."

"How did it get its name?"

"Nobody knows, but it was a long time ago. My guess is it had something to do with being unpredictable, not to be trusted." He smiled. "If we were naming it now, we'd probably call it Chinese summer."

We turned back at a place from which we could fetch my dock in one long reach across the wind. The easy motion of the boat and the hours in the warm, soft air were making us all drowsy and increasingly silent. But about a mile from home, Ross stirred himself and said, "Jon, do you remember those broadcasts of fables at Reeves?"

"Yes."

"They're still on the air. I listen to them. Most of them are in the classical form, but now and then some have had direct dialogue. Remember that?"

"Yes."

"Well, there's an interesting thing. They read five or six fables on each of these programs. For some time, one or maybe two would be unconventional, would have direct speech. But for almost a week now there hasn't been an unconventional fable."

I wasn't following all this very closely. Morana, sitting on the stern thwart, had the tiller. With my head resting in the angle between her leg and the thwart, I was down on the cockpit duckboards, knees up, trimming the sail to her steering. Now and then Morana took her right hand from my shoulder and touched my face.

I said to Ross, "Maybe the authors have run out of inspiration for a while."

"Maybe," he admitted, "but the unconventional fables stopped the day Farrant's government fell."

"You see a connection?"

"Over the radio the man who claimed to be young Tor said it was a time to watch and work and be quiet. He could have been referring to the series of attacks before the King's murder. I think the unconventional fables may have been signals."

"You mean they were in code?"

"No, nothing as systematic as that. I think they gave

the word to certain people to report somewhere for in-structions, or to carry out some action already planned."

I was doubtful and asked why you couldn't do the same thing with the classical fables. "You could," Ross said, "but they're so stylized and so familiar you'd have to use a set code. That has disadvantages over the radio if you want something quick and secure. No, probably the un-conventional fable form itself was the principal signal. Then it would be simple to drop two or three necessary specifics into it. There would be so few of them, and they would be so arbitrary no outsider could read them."

I thought this was all thin and fanciful, but I didn't say so. Morana brought the boat in to a nice upwind landing, and we dropped the sail and stowed the gear. Tomorrow the craft would go into the boathouse until spring. Dorna and Ross both said goodbye to Morana then; they wouldn't see her again before she left.

That night rain came in on the heels of Ross' Indian summer. The storm in turn blew off in the small hours, and I got up to a bright, still day of ringing cold. The rain puddles were solid, smooth ice.

This was Morana's last day, and she had a full round of appointments and conferences. I didn't see her until late afternoon when she came to my house. There, in the comfortable, slightly shabby main room we did what we had done twice before in the last few days—sat with our backs to the wood fire and watched the twilight slowly eat up the gold and then the crimson over the bay, and finally turn it all dark.

It probably wasn't the best prescription for this evening, but when Morana came in, obviously low in spirit, this was what she said she wanted. It did save her from talk-ing until she was ready. She didn't say a dozen words in all the time before I put on lights and we turned into the room.

Then she said, "You'll have to bear with me, Jonno. I'm not fit to be with. It's partly Farrant. All afternoon with that precise, nice—oh, I don't know what to call him— little man. 'Please do this. I hope this can be arranged this way. And on no account do so-and-so.' But he'll do well enough when he gets to New York. He's frightened now, and I don't blame him. I think I am, too—differ-ently."

We sat down to a supper of fish stew, mushroom ome-let, cheese, and a carafe of Camian white wine. At the end we took the rest of the wine and the cheese over nearer to the fire. Morana was more at ease now, but not more cheerful. "We've all done the best we can," she said, "but I have a sad feeling it isn't enough, that nothing's going to work. Our troubles come from what used to be our strengths. I'm afraid they're too old and habitual, too far gone for us to cure them. And we've seen to it that we have no friends. Maybe we'll have a respite until spring, but then . . ." I agreed with her. I didn't need to comment. A nod was enough.

"You don't know young Tor, do you?" she asked.

"Only by sight. He's a handsome man."

"Most of them are, all branches, men and women—when they're young. Some turn out to be dull and decent like Tor Twenty-one. Others don't." I knew the history of the Tor family was spotted with original kinds of eccentricity—some of them reputedly ugly—although the facts were hard to come by. Morana was saying, "I do know young Tor. Better than my uncle does. It was certainly Tor speaking over the radio."

I knew now I hadn't really doubted it. "Do you think he poisoned his father?"

"Perhaps not. At least he went along with it after it was done."

"What's he like?"

"Charming and plausible. Physically impressive. Selfish. Thoughtless. And ambitious, too, but I don't think there's much real determination to go with it. He'd make a willing tool—if he didn't know he was one—and he'd turn in your hand unless you kept a tight hold on him."

"Do you know anything about his cousins? I hear gossip about them sometimes."

"A little. I spent part of a summer in Winder when I was fifteen or sixteen. There are three of them. Two are brothers, and they must be in their thirties now. The other is from a different branch, and he's a few years younger." She paused, and then added, "I haven't thought of that visit for a long time. You forget how strongly some of the Winder separatists feel."

That was quite true. The rest of the country never heard much about them, but for centuries there had been stubborn, isolated little uprisings of Winderese who wanted independence, or joint sovereignty. The problem was the residual price of having solved a greater difficulty long ago.*

* See Appendix VI: Winder, pp. 221–22.

Morana watched me pour the rest of the Camian wine into our glasses, and said, "The Tor families in Winder now are in a hateful way. They don't amount to much in Winder anymore, except for the family name."

Morana led me to see an unfamilied arrangement of a different kind—people who were once fine shipbuilders and good fishermen, and had come gradually to be nothing. Long ago they counted on preferment from their relatives in the new Tor monarchy. To a certain extent they got it, but not on the national scale they wanted. Very slowly over the generations they receded, keeping largely with themselves, turning their energies away from what they could do and building toward the elaboration of a theory of betrayal and sectional bitterness.

The two Tor brothers Morana had known were certainly wild, mostly as savages are. They grew up on the mainland, near the base of the arm of islands that forms the Winder peninsula. They loved that desolate, foggy wilderness, and knew all the rocks, and crevices, and the high tops. They took their boat into the sea caves and through the shallow channels, the ones where the ebb tides run away from each other and the incoming tides meet and fight over the spiny stones.

One of the two, Ingo, used to sail up to Sulliaba now and then, where he would stay for months at a time. The other, Tirk, worked intermittently at the government shipyards.

"But, Jonno," Morana said, "that was a long time ago. They were handsome men. Ingo was taller and heavier, but they both had thick, black hair, and bold, narrow faces. They would try to frighten me with stories about how they were wreckers and pirates. They did frighten me, but I remember I didn't believe them."

✠

When we put down our glasses for the last time, empty, and stood up from the low table, I wasn't sure which way we would go. It might be down the stairs and out, or it might be to my room. Morana could read my wish easily in my face, but she gave no indication of her own. I didn't ask her. Words now could lead to a scene of unmeeting wishes, and a kind of exasperated frustraton which we would hate to give each other as a farewell present. She would let me know without any of this, if she didn't want me now. When I took her arm, she moved closer to me and came with me, very quietly, to my room.

In our recent days together we had made love here in a number of different moods. First we had simply been passionately needy of each other. Other times we were languorous and savoring or sportive and gay. Once she deliberately teased me and then resisted until we were entwined in a flame of violence.

But all of those were now in a separate compartment of our lives, one to be reopened someday, we hoped. As we lay beside each other in the warmth and the half light, our arms lightly around each other, Morana said softly, "Jonno, I don't want to go to New York. I have a feeling, foreboding." And then trying a little joke, but sounding sad, "Now I have *apia* and *ania* all in one. I don't want to lose you."

Tonight our feeling for each other was intensely gentle, even elegiac, if you can use the idea in connection with anything so leapingly and incandescently of the present moment as physical love. Just the same, and surprisingly, when we rose from each other and set about getting ready for Morana to go home, our melancholy was gone and we were cheerful.

When Morana finished dressing, she came to me, put the palms of her hands on my cheeks, and kissed me on the mouth. "You don't need to take me home, Jonno. I can find the way by myself."

"No, you can't," I said. "I won't let you. Besides, somebody might steal you away."

✠

Morana's plane was to leave at eleven in the morning. I drove her out to the airfield in the only vehicle that Lang House possessed, a light, well-sprung cart which was almost never used. My pony, Lok, tolerated the harness and the shafts, but he let me know that he was shamed and this service was an indignity. He shambled along at a reasonable pace, head and tail down, until we were about a mile from the airfield. There, where some small roadways joined, he saw two or three other contraptions like ours drawn by ponies as dejected as he was.

Lok was very quick. His head and tail came up and he

pulled his legs in under him. He began to reach and drive like a trotting horse. When he had the field clearly beaten, Lok whinnied once for all the world to hear, and brought us up to the airfield shed in frantic style. Morana, laughing and tearful, jumped to the ground, put her arm over Lok's neck, laid her face against his bony head, said something into one of his active ears, and then gave him something to eat which he thought highly of.

This was an airfield, not an airport. The only buildings were a closed shed for passengers and an open-ended shelter for the fuel pump and the service truck. The military were supposed to have some bases that would handle big conventional transports and jets, but I hadn't seen them. This airfield was a field, a big one on smooth, solid ground and with good turf. Way out in the middle of it was a concrete and macadam X, one strip running northeast-southwest and the other northwest-southeast. From where we were, we could see the purple and orange DC-3 of St. Anthony Airways lined up for a northwest takeoff.

Morana would make two changes of planes before she landed in New York. In St. Anthony she could choose between BOAC and Air France, where either would take her by jet-prop, through a long and unpredictable series of ports of call, to some major city in South America, northern Africa, or southern Europe. Between here and St. Anthony the DC-3 would fly over the ocean most of the way because neither Sulliaba nor Mobono permitted planes to or from Islandia to use its airspace.

We walked slowly out to the plane over the short grass, hummocky and yellow-green with frost. "Morana," I said, looking at her capacious Islandian winter clothes, and then thinking of wet, subtropical Mobono, and then of something else, "what kind of clothes do you wear in New York?"

She stopped in the middle of the field, looked at me in a startled way as though I'd pulled her out of a very different train of thought, and then smiled. "I dress like a good American girl, of course. What she wears, I wear. No matter what it looks like. Except—at the U.N., and public occasions, and receptions I'm so Islandian you wouldn't know me."

At a somewhat slower pace we went on toward the plane across the seemingly endless field. "Jon," she said, the first time in days she had used that form of my name, "until yesterday I hadn't thought of the Tor cousins in Winder for years. I told you I didn't know the third

cousin. That's true. But last night when I got home I
thought of something else. The night we were attacked at
the elevator, you remember the tall man?" I nodded.
"There is some resemblance, I'm sure. He could be the
third cousin."

At the steps to the plane we didn't linger. There seemed
to be fifteen or twenty passengers all told. From their
looks most were going no farther than St. Anthony. "Write
me sometimes," I said.

"Oftener than that," she said. "And you, Jonno?"

"You'll have a *cri de coeur* from me in every mail," I
said. "Seriously, of course I will."

We kissed each other, and then she went aboard.

✠

There were no episodes during the elections. The
Council was returned to office intact with what had to be
considered a strong new mandate. But there were two incidental surprises. One was the size of the majority, better
than two-thirds, that favored making Tor's sister Queen
forthwith, thus retaining the monarchy but changing the
dynasty in the next generation. We took this to mean
that the people believed young Tor was deeply implicated
in his father's murder.

The other surprise was the rate of voter abstention in
the industrial suburbs. In Suburra, for instance, forty percent didn't vote, as compared with five to six percent in the
country generally. No one knew quite what to make of
this, except that it was disquieting. Commiter and Ross,
with long experience of periodic American elections, were
clearly disturbed. Ross told me, "Even in presidential years
we don't get anywhere near the percentage of turnout you
do, but in any national election the figure doesn't vary
too much from one part of the country to another unless
there's a blizzard somewhere, or unless there's a very hot
local campaign. I've never heard of a discrepancy like
this. Is it protest abstention? Are these people disaffected
with the government, but not quite ready to go along
with young Tor?"

For the election itself I was on the Frays as I planned.
With several feet of snow on the ground, it was a white,
gray, and green world, very beautiful and very cold. My
brother Atta had just come back from a dangerous and

horribly difficult trip into the Karain. I'd known nothing about it. His face was raw and sore from exposure. A place on his nose and another on his ear looked to me like frostbite, but he said no, not quite. He'd snowshoed through the Mora pass and then hiked down into the Karain. Coming back, he ran into trouble—first a mountain blizzard and then days of clear, deadly cold and fierce winds.

There was no wind now as he talked about it, but it was cold enough so that we all sat near the fire, my father and mother, Atta, and I. "Things have moved along since you were there, Jon," Atta said, "but the direction is the same. Sulliaba is widening the trails to the passes and cutting new ones. Where there's solid ground you can find clearings under tree cover for supplies and, maybe, other things. I didn't get into the real marsh country. Nobody I saw knew much about it. But it looks as though Sulliaba thinks it can get motor supply and even tanks up to the northern slopes. The men I saw—you know most of them —have no doubt that Sulliaba will attack, and will do it with small units of mountain troops before the passes are clear. Then they can wait on the weather. We've nothing there but border posts, and they're down in the throats of the passes. We need a system of manned positions along all the slopes."

I thought about this until I could see the geography Atta was talking about—the difficult buildup over the marshes to begin with, the vulnerable supply line there later, and the early taking of the passes. This all made sense, if something else went with it. In fact it seemed highly probable, and I said so, but added, "Sulliaba will want a pretext. I think the attack will come after some signal or event inside Islandia. I've no idea what. Did you learn anything about Mobono?"

"I didn't get that far east, but I did learn some things. Again, they bore out what you found. Mobono won't ally with Sulliaba, and she isn't moving up supplies. But if we start losing, Mobono isn't going to be left out. She'll invade us from her side and scavenge. There's a lot of Carran and even Miltain she would like to have. Jon, you've got to convince Dorn to man the passes in strength. If I hadn't known you were coming here for the elections, I'd have gone straight to you in The City with this. We need men with rifles right now, and soon we're going to need heavier stuff than that."

"Dorn won't need much convincing to give us what he

can," I said. "I'll see him about it tomorrow. By the way, were you able to hear young Tor's speech here?"

"Yes," my father said, "clearly and poisonously."

Atta laughed shortly, and then asked me, "Has Hanno said anything about where he thinks that transmitter was, or is?"

"Yes. He says it's in southern Farrant. Almost in Dole."

"Where? He's lying to you, or someone's lying to him. It was almost due north of here. Just a little west. Over the border. Why would he . . . Oh. Just a minute." He left the room, and we heard him pulling drawers in the library around the corner. When he came back he had an outline map of the country, a protractor, and a rule. He spread the map on top of the piano, and then began plotting points and connecting them with pencil lines. Soon he said, "Yes, we both did the same thing. Each of us took the reciprocal reading so he could put the transmitter in a place he thought it ought to be. This is so rudimentary our American friends wouldn't believe it. Both of us were wrong, the only way we could be, by one hundred eighty degrees. I have only one loop antenna, and it's on top of a pole so I can't move it around. I merely made the wrong guess. But Hanno could have taken two or three bearings, and didn't. I wonder why. But our two bearings reversed will do it. Look at this, Jon."

I went to the piano and stared down at the map. For a little I saw nothing intelligible, but then I began to understand what Atta was talking about. There were two large dots—one in the Frays and the other in Suburra—the places where directional readings were made. Through the point in the Frays, Atta had drawn a line extending north into the Karain and also south into the ocean, passing east of The City. From Suburra, just northeast of The City, a second line ran to southern Farrant one way and southeast into the sea the other.

The two lines intersected near the west side of the small bay on the south coast which gives a harbor to the town of Shores. The place was seventy-five or eighty miles southeast of The City. Atta put a circle around it. He said, "I don't have Hanno's compass reading, so this isn't accurate. But it's close. A reading from a stationary loop tells you the line along which the main strength of a signal is traveling, but not which side of the source you're on. For that you need a cross bearing, and Hanno and I give each other one." He put his pencil on the intersection. "That's

about where Tor's transmitter was. What do you make of
it?"

I looked again at the map, trying to remember all I
knew about the west side of that small bay. There was
reasonable shelter from the long southern seas, no rocks,
and a gradual pebble beach. I said, "I think the trawler
put it ashore for him."

✠

The winter wasn't any longer in days and hours than
any other, but it seemed longer than all the other winters
of my life put together. Time and events had somehow
got stuck and were standing motionless in the gray cold
weather of The City. This was me, of course. Actually,
some things did happen.

Dorn got troops into the passes. Not as many as Atta
wanted, but the units were good and they were equipped
with recoilless rifles as well as machine guns and regular
rifles. Some field pieces and anti-tank guns and anti-air-
craft guns were moved up to the top of the Frays elevator
and held there with their crews, awaiting some modera-
tion in the weather.

Once Dorn had my information, he didn't need any per-
suasion. "Your brother is a good man," he said, "I'm
glad he's where he is. If anybody can hold the passes, he's
the one. And they're essential. They're the key to central
Islandia. If they go, then so do the Frays. We can destroy
the elevator and give an enemy a hard time getting equipment down from there, but we can't stop him for long.
We have to hold him in the passes. We can do this as
long as our aircraft can get at his supply line, the part
across the marshes particularly. But"—and here Dorn
looked out the window at the dark clouds and their depending scarves of mist—"if Sulliaba has people who can
really use all those MIG's it has, we won't have an air
force more than a few days."

Commiter kept Mora informed about what was—or
rather wasn't—happening on the Islandia Bay proposal.
Washington was interested, but it wanted us to apply to
the World Bank and the International Development
Agency. We had approached Washington at a time when
the American foreign payments' deficit was not only a real
and troublesome fact, but a painfully acute political issue

as well. Various measures, direct and indirect, were being taken to cut down the rate of American investment overseas.

One evening when Commiter and I were dinner guests of Mora, we went into the subject without any diplomatic formalities. "My government has a serious problem," Commiter said, "as long as the dollar is tied to gold. What would happen if we stopped supporting gold is guesswork, but at least it would solve your problem.

"Just the same, even as things are, I think you can probably get the kind of arrangement you want. I understand perfectly well why you want it that way. If you've got to let some foreigners in on some terms, you want a clear agreement with one powerful nation whose presence here will give serious pause to your northern neighbors and their friends.

"You know as well as I do that over the years you haven't given my country much cause to love you. But even so you haven't treated us any worse than you have everybody else. And the United States can find some good reasons for not wanting Islandia to sink. It's one thing not to have any commitments in this continent when Islandia is a going concern, which is still the case. But it would be something else to have all Karain under the influence of Russia and China, whether they were friendly to each other or hostile. That's what will happen if Sulliaba and Mobono overrun you. No, I think you'll get your agreement, but it may take some time."

Mora smiled bleakly at this and said, "Mr. Commiter, you're too good a friend and too well informed not to know that this is one of the few occasions in our history when time is an enemy and not an ally."

"In that case," Commiter said dryly, obviously completing a maneuver, "I suggest a prompt and cordial invitation to the new cruiser *Bangor* and her escorts. She'll be leaving American waters in a few weeks."

Mora flinched visibly, but he nodded in agreement. "Yes, I remember. If Dorn agrees, I'll send an invitation—a cordial one."

✠

Morana wrote me regularly as she promised. Apparently there would be no difficulty about our acquiring membership in the United Nations. Aside from this, there was little comfort in her letters because she kept putting off the date of her return. The reason was Lord Farrant, who was having trouble with New York. The place so unnerved him that he nearly took a plane for home after three days. Things began to improve after his wife arrived and he was settled in an apartment with her and his two regular Islandian assistants, but it was slow going. Morana wrote of him with a mixture of affection, irritation, and amusement as her estimates of the length of her own stay grew from the original six weeks to seven, to eight, and finally to nine.

The Council installed Tora as Queen the week after the election results were certified, but we heard nothing from or about her brother Tor. The silence surrounding him was so complete the earth might have swallowed him, and we wished it had, knowing very well that we could have no such luck.

Ross I saw not at all in those days, but Dorna did, and I heard of him now and then through her. She said he was enjoying his own courses immensely now that he didn't have to worry about stepping over some implied but never stated limitation on his subject matter. Also, he was working with the University authorities on plans for a steady expansion of the curriculum. "I think I'm his best student now," she said. "I commute to Reeves for his classes. My family doesn't know whether to laugh or be impressed."

"Dorna, is he going to become . . . ?"

"Don't ask that, Jon. We don't know yet." Her playfulness fell away, and she looked at me as her great-aunt probably looked at my grandfather when she told him obliquely that she would be marrying a Tor. "Yes, it's that way. You were going to ask—or, am I, Dorna, going to become American? We can't think about that problem now. He wants to use what time there is for teaching and planning. And, Jon, I help him some."

Though I didn't see Ross, I did have a note from him at last about a week before Morana finally returned. He spoke mostly about his teaching and about how pleased he was with the progress on new courses of study. But at the end he wrote, "You remember the conversation we had in your boat about fables over the radio? You weren't impressed with my suspicion of the nonclassical ones. You were probably right but, as a matter of incidental interest if no more, the direct discourse fables are back on the air again for the first time in months. I hope there won't be episodes to follow."

✠

At the airfield the frost was out of the ground and there were few muddy spots left. The breeze from the north-west wasn't carrying the news of real spring quite yet, but it had information in it about melting snow and wet earth open to the air again. Here, last year's grass was yellow and dry, no new green was showing under it so far, and the ground was full of water. I remembered my grand-father saying this was the time in New England to burn over a field, if the wind was down and you had beaters with rakes and shovels. I've never seen it or heard of it in Islandia. As my grandfather described it, there was noth-ing but an edge of fire that moved out over the old grass in arcs and demilunes, like ringworm patterns.

Now high in the northeast there was a bright, glinting speck that grew until it took shape as the purple and orange DC-3 of St. Anthony Airlines. The plane passed to the southeast, banked and turned, and came in up the wind. It stopped well beyond the X crossing of the land-ing strips, and on the leg farthest from the airfield buildings. When the door of the plane opened, I was on rough, slightly squelchy ground about 150 yards away and walking at a good pace. The first person in the door was Morana. I couldn't see her face at that distance with the sun on the purple and orange plane, but I knew her shape and her style. I raised my hand and waved. She waved back and started down the steps.

Just then a file of riders galloped around the tail of the plane from the far side and stopped in line in front of Mo-rana. I think there were five of them. The three in the middle swung down from their ponies and took Morana by the arms as she came off the last step to the ground. She looked at them, wrenched one arm free, and began to fight. For a second or two I saw her kick, scratch, and try to bite. After that nothing was clear except that the two men still mounted had the passengers and crew covered by handguns.

I was running, shouting, and stumbling. The line of ponies was between me and what was happening. I could see a tableau while one of the ponies raised his head to swallow, or a swirl of feet and legs when I was picking myself up from a fall and could look underneath. First they were sliding a long, loose gunnysack over Morana's head and down to her feet. Then they wrapped her around into a bundle with strips of sacking, and finally slid her face down into some kind of harness over the shoulders of the biggest pony.

Then the line of riders moved off around the plane, leaving the way they had come. I passed the plane, too, and ran on after them without hope or plan. All that occurred to me was to run, and keep on running and running. In the end I wasn't running anymore, scarcely walking, and I shambled to a stop nearly foundered. I was trembling all over the way a run-out pony sometimes does before he collapses.

Standing spent in the great expanse of empty field, I slowly began to feel again—nausea, desolation, fear, and finally anger. Also, as I began to think a little, I saw that what I had done was even worse than futile. If I had used what strength I had in running the other way, by now I would be almost back in The City where something possibly could be done. As it was, I had given the kidnappers an hour or more of extra time without even learning the direction they took when they left the airfield. With a shaken spirit and heavy feet I made the best speed I could across the endless turf toward my cart and my pony.

✠

The familiar, quiet activity of The City calmed me some—people walking, riding, exchanging a greeting in the pleasant early spring afternoon. First I went home, unhitched Lok, and fed him. I didn't know how soon I might need him. Then I forced myself to eat for the same reason. After that I went across the inlet to Dorn House and was not surprised to find none of the family home. The Council had no formal sitting today, but Dorn was keeping long working hours in his office, and his boatman told me he thought Lord Dorn was there.

I went into the Council building through a small side entrance and followed a series of back corridors to Mora's office. The door was closed, so I knocked. There was no answer and I couldn't hear anything from inside, but I sensed there were people there. I knocked again. And again. Finally the door opened a few inches. On the other side of the vertical slit I recognized Mora's secretary.

He knew me, too, and said, "Isla Lang, this is not a good time. This is an important meeting. I am instructed to admit no one. I'm sorry."

He started to close the door again, but I held it toward him. Just then I began to see. This was the signal I had spoken to Atta about. Except it might be a cluster of rockets. I looked at the slim, elderly man on the far side of the door, thinking what to say. He had been Mora's secretary since before I was born. There were rumors that he was an *apia* indiscretion of Mora's father. Whatever the truth of that, I knew him—as did everyone else—for a gentle and disinterested man.

"Runan," I said, "I have important information that may concern this meeting. In any case, Isla Mora could come here to the door. I would tell him in one minute, Runan." I wished I could tell him in less time even than that.

Runan went into the room, leaving the door as it was. Within seconds he was back, and nodded to me to go in. Dorn was there with Mora, and so were three military men I did not know, an army colonel, an air force colonel, and a navy captain. I took them to be staff officers.

The expression in Mora's eyes told me that somehow he guessed the substance of what I had to say. I went through my account haltingly and painfully, criticizing myself bitterly for wasting time trying to pursue the kidnappers. Mora said, "Sit down with us, Isla Lang. We can use your help. This is literally a council of war. And don't reproach yourself. You did what I know I would have done. Besides, nothing could have been accomplished here in The City." He sat back in his chair, his hands grasping the arms. "Isla Dorn was about to summarize what little we know. Dorn?"

Dorn's eyes showed hurt as Mora's did, but being on the blue side of gray they sharpened and glowed with an evident anger. His voice was matter-of-fact. "Dorna, also, was kidnapped late this morning on her way to take the monorail to Reeves. Hanno has disappeared, and we know nothing but the fact.

"We have some information about armed insurrections in the Winder shipyards, and in the industrial suburbs of Doringata and Suburra. I assume there are others. There must be. Small bonfires here and there won't bring in the outside help.

"In Suburra the rebels have the printing office and the radio station. The printing office can wait, but we want the radio station back now." He looked at the army man. "How long, Colonel?"

"About an hour," the colonel said, "if we start shooting."

"How many men are in the building?"

"Maybe a hundred and fifty."

"Can you cut off their power from outside?"

"Not entirely. There is a generator in the building that will run the transmitter."

"Have any shots been fired?"

"Not to my knowledge, sir."

It was a few minutes before three. Dorn said, "If they can help it they won't go on the air before four because nobody will be listening." Then, addressing the army officer, but looking at Mora, he said, "Colonel, instruct the officer in command there to give the rebels these terms. All who leave the building, peaceably and unarmed within one hour, will be let go free without questioning. At the end of the hour the place will be taken by whatever means are needed. If the station attempts to broadcast, we will open fire with artillery at once." When Mora nodded, the colonel rose and left the room to send the order.

"I hope they haven't any hostages there," Dorn said, "but it can't be helped." Then he spoke to me. "Jon, we've put your brother in direct command of all forces in the Frays and we're sending him two more battalions. We did this about an hour ago and had to use the heliograph because most of the provincial telephone lines are cut. Your father took the signal. He told us Atta was in the mountains now with a camp somewhere in the high valley between the Mora Pass and the Lor Pass. He'd no word of any fighting there yet. We've put guards and patrols along the monorail, but they won't be much use."

When the colonel came back, Dorn asked each of the three officers in turn to give his estimate of the situation from the standpoint of his own service, and to report on the readiness and present disposition of his forces. They did it well and honestly. What it amounted to was, if Sulliaba stayed out, we had a hard, long-range social problem which we already knew about, but nothing military which we couldn't handle. If Sulliaba came in, however, then all the factors, including the domestic ones, changed value drastically against us. It was close to what I had thought myself, but hearing it in military language made it worse.

It was now very nearly four o'clock. At a sign from

Mora, Runan turned on the radio in the far corner of the room. Nobody stirred and there was no sound from the machine. If it would only stay silent. Then, a voice came into the room, one I didn't recognize but that was oddly familiar.

"Good afternoon. This is Islandia radio coming to you now for the first time under the auspices of your ancient and legitimate government which has been dispossessed since the disappearance of the last Alwin. I am Tor Mergil speaking to you in behalf of my cousin the King, Tor Twenty-two." Morana had been right. This was the voice of the third cousin, the man at the elevator. "The King is with his troops whose arms are everywhere overwhelmingly successful. The King sends his good wishes and affection to his countrymen, asks them for their support and loyalty in this struggle, and assures them the future now belongs to a vigorous, growing, and progressive Islandia. The King also asks the recognition and support of other nations in this long overdue enterprise."

At this point, muffled and remote because Mergil must have been deep down in the building, the radio brought us the explosion of the first artillery shell. Moments later, sharper and louder, the airborne report of the same shot came to us through the open window. It was an eerie experience. Then as the rate of fire increased and other guns joined in, the noises from the radio couldn't be identified any longer with those from the outside world. To hold some kind of concentration I found myself accepting the shocks through the window as real and the sounds through the radio as anticipations.

None of this could bother Tor Mergil. For him, at the source, there was no time slippage. When a shell hit, he knew everything important about it in an instant, except perhaps whether or not it had killed him. He raised his voice.

"The King expects the fallen government to fight determined local actions and to achieve some temporary successes. You probably hear gunfire over your radios now. That is the effort of Mora and Dorn to stop me from talking to you. They may succeed for a short time." (I was aware now that the shelling had stopped.) "Whatever happens here now, the King will speak to you tonight . . ."

The radio gave squawks, and piercing noises, and then nothing. Finally there was a sharp rap, as though someone had struck the microphone to see whether it was alive. Then came another voice, young, baritone, and full of the inflections of Camia. "This is Islandia radio again, under the control of its lawful government. The noise you just heard was a rebellion falling down. I am Lieutenant Gromar of Camia, and my orders are to say Queen Tora and her ministers will speak to the country at six o'clock. You can count on this."

As Runan turned off the radio, Mora said with a trace of a smile, "I like the sound of Lieutenant Gromar. Wouldn't it be nice if the rest of it could be that easy. Dorn, you and I must go and encourage Tora. This will be an ordeal for her."

✠

There is nothing I want to say or remember about that night.

When the Council met in the morning, in closed session, Mora sketched the international situation. Sulliaba had recognized Tor's claim immediately and was attacking in the north. Mobono was still quiet in word and deed. Radio Moscow said nothing of Tor, but was savagely attacking the Mora regime. Radio Peking was contemptuous of both sides. The Western nations generally, with the exception of France which was silent, were saying things favorable to Mora and Dorn.

At the United Nations, Farrant would ask today for a hearing by the Security Council. Mora didn't think he would get it or, if he did, that the Council would take any action. Russia, and perhaps France and other nations, would argue that Islandia's application for membership was still pending in the General Assembly, leaving room for doubt about the legitimacy of its government. If Tor's claims proved valid, he had every right to ask for assistance from the friendly state of Sulliaba.

"This is sophistry," Mora said, "but it is also politics. We must face the fact. that we are on our own. In the past we liked it this way and had trouble declining unwelcome assistance. Now that we want help, we are not likely to get it. To be sententious, this is the way of the world. And it must be admitted, we asked for it. Now we know what we must do, we can set about doing it—as we have before." He held up both hands to stop the applause that was beginning. "Save your strength," he said. "Isla Dorn has a use for it."

Dorn was brief and sober in his account, and startling in his prescription. Yesterday, as soon as Atta heard Tor Mergil's broadcast, he moved strong advance parties north of the Mora Pass out of Islandia and into the Lor Pass. This country does not belong to Sulliaba. Technically it is part of the tribal lands of the Bants, but it is very much like Tibet. Since the Bant tribes vary from grassland high-plains nomads to tropical forest dwellers, and have no Yak and mountain goat culture, as Ross calls it, the bitter land around the Lor Pass is empty. Atta's detachments there were holding well under pressure. If it seemed that the Lor Pass could be kept and not outflanked, these troops would be reinforced. If not, they would retire after a strong delaying action to the main positions in the more formidable Mora Pass.

Our air bases in Deen, Camia, and Upper Doring were bombed in the early morning with no damage to aircraft but a good deal to runways and buildings. Tor's people had seized government installations in five additional and widely spread locations as well as the University buildings at Reeves. Dorn said he was certain Sulliaba would not wait long before mounting a second invasion, this one from the Sea. The most likely target was the west coast somewhere between Farrant and the southern Doring plain.

"Now," Dorn said, "this government proposes that the Council select a small executive committee of members to discharge its duties here and that all other members return home to take direct charge of their provinces." At this, there was a collective tightening of faces and a leaning forward.

Dorn scanned us carefully. "Thank you," he said. "I'll be as plain as possible. There is a rebellion. We must contain this without killing. We have enough inherited bitternesses. We don't want to start new spirals.

"We are also being attacked from outside, and we know that there is at least temporary cooperation between Sulliaba and our own rebels. To stop Sulliaba we need every trained man we have. And the cost, if we bring it off, will be hard and bloody fighting.

"Our only chance, as your government sees it, lies with you, the Islar."

A page handed Dorn a sealed message which he opened and read, and then dropped on the table beside him.

"More attacks on the airfields," he said. "It's useful to look at this from where Tor sits. You would think he would use what men he has in small commandos for guerrilla fighting and sabotage all over the country. That's how he could hurt us most, but he isn't doing that. I suspect it's because most of his people—industrial workers, some civil employees, and a few students—aren't at home in the countryside and are not liked there. They wouldn't last long or do much.

"Instead, Tor chose to deprive us of a selected number of plants and installations. This is shrewd and it is working well for him. The places he picked are important. And he has forced us to disperse large numbers of troops. This isn't a bad substitute for guerrillas. And I'm sure he hopes we will attack his garrisons, achieve a lot of killing on both sides, and create a sympathy for him in the country that he can't make for himself.

"We're not going to do this. The places he has taken are critical, but we can get along without them for a while. We have to anyway—call it a positive loss—because it would take us half a year to set things working after an assault.

"There is one exception, Islandia radio. We had to have that back at once. Tor needed it for one signal to Sulliaba, and to show the country he had his hand on a legitimate thing. He did them both. Of course, he would have liked to hold the station longer. But I have to admire his cousin Mergil. His men were a picked lot. They *are* capable of performing on their own. Mergil used our terms to free almost all his men, and he still did what he came for. When we retook the station there were six prisoners, two wounded, and none killed.

"But for the rest, Tor has voluntarily imprisoned his forces. This serves his purpose very well at the moment. As for us, we want to keep him sewed up in his prizes, but we don't want to do it with regular troops. So we ask the Islar to return home, raise local forces through the provincial police, and relieve our army units quickly. We will see that you get equipment of a sort."

✠

I wasn't put on the Council's resident executive committee. Five senior members were picked, all from provinces

Tor had avoided. There wasn't much for me to do in the Frays, except get in the way. Tor had no citadels there. The place was an active war zone, and neither Atta nor my father needed counsel from a mind as divided as mine.

Before the Council disbanded I tracked down Isla Brome of Alban and talked with him for a few minutes. Then I walked home, carrying rolled up under my arm a very large-scale map of Islandia which I pilfered from the Council supply room. I spread the map on a drawing board, clipped the corners down, and began to lay out lines with great care along the bearings Atta and Hanno had given me.

The information from Hanno was the puzzle. After my talk with Atta at the time of the elections, I went to see Hanno. He was open with me, or seemed to be. I asked him for the compass readings that had given him the location of Tor's transmitter. He said he didn't remember offhand, and sent for the file. With the record in his hand, he said, "Our base points were Suburra and Reeves. In the event, it gave us a narrower angle than we would have liked, but it was enough." He handed me the paper. "We've had people searching the place for Tor and the transmitter. We haven't found him or it, and we got there about seven hours after his broadcast." I wrote down the figures, gave him back the record, and thanked him.

The interview hadn't made any sense at the time, and didn't now, assuming that Atta and his machine were not hallucinating. On the whole I thought it more likely that someone was lying to Hanno because it was certain that at least one of his readings was false.

The size of the map I was using, helpful in many ways, did give a misleading impression of precision. I had all the compass readings down to minutes and seconds, but they couldn't be that accurate. The Reeves bearing crossed Atta's line at a place not far inland from the easternmost reach of Islandia Bay, a long, shallow neck of water. The Suburra bearing, as before, crossed just west of Shores Bay near the south coast. The two places were forty-five to fifty miles apart. I was leaning over the map trying to make the shadings and contour lines yield me the meanings of the two indicated positions, when I heard voices downstairs. A few seconds later Ross came into the room.

He looked depressed, grim, and very tired. He said, "They threw me out—the students. They aren't bad kids, any of them. They just want change. Some of my own students are the leaders. Banch was back again. They've tasted some change, and they like it. But they won't listen to me now. They can't see that they're going to be sold out whatever happens."

"What's the situation in Reeves now?"

Ross came over to the table beside me and stood looking down at the map without seeing it. He said, "Maybe a third of the students have seized the University buildings and grounds and are holding them. The others are going home. A few who live in Reeves are joining the local levy the police are going to organize. I'd join it myself, but I can't just sit still in Reeves. I'd go crazy, or run amok. There's got to be something somebody can do about Dorna and Morana. That's what's eating me."

His eyes at last began to see the map. "What's all this? Nothing's happening down there."

"Someone has gone to a lot of trouble to make us think Tor's broadcast came from over here," and I touched a place on the west coast just north of Dole.

He bent over the map. From the markings there he read my whole process of elimination and guesswork with incredible speed. Straightening up from the table, he said what I had not yet even put into words to myself, "You think one of these two places is Tor's personal headquarters—or hideout. And it's a good bet that where Tor is, there are the hostages. Have you a plan?"

"Not yet. I can't make one until I talk with Dorn. I was just about to go over there."

"And I should see Commiter," Ross said. "I'll be back in about an hour."

✠

Early next morning in one of Dorn's boats we set off as a party of five—two of Dorn's men, Ebur and Tresk, who were sailors from Dorn Island; my own man, Hettin, who asked to come; Ross and I. The weather was chilly and cloudy. We had a journey of some forty miles by water. Ebur said he expected rain but not too much wind.

The evening before when I told Dorn what I knew, what I guessed, and what I meant to try, he said, "You may be right. In your place I would do the same thing. I wish I were in your place. So does Mora." He shook his head. "We're not. What do you want me to do for you?"

"Nothing. I want your permission because I am a mem-

ber of your government. And I want you to know what
we're doing. That's all."

"I ought to be able to do a little more than nothing,"
Dorn said. "Not troops, of course. I wouldn't send them if
I had them to spare. Too dangerous for two hostages.
Tor knows he can't influence our actions as heads of gov-
ernment by this. Mora and I are sure that the hostages
are for Tor's personal protection. That's a bit different."

"You say two hostages," I said. "You don't think Hanno
is one?"

"Hanno may be a prisoner but, if so, it must be for other
reasons. At this point Tor couldn't buy a five-minute re-
prieve with Hanno."

Then Dorn gave me two of his own men and a boat,
advising against the use of mine. "That rig of yours is
known all over the bay. Also, your boat can't reverse direction, and where you're going you may not be able to
turn around." I thanked him and then told him I had had
a short and very general talk with Lord Brome of Alban.
On the basis of this we agreed on a rudimentary arrangement for emergency communication.

Ebur knew his weather very well. Hour after hour we
moved slowly southeast across a light southwest wind
through intermittent rain that was always cold and sometimes heavy. A stiffer wind would have steadied the boat
and made us all easier because we were running cross-
grain to the swell left by the last five days of northwest
weather. None of us was sick, but the motion was irregular and galling. We all felt better when we turned to port
into the long gooseneck of the eastern reach.

This was a part of the bay I'd never sailed in and knew
little about. Ebur said, and my chart bore him out, that
for the first several miles the water was shallow but adequate at all stages of the tide. In the bay the tide fluctu-
ation is very high for a body of water so nearly sealed off.
It runs from about eight inches to a foot. Compared to
the great tides off Winder of eleven to sixteen feet and
more this seems small, but it is enough to create currents
of six to eight knots in and out of the mouth of the bay.
Unless they are powerful, ships and boats negotiate the
entrance to Islandia Bay only with the tide or at slack
water.

Any tide was important to us when we began to follow
the gooseneck around to the northeast. Here, at high tide,
the water covered everything to a minimum depth of five
or six inches according to the chart. At low tide the place

was mostly mud and sand flats with pockets of trapped water. There were two winding channels with water enough for our boat at any time. But the chart was honest about them. It read: directions and threads of channels variable.

We were fortunate in our timing or, rather, Ebur was accurate in his estimate. We reached the flats soon after dead-low water and had the incoming current behind us. Also the windings of those variable channels were plain to see, even through the rain, against the tan and the light chocolate of the exposed sand and mud. Whenever the rain slackened enough so that it didn't splash and dance on the surface of things, we could see the flats bubbling and working in response to some kind of marine life down below.

Ebur stowed the sail and sent me forward with a light pole to fend the boat off from the channel banks. He and Tresk, with longer heavier poles, took positions on either side of the boat aft of amidships and thrust us forward. As soon as I began to sense how to keep the boat away from one bank without grounding it on the opposite one, we made surprisingly good speed. And the incoming tide kept gaining in strength. Even so, it was getting on for dusk when we came to the end on a reedy, marshy stretch of shore, our bow on sand beside a solid hummock of marsh grass.

The place was silent except for the lapping of the water and the rustle and hiss of the reeds in the slowly increasing breeze. The rain had stopped, and the overcast was lifting but hadn't broken yet. There were no birds at that hour. On the way in we had attracted gulls and some marsh birds like small herons, but they gave us up when they were sure we were giving them nothing.

Ebur was to stay with the boat. Though he disliked the spot for obvious reasons as a sailor, he said he would stay put until the ebb tide of tomorrow afternoon. That would give us time to find the nearest of our points; to send news if there was any, or to come to the boat if we had quick success or sudden trouble.

"Isla Lang," Ebur said, "it's not as bad here as I've let you think. I don't like being controlled by sands and tides. I'd rather have open water, but that's habit. The main risk here is wind, and this is a time for wind. A strong onshore wind, with the tide, could move me inland thirty feet and strand me. An offshore wind could beach me where we are now.

"When you go ashore, I'll drop back into the channel and anchor. If you aren't here, or haven't sent me a message, by mid-ebb tide tomorrow afternoon I'll go out to open water and make camp on the north shore at the beginning of the east reach. When do you want me to come back here after that?"

I liked this place even less than Ebur did, and, unless it was tomorrow, I didn't want to come back here at all. I said, "Why not the south shore?"

Ebur, who was not a tall man, nor a heavy one, but immensely strong and quick, was deliberate and sure in his opinions. He said, "I know what you're thinking. From the coast it would be better for you to go to the south side of the reach and not here. It would be better for me, too. But I think the danger to the boat from Tor's people is greater there. And you couldn't find me anyway. No, this beginning and ending of things here is what we know. This is the place."

I didn't want to agree, but I didn't think of anything else, and time was going by. I was about to say all right when Ross touched my shoulder. "Jon," he said, "and Ebur, forgive me, but you've mired yourselves in this mud. You're not thinking. All we have to do is turn the plan around so Ebur can come to us on a signal. Smoke by day, torch by night. Ebur makes camp on the north shore and stays there. When we reach the south shore we let him know. And, after tomorrow, nobody has to come here again."

Ebur liked the idea, and we worked out signals indicating different degrees of urgency. When I thanked Ross, he said, "I'm surprised you and Ebur didn't think of it. Particularly you. It's not foolproof. Ask Tristan and a few Greeks. But for an American it's a divided tribal memory. Half Paul Revere and half Chief Cloud-in-the-Sky. I think I like it better than this swamp."

✠

For the first hundred yards the going was treacherous and the weight of our gear made it worse. At times, for several yards together, we could make zigzag progress stepping from hummock to hummock, but more often we had to go down into the sticky mud and sand, climb a hummock, and then go down again. It was slow, very tiring, and hard on the nerves. Neither the chart nor the corresponding map showed quicksand, but that didn't prove anything. They didn't indicate this bog at all. Each time you put a foot down in the ooze you couldn't help wondering if you would be able to pluck it out again.

When we began to feel solid ground underfoot, and the reeds changed to dune grass, we stopped to get our breath. Tresk gathered a large handful of grass, wiped the muck off his boots, and then said it for all of us, "Now I feel better."

The light was almost gone where we were, but the clouds were running fast and there were rents in them through which shot almost horizontal sunlines exploding in bursts of crimson and purple on the twisting cliffs of vapor. We set off to the east in improving spirits.

The dune country came to an end after about half a mile. Then the land began to rise evenly and slowly, and we could tell from the footing and the increasing variety of vegetation that there was now some loam as well as sand and clay in the soil. We hoped to reach trees, at least scrub conifers, before we camped. They would give us some shelter and a fire for breakfast.

In the windy dark we guided on Tresk whose night eyes were much the best among us for this kind of groping. We stumbled and tripped, and so did Tresk, but he didn't miss the blacker blacknesses that meant a hollow nor the lighter ones that meant an obstruction, like a boulder or a sudden ridge. But suddenly, when the clouds tore apart and a glint of moon and stars came down to us, it was Ross who raised his head and his arm, crying out, "There!"

We all saw it, to our right. A cluster of half a dozen stunted fir trees partway up a small hill. They would do for what we wanted. We spread our groundsheets under the low branches, took a peg of brandy each, ate sparingly from our supply of waybread and cheese, and finished with water from the flasks we carried. Then we rolled ourselves up in our parkas and light blankets. The sky was almost clear and very bright.

I woke in the dawn just before sunrise in response to the feeling that I was being looked at. Some fifteen feet away a huge black dog, with a white shield from his throat to the bottom of his first ribs, sat regarding me out of yellow and green eyes. When he saw I was awake he yawned, opening his jaws and their impressive red-and-white furnishings almost to a straight angle. Then he trotted another ten feet away and sat down again. In motion he showed himself to be a magnificent animal. His short, smooth coat had the gloss of a seal, and something about his big feet suggested they were webbed. He was neither heavy nor thin, just large, and you couldn't see the play of muscles and tendons but you could see where they were.

I poked the others awake, and we set about the day. Tresk set off to find water. I made a small cooking fire from fir cones and dead branches. Saving our meat rolls, we had bacon with waybread, and cheese, and tea. Then we packed up and started off. The sky was clear, and the breeze was soft and warm out of the northwest. By the time the sun was fifteen degrees above the horizon every growing thing around us was silently shouting that this was spring at last, real spring. We smelled it from the grass, the earth, and the trees—delicate, insistent, complex. Each breath I took told me I was a child again, knowing this magic sweetness for the first time, and that I had no troubles my father and mother would not take away.

Meanwhile, the black dog came along with us, sometimes thirty feet to our right, sometimes about the same distance to our left. Ross, who tried to approach the animal several times, achieving only a kind of grave and peaceful lack of success, said finally, "That's no dog. He's Fenris, Junior. He's kept in harness by cobwebs sealed with grasshopper spit. When the time comes he'll break loose. I hope I'm not in his way."

With no verifiable landmarks and no sextant, proceeding by hand compass and dead reckoning, it is unbelievably difficult to be sure you have found on the land the place that is indicated by the crossing of two lines on a map. Except for distance and general direction, the map was not much help. The bland character of the country had something to do with this. The cartographer had no important streams, gradients, or configurations to show. He left us in *terra incognita* with two faint, far-apart elevation lines to keep us company.

We never did identify the exact spot, but by the time we were through we were certain we hadn't missed it. We went back and forth over the area for two hours, as Ross said, "like a foursome of demented golfers looking for a ball in the rough." Tor's transmitter wasn't here now, and we were all convinced it never had been. There was no conceivable reason to put it here, not even concealment.

Before starting south we ate again. Perhaps it was just

one meal too many of waybread and cheese, but I suddenly felt depressed and futile even though from the very beginning I hadn't expected to find anything here. I couldn't help thinking of Atta and my father and the desperate fighting in the ice of the northern passes. The odds against us all were too high. We had been feckless too long. Islandia was close to the end of her history. And here we sat on the warm grass of a field in nowhere eating bread and cheese.

Ross sensed my fall into doubt and irresolve. He may have come partway with me, though he didn't show it. "Cheer up," he said. "This morning was necessary. Now we can start to work. If you're worrying about your brother, I wouldn't too much. I think he'll make Sulliaba behave like the merchant en route to Madras." This was said in English, the first time Ross had used it since we left The City.

Ashamed of myself, and reluctantly grateful to him for prodding me, I answered in English, "What happened to him?"

"Nothing good," Ross said,

> "While threading an intricate pass
> In the dark of the night
> Turned so hard to his right
> He found himself facing his ass.

"Let's get on our way," he said. "Walking will be good for my nerves, too."

✠

A few minutes after we started out again, there was a sudden rustle and flurry in the grass in front of us. A big rabbit broke cover and bounded away to our left. Fenris saw him but did nothing except cock his ears. Ross was right about the dog. He seemed to be held by some invisible leash.

Not so Tresk. In an instant he had out a leather sling, put a stone in it, whirled it, and threw. The stone took the rabbit behind the ear at the base of the head and killed him in mid-leap. We would have more than waybread and cheese for dinner tonight. I didn't even know Tresk had a sling. On the mainland the thing is unknown ex-

cept as a toy for children, but I had heard or read somewhere that it was still used as a weapon on Dorn Island.
After Tresk collected the rabbit, I asked him about it.

"Yes," he said, "we all grow up using the sling. It's very
cheap. There's nothing to buy. You can fill the pot for
nothing. Also, it is quick and quiet. Range? Well, more
than most pistols but nothing to compare with a rifle. You
can throw a stone a long way with a sling. That's one
thing. But if you hit a target the size of a man at a hundred yards it's luck."

"Are there many on Dorn Island as good as you?" Ross
asked. "That was some shot."

Tresk obviously was pleased, both with his performance and the admiration it was getting, but he wouldn't
set himself up for something he wasn't. "The throw felt
very good," he said. "I didn't think. I didn't aim. I just
threw, and this time I hit. The next time I'll miss. Our
dinner jumped up to meet the stone."

As we went southeast along Atta's bearing, if we were
on it, the country changed again. The trees were bigger.
There were more deciduous hardwoods, varieties of oak
and beech, and fewer conifers. We saw no houses during
this time—not surprising because we were following a
compass reading rather than the ways people walked and
rode—but we were getting into farmed land. Some of the
fields we passed had the stubble of winter wheat on them.
Others were ready for plowing, dressing, and planting.

These small things made a great difference in our spirits.
This wasn't like my solitary trip through the mountains
when I had to hope I wouldn't see a trace of another
person. We needed evidence of a peopled world, even if
we stayed away from the inhabitants. Now we knew we
hadn't sloshed off Ebur's boat into a void. The works of
our countrymen were visible. Somehow we had made a
meeting with our intention. And we had a real dinner to
look forward to.

We began to talk to each other. Not one to one, but
each to the rest as though the four of us now had an iden-
tity. Hettin, who had been almost mute for the whole trip,
now began to speak of how the land here was farmed,
why one field was made ready before another, and what
complementary crops were grown in alternate years to
keep the soil fertile. I knew Hettin was not a native of the
Frays, but it occurred to me then that I'd never known
where he came from.

"Hettin," I said, "you sound as though you'd lived here once."

"I was born and raised not many miles away," he said with what I suppose was a smile, though not a happy one. Hettin was a thin, wiry man with a lined face and watery eyes. He looked almost any age you might guess, except that he was younger than any you would guess. His wife, I knew, did come from the Frays. In the past, before I became Isla, I saw little of him. Recently, at closer quarters, his habitual energetic, melancholy good humor had puzzled me. He surprised me by asking to come on this venture. Now I was curious, and knew very well I couldn't ask.

Shortly before four o'clock we finally saw a house. Even though we had no intention of going near it, the familiar sight gave solidity to the improvement in our joint state of mind. The place was perhaps half a mile away and on higher ground. The afternoon sun drew a warmth of color from the gray stone walls, and it was a pleasure to look at it across the well-marked fields and see the tones change with the passing of the occasional clouds.

But then, not all at once but gradually, unease came back among us. It wasn't a stop in conversation because we weren't doing much talking. There was a sense of constraint, a tightening of arms to the body, a peering for something. The scene was not right. I began to feel I was seeing something that wasn't there.

Hettin identified it. "The house has no roof," he said. "I think it's gutted. We're below it, and the ridgepole wouldn't have showed much from here. But that's what it is."

We took this in silence, recognizing it for fact. Then the other three turned toward me, and waited. After a moment I understood. Here was another fundamental change in our society of four. As soon as Hettin spoke, we became a military unit. They expected decisions from me, and orders.

I said to Hettin, "In the parts of the country I know better than this fires are almost unheard of. Do you think this is accidental?"

He shook his head, and that was all. Beside me, Ross was looking at the building, his hands cupped close around his eyes. He could concentrate his sight this way, but not lengthen it. When he took his hands down, he said, "Maybe field glasses would have helped. Probably not much. I was looking for a heat column. I can't see one. But there's enough wind across the place to blow it away unless there is a live bed of coals down inside that hasn't ashed over. If there was a fire, I'd guess it was at least twenty-four hours ago."

"We'd better look at it," I said.

The distance on foot was a lot more than half a mile. We worked our way around fields and between them to avoid leaving tracks on any dressed ground. When we were about a hundred yards from the house and still below it an eddy of wind brought down to us a breath of heat full of the smell of wood ashes and burned fabric. We circled the house to the door on the far side and looked in.

The stone walls everywhere were intact, including four interior dividing walls. Except for them, there was nothing. The thick stone circumference had been a furnace, an oven, and a kiln. The outside walls were still uncomfortably hot to the touch at shoulder height. Inside—and none of us was able to stand on the lintel for more than a few seconds—was an evenly sloping, grayish-white mound, no more than ankle-high at the doorway but about even with my hips at its peak in the middle of the house.

Air was still being sucked through the door by the heat. And now that there was no flame to consume it entirely, air was eddying down over the roofless walls. The currents met over the ashes, shifting them and spinning them up into tops that danced for a few feet and collapsed. From underneath, pink in the daylight, the live coals blinked at us through the moving ashes.

As we finished our turns of looking, Hettin cut a small branch from an apple tree near the house. The stick dripped the clear, thick water the tree was pumping to all its dependencies. Hettin leaned over the sill and drove the wet branch down into the coals. There was not even a hiss from the sap. The cooked piece of fresh wood exploded in flame, twisted rigid, and then dropped as ash on the rest of the ash. We moved away from the house to the orchard.

To me, Hettin's demonstration was an oddly frightening conclusion to a depressing experience, and I knew I wasn't the wiser for any of it. Meanwhile, I had forgotten all about the dog, but now I heard him for the first time. He was standing in the far corner of the orchard, nose pointed toward the sky, howling.

Ross and I walked toward him, and this time he didn't move away. When I put my hand on his head, he became quiet but he was still trembling the length of his body. Slowly, as I stroked him, the tremors decreased. Finally he sat down with his side and shoulders close against my leg. Ross and I didn't need words for what we both now knew. Neither did Tresk who had just joined us. There were human ashes in the house along with those of wood and cloth.

I looked around for Hettin and saw him trotting toward us from beyond the orchard. He beckoned to us. When we reached him, he said, "There have been horsemen here. A troop of maybe six to eight." We followed him into the meadow grass. There we came on a plot about fifty yards in diameter that was well trampled in the middle and showed signs of grazing on the edges. And there were fresh horse droppings.

"The ponies were hobbled here," Hettin said. "They stayed for some time. At least an hour. Probably much longer than that. They came from the north while it was still raining, or just after, and then went away to the south in fair weather."

Hettin showed me the tracks, and I had to agree with him. Those on the north were certainly headed south. They were sliding, undefined gouges in the turf made when the sod and the ground could hold no more water. The tracks to the south were much firmer, and from the bite of the hoofprints there was no doubt about direction. Also their spacing and grouping said the party arrived at a gallop and departed at a trot.

It was now late afternoon with perhaps an hour and a half of full daylight left and another forty minutes of twilight. Our first need was to eat and get a little rest, and I was sure none of us wanted to do either of those things here. I had a notion, too, that our cooking fires should be out before dark. To the east of us and slightly south the ground continued to rise slowly until a wooded knoll made a horizon about three-quarters of a mile away. By a small circuit due east over rock outcroppings and through bushes we could reach the wood without leaving an obvious trail. We set out for the knoll and the dog, Fenris, came along, this time among us.

Tresk set about the rabbit, Ross and Hettin saw to the fire and the water, while Fenris and I sat aside. I did my best to think, and Fenris did his best to help me with his heavy head on my leg. And he did help me by keeping me aware of him. He was our only witness to what had happened in the burning of the house. He had told us that with no mistake. If the events at the house concerned us, then Fenris and what he knew were important to us far beyond our sympathy for him and our pleasure in his company.

It is very hard to make a plan that accounts for random and possibly irrelevant facts in an endeavor that may be unreal itself. You have to move yourself back from the present instant as far as you can and try to look at everything as you saw it when you decided the effort was worth making. I did that. By the time the rabbit was cooking, I decided that anything unusual we came across was evidence that our first guess was right. But I wanted to test the others on this.

First I asked for a check of weapons. In addition to Tresk's unexpected sling, we had three rifles, a double-barreled shotgun, and Ross and I each had a Colt .38 pistol. One of the rifles was a pump-action .22, and the other two were .30 caliber with bolt action. The assortment didn't amount to much in the way of firepower, but the elderly pieces were in good condition and well sighted-in. In any case, we couldn't fight a pitched battle. Without more talk from me we loaded our pieces, including cartridges in the firing chambers, and turned to our first good meal in a long time.

In the middle of the rabbit stew I put the question. "What do you think, each of you, about that burned house? Does it mean anything for us?"

Tresk spoke first, saying, "The dog thinks it does. I know it's not sense, but look at him now. Isla Lang, you went up to him when he was howling and told him with your hand you understood what he was grieving about. But that wasn't why he quieted and came to us. He knew from you somehow that we were connected."

Hettin said, "The tracks go in our direction, and they are true. There was no circling back. We would have seen it one side or the other."

Ross looked distressed, and I could understand why. It was one thing to be a foreigner of good will at Reeves without any involvement. He could say and do what he pleased and the risk was limited to him. Now he had a strong personal commitment, but he was still a foreigner and I was asking his advice about something that concerned Islandia as well as Dorna. Just the same, I meant to have his opinion.

He walked around the question at first, saying, "When I came to Islandia I would have agreed with Hettin, but not with Tresk. Now I agree with them both. For myself I have to assume that anything headed for our destination does concern us until we know for sure that it doesn't."

"We seem to be of one mind," I said, "including Fenris. Then we will follow that trail—tonight."

✠

Across grassland the track of six or more ponies is not hard to follow, even at night. Before long we had a moon to help us, and we made good time. On rough ground or in woods, when we were at fault, Fenris took over. He was now a different animal. As soon as he knew we were following the horsemen, he put his nose and his own will in line with us. Loping along on his big feet, he didn't outpace us, but the looks he gave us over his shoulder every now and then clearly said he wished we could move faster.

The weather was clear and still, and grew quite chilly, but as dew began to form the air became alive with the moist, night smells of spring. In some of the hollows patches of ground fog were forming. From above, these looked like mounds of soft, new snow. When we were down in them we moved through a kind of faint luminescence that seemed to be made by the mist itself.

About once an hour we stopped for a few minutes' rest and then Fenris would grow uneasy. Sometime not long after midnight we passed a place where the horsemen had made camp. From then on Fenris grew increasingly eager, so much so that I said to Hettin, "He seems to think he has a fresh scent."

"We should have looked harder at that campsite," Hettin said. "They may have spent some time there. And from what I can see on the ground, they've been moving slowly."

As first light began to show in the northeast we made a longer stop than usual and ate a cold breakfast. We needed a place to sleep for an hour or so, but this felt too exposed. Just ahead a wooded ridge might be what we wanted. I asked Hettin how far we had come and he said he couldn't tell.

"But I think I know where we are," he said. "About ten miles from the inland tip of Shores Bay and something like eighteen from the place you marked."

We were shouldering our gear when an eddy of air down from the ridge shocked us all into frozen stillness.

There was woodsmoke in it. Moving nothing but our heads, we searched. There, seeming to come out of the ridgeline itself, was a climbing, shifting thread of gray distinguishable only by its motion from the dawn sky. In careful silence we unslung our packs and set them back on the ground. From a piece of light line I improvised a leash for Fenris, slipped it over his head, and gave the end to Tresk. Then by hand signals I indicated that I wanted Ross and Tresk to stay with the gear while Hettin and I reconnoitered.

We crossed the small stream from which we had taken water and started up the ridge through sizable trees. The going was clear but steep. Because people don't normally build campfires on the very summit of a hill it seemed likely that the smoke was coming from a sheltered hollow just beyond. A mounted party could have reached it easily by a short detour to the left where the ridge was lower and easier.

After the first few yards I knew the footing was good enough so that we wouldn't give ourselves away by our own noise, but the woods were the kind squirrels like. At any moment I expected to hear overhead the chattering, scolding relay of warning from one informer to the next. But the squirrels that season were elsewhere, or that morning they were slugabed.

We took the last stretch first on hands and knees and, finally, by a use of the belly muscles that comes more easily to worms, snakes, and nautch dancers. The crest, where we reached it, was a rough, flat face of rock wide and long enough to seat a family dinner of three generations. The smoke of the fire curled up over the far edge of this table.

Hettin and I exchanged finger pointings. They meant we thought there was a vertical rock face that served as a chimney for the fire. We moved slowly off the rock to the right where a screen of seedling firs offered some cover from below. Under our chins there seemed to be a drop of a number of feet, although we didn't immediately put out our heads to look. In front of us and below us was a slope of grass and bush dropping off to our left, conforming roughly to the ridge.

First we saw the ponies, seven of them, loosely hobbled out on the grass. Then we heard the snick and crackle of the fire taking hold of the bark of new, dry sticks. A voice said, "Why not stay here?"

An answering voice, and a familiar one, said, "Because

we have been in motion. The best way to stay undiscovered is to keep on moving, just a little."

"Why not go straight to Tor?"

"A good question. I'll tell you before you guess the answer." By now Hettin and I could look down through the evergreen feathers. The fire was at the base of the rock, as we thought, and there were four men around it. Hanno was speaking. "When Sulliaba lands, I will be in charge of things, not Tor. Tor does not know this, but he may suspect it. We should stay out of Tor's way until then."

Now for the first time I got a good look at the owner of the second voice. He was Banch, the student from Ross' class who had spoken the day I was there. He said, "Then what happened at the house—the death and the fire—the real reason for that was to make sure that Tor would do no more than suspect until it was too late?"

"No," Hanno said, "that was an accident as you saw. The thing wasn't important enough for killing. But that man, Tamir, did know, and it was clear he was becoming Tor's man. He would have told him."

"How long now before Sulliaba lands?"

"Not long," Hanno said, "but you can't be sure to the day and the hour. It's a long voyage the way it has to be made, and there's always weather."

At this point, tardily, I began to wonder about the other three men, and just to put the question was to know where they were. I didn't like the answer at all. They had gone back over the ridge to the stream for water. Just as I realized this, there came up the ridge from behind us a confusion of sound, not loud or informative but enough to make Hettin and me stiffen where we lay.

Hanno and his people down below didn't seem to hear it. Their fire was still blazing hard and two of the men were setting out skillets and pots with a certain amount of rattling. Then the sound from behind us stopped. In itself there was nothing reassuring about this. I was ready to give Hettin the signal to withdraw and look to our friends when, out of the far corner of my eye, I caught a flicker of quick motion down below the ponies where the grass and brush gave way to the trees of the ridge. I remained still, suspended. Twice more I had a glimpse of the motion but not of what was moving. Then it came into the clear.

Flat to the ground, making a silent black streak as a paintbrush does on paper, Fenris was charging the camp below. They didn't see him or hear him. The dog ignored

everyone but Hanno. Finally, Hanno saw what was coming
at him and jerked an arm up to protect his throat. Fenris
mangled Hanno's wrist in two slashing bites and then, still
unable to get at the neck, began savaging Hanno's face.

Banch, Ross' student, was drawing a pistol. At this moment, right next to my ear, Hettin fired his .22. The high-
velocity, steel-jacketed bullet, appearing to take the young
man in the upper arm, spun him sideways and shook the
pistol out of his hand. All of them now, except Hanno,
looked up across the fire toward the rock in fear and surprise.

"Fenris! Hold!" I shouted. To my amazement he did
hold. It certainly wasn't the name, which he didn't know
yet. But he was a trained dog, and in the last twenty-four
hours he had accepted me. To Hanno I said, "Don't move
or the dog will kill you."

Motioning Hettin to stay hidden, I stood up, switching
my own rifle off of *safe*. I knew this was dangerous. I felt
naked and very tender both back and front. I was
likely a dead man if Ross and Tresk were not in control of
their situation. But I had to assume that they were, and
I had to let them know we were in charge here. Looking
down, trying to ignore my own fear and the ringing in
my head from Hettin's shot, I still could see that Hanno's
people were in bad case. The retribution was too quick
and complex for understanding. The reappearance of the
dog, his obedience to me, the ambush—all suggested an
overwhelming combination of knowledge and force. They
were in shock.

Standing above them, as frightened as they, I had a
wordless sense of my temporary advantage. "Stay just
where you are," I told them. "You are surrounded and
covered. Your three companions who went back to the
stream for water have been accounted for . . ." As I
spoke, down out of the woods near where I first clearly
saw Fenris, there came four men. The two in front, their
arms stiffly out from their sides, I'd never seen before.
The two behind, by their shape and walk, were Ross and
Tresk. Except for one man I now had the sum. ". . . And
one at a time you will do as I tell you."

Ross halted his party within speaking distance, but out
of our line of fire. "Isla Lang," he said, "the other man is
dead. They tried to rush us. Tresk used his sling."

We set the uninjured men to dressing the wounds of
Hanno and Banch. Although Banch had taken a bullet
wound, he was in much the better shape of the two, and

had been extremely lucky. A high-speed, steel bullet doesn't tear up tissue too much but, even from a .22, it will splinter bone. Hettin's shot had gone through without touching bone. Hanno's face wounds were superficial, though ugly, but his arm was serious. Fenris' teeth had met in the middle of his wrist. He ran a large chance of losing his hand, and an even larger one of being hanged. I was compelled to admire his composure under the rough surgical first aid. The sweat poured out of him, but he did not retreat into shock and he kept his mouth closed.

When they had his arm bandaged and in a sling, he said to me, "I'd like to be clear about what happened. You must have heard the nonsense I was talking to Banch. Do you believe it at all? You could. You're just touchy enough."

"Yes, I believed it," I told him. "Once when you said it, and again when the dog confirmed it."

"The dog," he said, twisting his encrusted face into a sort of smile. "There's nothing wrong with him. But what can you know from him? He behaved in the manner of a good dog. Does that tell you anything about the house or the man in it? Did you know he was your man Hettin's cousin? Does all this tell you anything about me? I have behaved in the manner of a security officer. Does it tell you anything about yourself—that you are about to behave in the manner of a fool?"

This was a courageous and resourceful performance, and for all I knew it might be valid. Hanno impressed me, but not to the point of indecision. "Hanno," I said, "it tells me just one thing surely. This operation of yours is over. I've had a feeling for some time that my continued existence depended on your notion that you could make a tool of me. The only thing I want from you now is to borrow your field glasses." With his good arm he unslung them from his shoulder and handed them to me.

I drew Hettin aside, wrote a note which I gave him, and told him to pick the best of the seven ponies. He was to ride as hard as he could to the town of Shores and deliver the note to Lord Brome. He loped away at once, with no questions, and I put that problem aside.

Fenris, who had brought down his enemy, now stood beside me relaxed, his pink-and-red tongue in his open mouth tented at one edge where it hung over a biting tooth. I looked at the five men of Hanno's company. Tresk had disarmed them, but there they were. What to do with them? Except for Banch, they looked to me like

professional malcontents from the lower ranks of the Civil
Service and government industry. They seemed hardy but
unreliable, even for Hanno.

I said to them, "You are all free to go. On foot. And
north. Tresk will give each of you a saddlebag of your
own provisions. You would do well to bury your dead
companion in passing." I put my hand on Fenris' head.
"Remember, I advise you to go north. I repeat, that's advice not an order. If we meet you again, we'll kill you to
be rid of you. If you escape the dog here and fall into the
hands of Tor's people . . . ?"

Four of them picked up their saddlebags and started
back over the ridge. Banch stood where he was, the bag of
supplies at his feet. I looked at his young face, drawn but
unlined, and in a way, unconcerned. I felt a surge of pity
and hatred for him that came out in contempt. "Well,
Banch," I said, "Hettin didn't shoot you in the leg. You
can walk. Are you too good for your associates?"

He heard my voice, but obviously not my words. He
seemed to be returning slowly from a far-distant point in
his own interior geography. He said, "I didn't know anything except the dog and Hanno. The dog answered the
questions Hanno lied to me about. When you shot me, I
was drawing a pistol. You thought I was going to kill the
dog. No. I was going to kill Hanno."

The trouble was we had no time. The note I gave
Hettin told Brome that he had about forty-eight hours, if
that, to set up a defense of the sea beaches just west of
Shores Bay, the only place along this stretch of coast
where a landing could be made. That meant we had to
accomplish our job sooner than that. I resented this delay now, but I saw that what Banch had just said could
be so. I decided to spend a little more time in the hope
of gaining a lot.

"Why were you going to kill Hanno?"

"I joined Tor's party," Banch said. "I don't know about
the others, but I thought Hanno was for Tor not for himself. Tamir, the man who died in the house, was supposed
to be Tor's man. His house was used as a post by Tor's
people. Hanno thought Tamir was his man, and found out
he was wrong. So Hanno murdered him and set fire to the
house. Hanno was the only one to go inside. It was soon
after the rain stopped. The rest of us stayed with the
ponies. I saw the dog go into the house after Hanno did,
but I didn't see him come out. Suddenly we saw fire and
smoke coming out of the door. Then Hanno came out with

his cloak wrapped around his head. We tried to get in after Tamir and couldn't. Hanno told us Tamir seemed to have a stroke, or an attack, and fell against a shelf knocking down a large container of kerosene. Hanno said this broke on the floor and the kerosene reached the fireplace while he was looking to Tamir. He said Tamir fell when he was coming down a steep set of steps and that he was dead from the stroke and the fall when the fire started.

"When the dog told me the truth, I was going to kill Hanno. I joined a revolution under Tor. I don't like Sulliaba, but a revolution needs outside support. It doesn't need treachery and murder inside. Now I'm no longer for Tor. There's too much Sulliaba. You can try me for treason later. Let me come with you."

I turned to Ross. "You know this man. What do you think?"

Ross looked at Banch coolly, without hostility, and said, "He's intelligent. He's also a troublemaker and rash. But he loves his country, and I think he's honest."

That was very close to my own opinion. Actually I suspected that Hanno, too, might have been telling me a version of the truth. Hurriedly I wrote another note, and said to Banch, "You can't come with us, but you can serve just the same. Deliver Hanno unharmed, along with this note, to Lord Brome in Shores and you will find yourself in less difficulty than you have any right to expect. Take one pony. Hanno will need it. Tresk will give you back your pistol when you start. Now, get along."

Hanno rose slowly to his feet. After a little, mounted or walking, the journey was going to be agony for him. But he had that ahead of him in any event and he didn't seem to be thinking about it. Instead he looked at me out of his battered face with an expression somewhere between amusement and admiration. "Isla Lang," he said, "sometimes you show more sense than I give you credit for. Good luck. You'll need it."

╬

Mounted now, and leading two ponies, we rode steadily at a moderate pace for some two hours. We came into rich, level grain country where the plantations were separated by stands of tall hardwoods, much like colossal hedgerows hundreds of feet in depth. We rode always along an edge of a wood, with Fenris padding along just ahead. As long as he was undisturbed, so were we. His nose and ears were my confidence. If it hadn't been for fatigue and anxiousness, that ride would have been a delight. As the sun climbed, spring clamored again, stronger and headier than the delicate version that came to the lighter soil and thinner air of the Frays.

Shortly before ten o'clock we turned into an extensive and dense woods along the course of a small brook flowing slowly southeast. If we were to be good for anything, we had to have food and some rest. We stayed well away from the stream and didn't go too deep into the woods. Tresk took the ponies upstream to water at a place where he found overlaid animal tracks of various kinds including deer.

Our composite guess was that we were within two miles of the ocean and a mile and a half of the intersection on the map. On our way we had seen houses and barns here and there, and we had also seen the smoke of outdoor fires where men were burning piles of rakings and winter deadfalls. We made a cooking fire and ate a good meal from Hanno's supplies. Then, because I wanted to do the first reconnaissance, the others kept watch while I slept.

Three hours' sleep is a great deal better than none, but you don't feel that way when you first wake up. I got up with all my muscles loosened and my joints begging me not to be pulled back into place just yet. But five minutes later, when I started off on foot with Fenris, my body stopped complaining, and I felt fresh again.

The wood we were in ran north and south, and we stayed inside it moving toward the ocean. There were beginning to be clouds in the sky and the light breeze seemed to be shifting some from northwest to west. There could be showers later. At the first intersecting stretch of trees I turned east toward Shores Bay, and then south again at the next one. By this time I was walking very slowly just inside the edge of the woods. Finally, I stopped altogether and took out the map. If we had made camp where we thought we did, then I must be very close to what I was looking for. The trouble was I didn't really know what I was looking for. I could easily see it without recognizing it. I got up and went on past one more east-west line of trees that blocked my view.

In front of me now was not another hedge of trees, but a horizon of white. It looked as though it rose out of the ground, but I knew it didn't. This was a fogbank that often rolled in to within half a mile of the southern coast at this time of year. The shore was there, maybe half or three-quarters of a mile away. The map showed an elevation of fifty feet just this side of the narrow beaches, and from what I could see the land looked arable all the way.

The ground sloped gently down to the southeast. In the middle distance was the now familiar grouping of this part of the country, a smallish house and then at some distance a large, very tall barn. I unslung Hanno's glasses, lay down among the leaves, and began to study the scene.

Here again I was at some disadvantage. Each region of Islandia does things somewhat differently from others. In the Frays we have no great barns with curving roofs like the ones in Alban, and we pitch our house roofs much steeper. If you don't know exactly what should be in front of your eyes, it is harder to notice something that shouldn't be. This was my case. But if something is really wrong, you ought to be able to sort it out.

After half an hour of painstaking searching—and Hanno's glasses were very good—I could find no sign that the place was not the farm it appeared to be. The horse stalls were on the side of the barn toward me. I couldn't see inside, but in the sun just outside the entrance a middle-aged man sat at a bench working on harness. I watched him test stitching and rivets. If he didn't like the state of the sewing, he set the piece aside. If the trouble was a rivet, he prodded the leather for soundness, worked a new hole through the adjoining pieces with an awl, forced a stem and heel in to seat, slid a spreader over the peg, put the heel on a pounding iron, and then with a hammer splayed the peg over the spreader. It was beautiful.

The cow stable was on the far side, but I could see part of the enclosed yard. The cows evidently had not yet been let out to pasture because the ground of the enclosure was trampled and mired from the passage of the animals to and from and around the well. In one corner was a large, well-seasoned mound of straw and manure. As I watched, an empty, ox-drawn manure wagon came slowly up from a field to the east and entered the yard. The driver backed the wagon into position by the manure pile. Then he and his helper climbed down, took their dung forks and began to throw in another load with the slow rhythm of men who know how farm work is done.

I took the glasses down from my eyes virtually convinced that this pleasant place was innocent. And yet, if my bearings meant anything, this satisfied their conditions almost exactly—within the likely error of the bearings themselves. I considered and discarded the idea of trying to work my way closer. Not in daylight. There was no cover at all. I tried out the notion that the lack of cover itself meant something. But this was no good. All the farms we had seen were arranged this way, some with a few trees around the house and some without, but all in the middle of open fields.

Looking at the whole scene without magnification, I was ready to admit that there was nothing here for us, when a cloud, the deepest and largest yet, began passing across the sun, suddenly darkening the landscape. In the house a light went on. I saw it happen, felt that it probably was needed, and for several long moments afterward thought no more about it.

Then I remembered I had seen the light *go on*. A kerosene lamp, or a candle, does not do this. It starts dim and grows gradually to its full brightness. This light had answered a switch. It was an electric light, and this gave a different meaning to things. Except in some government installations and a few of the consulates, there are no electric lights in Islandia. Electricity meant a generator, and the likely place for it was the barn.

Now that I knew what to look for, I took up Hanno's glasses again. On my side of the barn I could see no exhaust vent for whatever engine was running the generator. Even so, there must be a cable between the barn and the house, and it had to be buried. I had searched the airspace often enough to be sure there was not even a rope hanging anywhere.

But I was too close to the ground to see whether a trench had been dug recently, particularly if the sods had been cut with care and replaced. You need height to identify a line of that sort. Then I searched once more along the foundation of the barn. This time I stopped at something I had seen before but had passed over because it was not unusual in itself. Near the northwest corner, rising some ten inches along the stonemasonry was a pile of earth and gravel. I refocused the glasses as finely as I could and studied the thing.

The part of the pile that was earth didn't tell me anything useful. There was less of it than I'd thought the first time, and what there was had been channeled and eroded. It would look much as it now did whether it had been there a week or a year. As I began to examine the gravel, the sun came out from behind the heavy cloud. In the stronger light the stuff didn't look so much like gravel. In fact it wasn't gravel.

With the certainty of this my hands began to shake. I had to lower the glasses until I was steady enough to see through them again. There was no doubt. The stones in the small pile were granite chips and fragments of mortar. They came from the thick-base wall where some one must have driven a hole with a stone drill and a hammer.

Fenris and I departed quickly and quietly.

✠

"Those are the only buildings?" Ross asked.

"Yes."

"Then there can't be much of a force there."

"No. Eight to ten men possibly. No more."

"Then is this likely to be Tor's headquarters?"

"Yes," Tresk said. "It makes it almost certain. If he wants a communications base close to Shores and the sea —and Hanno told us why he does—he has to do it by disguise. He has foreign equipment, so he is able to change his transmissions to FM, which we can't pick up. He needs a small farm, not a big one. It should be one that actually is a farm and is known as such. It should be a place that has kept to itself and never needed much traffic with the town. This is what Lang has just seen."

Ross wasn't entirely convinced, nor was I. But it was the only supposition we could make. Also I knew I had not been mistaken about the electric light or the drilling in the foundation of the barn.

"Then what next?" Ross said, looking at me.

I had no ideas then, only impatience. With each breath and pulsebeat I felt the moments going by and subtracting themselves from the time we had, whatever it was. I did have the sensation that something usable was trying to move up from the bottom of my mind into sight. But it wasn't going to emerge now. I was still too nervy, too much almost even for ordinary consecutive thinking. Just then I was a poor leader of anything, and knew it.

Tresk said, "They wouldn't lay a cable from the barn to the house just for an electric light. The transmitter must be there. And the house is small. Tor would be a fool to keep prisoners so close to a broadcasting machine, especially when one of them—Morana—knows about such things. I think it is the barn that concerns us most. Anyway we need a closer look at both these places."

This was sensible. The place was our only chance. We had to take it as a certainty.

So I said, "Agreed. How do we get a closer look?"

"I go and do it," Tresk said. "Right now. In another hour it will be twilight. Maybe it will rain. If I'm seen, it shouldn't matter. I won't be recognized. Either of you would be. Keep Fenris here."

It did rain. The dark came early. Hour after cold hour went by and Tresk did not return. Ross and I got what sleep we could in turns, speaking little, each refraining from increasing our total anxiety by not mentioning his own. But unease is contagious. Fenris took it from us and prowled around the camp, lying down only to stand and pace again. Then the ponies contracted it from him, stamping, jostling, and snuffing. In the early morning, an hour or so before dawn, the heavy showers diminished, and gradually the rain stopped but without any lifting of the weather.

With the first light, Ross and I ended our long exercise of speak-no-evil and faced our predicament. We fed the ponies, contrived a fire, and cooked breakfast. Fenris took some out of politeness, but he wasn't interested. Between sips from a sugared pot of steaming tea, Ross said, "Now we know one thing. You found the right place. What's your guess?"

Hot food does help at bad times. I was able to say, "I think *Punch* is right. *While There's Life There's Hope.*"

In the faint light, through the steam from his tea and the fog from the ground, I saw Ross smile. "Well played," he said, "considering the conditions. Go on."

"That's harder. You asked for a guess. Mine is that Tresk was taken, not killed."

"Why?"

"They don't know him. He had no firearms. They would suspect him, but no more. They would want to learn something from him. And Tresk would feel he was more useful alive in their hands than dead. A trap that will hold two may not be strong enough for three."

"It's a good try," Ross said, "and I'll go along with it. But there is a thing called the Reality Principle. I won't say this again and I won't act as though I'd ever said it. Just the same, before we begin we should admit the fact. This will keep our nerve steady and our resolve firm. Our chances are next to nothing, and we both know it."

"Yes, we both know that, and we should acknowledge it now. But all we really know is that we are five ponies, and one dog, and you and I can barely see each other from three feet away. We're depressed, not finished. Let's go," I said.

We took the ponies south through the tongue of woods and tethered them by water near the tip. Then Ross and I and Fenris began the series of checkerboard moves I had gone through yesterday. All the while I was thinking of the ugly matter Ross and I, for all our breakfast frankness, had left unspoken. How did Tor treat prisoners? I had told myself all along that Morana and Dorna were in no danger of maltreatment or torture because Tor had taken them for his own safety and not for what they knew. Also, I had made the assumption, I now had to admit, because Tor was an Islandian not a Sulliaban. Islandians, no matter how bad, didn't do such things. Put that way, the notion sounded as silly as it was.

As individuals the outlook for all of us was poor, but the prospect for Tresk was grim. In spite of what I had said to Ross, I could see no reason to expect that Tor would not put him to the question physically sooner or later. Knowing Tresk, I was sure he had not told Tor anything yet, but the possibilities were not good to think about.

As we trudged on through the wet woods, I realized that the growing weight of my fears and doubts was caused by Tresk in still another way. His loss changed us in kind, whereas Hettin's departure had done so only in degree. Three men still amount to an expedition. But two men walking through the dripping trees are just two men walking through the trees. This insight did not make me feel better.

This time I went well out into the final east-running band of trees so we could keep some kind of watch on the side of the barn I hadn't been able to see yesterday. By the time we were lying prone in the sopping brush, the cattle yard was full of animals shouldering each other and lowing while two men kept them moving to the well and then back into the barn. When the last cow was inside, the two men walked around to the front of the barn and soon reappeared driving the manure wagon. They then forked on the first load of the day.

The scene was completely peaceful. Fenris, restless no longer, lay with his head between his paws a few yards to my right. Above us the overcast was still low and thick, but it was moving with some speed and would probably break up in an hour or so. In front of us there was no sign of life for the next thirty minutes.

Then two men left the house and started for the barn. They walked without hurry and casually, but somehow awkwardly. My stomach tightened and my tongue went dry. Neither man was holding a gun, but through the glasses the unnatural way they carried their upper bodies was plain. I passed the glasses to Ross, who looked and said, "They're wearing pistols inside their cloaks under their left arms, and they're not used to them."

The men went out of our sight just before they reached the front of the barn. After several minutes they showed again with a third man—Tresk. They took position behind him, a pace to either side, and started back toward the house. Tresk was limping on his left leg.

Ross and I had rifles ready, he the .22 and I a .30 caliber. Through lips so stiff they would scarcely form words, I said, "If Tresk does not make a move, we do not fire. If he does, we do not fire unless they start to shoot at him."

Then out in the middle of the field I saw Fenris. I was just beginning to wonder how he got there without my knowing it, when I had a terrible anticipation of the catastrophe that was surely coming. Fenris would force everything. Within seconds we would be shooting.

But Fenris forced nothing. Tresk didn't even look at him. The guards seemed to call to him and whistle at him, but Fenris paid no attention. As on the morning we first saw him, he was aloof and quiet, padding along a few yards from the guard nearest us. When the three men went into the house, Fenris kept on going around the corner and out of sight.

Twenty long minutes later the same trio reemerged, took positions as before, and began the walk to the barn once again. Soon Fenris was there, too, flanking the party on the far side this time. Tresk still limped, but showed no signs of new injury. He walked stolidly, head down, going back toward imprisonment.

Almost exactly halfway between the house and the barn, Tresk suddenly stooped and spun to his left in front of the guard near us. Rising and striking in one motion with his immense speed and strength, he drove the heel of his hand onto the guard's jaw. Then, catching the man as he fell, hurling him against his companion, Tresk turned and ran a swerving, irregular course for the woods without favoring his leg.

The other guard, staggered and nearly felled by his companion's body, struggled to draw his gun. He had it in his hand when Fenris leaped at him, striking him on the arm, the chest, and the head. The pistol sailed through the air, and the guard fell backward to the ground. Fenris didn't seem to bite, but with bared teeth he stood over the man while you could count slowly to ten. Then Fenris turned for the woods, running as close to the ground as a shadow.

Not a shot was fired from anywhere. The people in the house didn't even know of the escape until the guards stumbled up to the door. Then two more men came out, one of them unmistakably Tor. Through the glasses he seemed very angry but not disturbed. I could see his lips move and curl as he told his men what he thought of them. Then he scanned the edge of the woods, shrugged his shoulders, gave the guards a few more words to remember, and waved everyone inside.

✠

Ross nudged me and pointed. A short distance to my right, as though he hadn't been anywhere or done anything, Fenris lay with his head between his paws. Ross and I moved back deeper into the trees. Within a minute I saw Tresk moving cautiously from trunk to trunk. I stood up for him to see me, and then realized that he was using the trees for support as much as concealment. He was limping badly.

"I can use it if I'm scared or mad," he said, as we helped him sit down, "but I mustn't let it stiffen. There's a mantrap just inside the front of the barn, and I fell into it last night." He pointed to his leg just above the knee. "It caught me there on the way down."

Tresk said about Tor, "He came to see me last night and wasn't impressed. Just now he had me brought to him, as you saw. He thinks I'm a stupid accident. He has too many things on his mind to take me seriously. Just now he doesn't have enough men to search for me even if he wanted to. He doesn't know about you, but he's too strong for us to attack him. He's not worried about anything, just impatient. The motor for his transmitter generator was going all night. And I overheard a little from the guards.

Parties of Tor's people will be gathering in these woods during the day. So we can't stay here long."

When I asked him about the barn itself, he smiled and said, "I didn't see much of it. I think the women are in a room at the top. I don't know how to reach it. We can't get in from the front. We could solve the mantrap in daylight, but we'd all be dead." He stood and began to bend and stretch his bruised leg. "On the back side there is no entrance, but there may be a way from the cattle stalls to the lofts."

"Tresk," I said, "you've seen Tor twice. What do you think?"

He stopped flexing and considered the question with his leg half extended. "Tor is quick and bold. And dangerous. And cruel. Not for pleasure. It saves work. He's proud and lazy."

"Do you think he poisoned his father?"

"Yes. It got something done. If Tor found himself in his own way, he might poison himself before he thought twice."

An expedition once again, we moved east through the hedge of trees to a point where the tracks of the manure wagon came close and then turned parallel. Here we were about seventy feet from the fence enclosing the stockyard behind the barn. The fence, if we could reach it, would give us real cover the rest of the way to the barn.

But the stretch from us to the fence was not good at all. The wheel ruts, of course, even when combined with the height of the short grass on the verge, weren't deep enough to give more than the illusion of protection. Even so, the hooves of the oxen and the heavy wheels had churned the entire track to a grayish dun color much like that of our parkas. It wasn't much in the way of camouflage, but it was the best we were going to get. The manure wagon was nowhere to be seen. We told Fenris to stay out of sight and could only hope he agreed. The time for us to move was now.

In single file, several feet apart, the hoods of our parkas up to keep our skin from showing, on elbows and knees to stay below the skyline and on ground of our color, we began the journey to the fence. I led and Ross came last. This put Tresk with his injured leg where it was easiest for us to help him, but it also made him the best target. Turning once to check positions, I saw Fenris at the edge of the woods looking after us. He lowered his head and went back into the trees.

I set a slow pace. Against the urging of every nerve and muscle in my exposed backside I made it wormlike, a wriggle more than a crawl. My mind told me that motion would betray us to the house, not our shape. And even if we reached shelter unharmed but seen, it would do us no good. We might better have stayed in the woods.

I looked ahead and saw we were halfway there, or nearly. The gate seemed so close I could feel the latch in my reaching fingers. Forty feet. Nine or ten strides. Three seconds. Less than that.

I put my chin back down in the mud and roots and hunched again. A long time later, at least five minutes, I reached up and pushed the gate open. We wouldn't know for some time whether we had been observed, but right now nobody could see to shoot at us. I rolled over for a moment to let some of the fear-cramps drain out of my back. Thesk sat with his knees up. Ross followed my example, and said, "In my country you can accomplish all this discomfort in the name of exercise instead of cowardice. You just stand in a doorway and at full length push the backs of your arms against the doorjambs for longer than you can bear it. They call it isometrics. Please remember, Lang, I'm now overtrained." He sat up and wiped the sweat off his face with a parka sleeve.

From here Tresk led us along the side of the barn and into the cow stable. Some fifteen cows, dark brown and white, in a long row of stanchions, were flicking their tails and chewing. They paid us no attention at all. A young bull in a box-stall snorted when he heard us, but he couldn't see over the boarding so he forgot about us. The place was sweet and warm and slightly spicy, I suppose like every well-kept cow barn in the world.

Tresk found what he was looking for on the inside wall in front of the feed bins, the wide slippery noses, and the fifteen sets of softly grinding teeth. There, a pitchfork stood against the wall beside the leavings of a pile of hay. Above it a square opening in the ceiling was the mouth of a two- to three-foot chute down which hay was thrown from the mow. Narrow strips of wood nailed ladderlike went up the wall into the chute, giving a difficult access to the hayloft. At the top the chute was closed by a fitted cover or a hinged trap.

I tried the ladder and found it even worse than it looked. Sometime in the past, when the edges were square, there was purchase for your fingers and toes. Now the rungs all were rounded down at the outer edges. This was

more like climbing a vertical rock face than a ladder, and
the fine chaff I found under my fingers said that this route
had not been used in a long time.

With help from below I got my head and shoulders up
into the chute. There, by forcing my chin onto my chest,
there was just enough height to put my back against one
side and use my legs as a cross brace from below. This
freed my arms, and I raised my hands up to the trap. In
this position a man is like Atlas holding the world on his
shoulders, or like someone trying to do a handstand with
his head and body both on the wrong side of balance. It
was awkward, uncomfortable, and gave no leverage at all
—another one of Ross' isometric torments.

I pushed up slowly and hard. The muscles across my
shoulders and upper arms, untrained for effort in this unusual direction began first to hurt and then to shake.
Nothing whatever happened. I was afraid now that the
trap might be bolted or, just as bad, hinged at the edge I
was trying to force. And I was acutely aware that the
manure crew would be back before long. So I stopped my
motionless struggle and shifted as far to my left as the
chute would let me. From here I drove the palm of my
right hand up at the corner of the trap. This time the
thing budged, showering down hayseed and chaff on me.
Two more blows and I was able to raise the tight-fitting
heavy cover. In another three minutes we were all in the
hay mow and had lowered the trap back into place by the
ringbolt in the top side.

What we were in now was really a larger, openwork
extension of the chute that rose all the way to the roof.
The timbers of the frame were near enough each other so
the hay wouldn't fall onto the trap of itself but still open
enough for hay to be forked through from any level. Just
beyond the frame, the hay stood at shoulder height and
rose evenly to a high point at the west end of the loft. We
climbed onto the hay and took our bearings in the near
twilight.

The place was conventional in its general arrangement.
There was a central nave east and west with lofts on
either side beginning eleven feet or so above the floor. The
spaces underneath the lofts were closed off. Normally,
these would be workrooms and storage space for tools,
harness, and grains. That's what they probably were here
for the most part, but we knew the generator was directly
under us and we could half hear, half feel the motor driving it. There was nothing unusual about the loft we were

in, and the one across from us looked just the same except that there was more hay in it, and the chute down to the horse stables was on the west.

Tresk pointed to the planking inside the main door. "That's the pitfall," he said. "Very simple when I see it from here. It's a big trapdoor on an axle. When the bolts are in, it's as firm as the rest of the floor. Last night the bolts were drawn. I stepped on the outer edge. It dropped me down five feet and put a wall in front of me."

Underneath us a door opened, and the full sound of the motor reverberated through the barn. Bang—chuck, chuck, chuck; Bang—chuck, chuck, chuckchuck; Bang—chuckchuck; Bang—chuck; Bang—

Up from his hay covering Ross said to me, "It's a one lunger, by God! Where did they get it? Fifty years ago in New England they used engines like this to chop silage. Running a radio off it must be chancy."

The racket diminished and then almost stopped as a door swung shut again. It must have been a very heavy door, or perhaps there were two with an airspace between. A man appeared on the floor, walked to within a few feet of the entrance, and then stood waiting.

Then both sides of the big main door (there was a smaller man-sized one cut into each side) swung open slowly, admitting first a shaft and then a flood of light. The silhouette of a man came into the barn. By his shape and bearing he was Tor. Then, from outside, unseen people pushed the doors to once more.

The cutout of a man now took on dimension, and he was Tor. The man waiting probably was an Islandian, but Tor spoke to him as an employer might to an expert. "What power are you running at now?"

"Three-quarters. What you asked for."

"It's not good. How long can you give me full power, with the fuel you have?"

"Two hours."

"That should do it. Give me two hours. Then disassemble and pack. Be ready to leave by sunset."

"What of the guests I . . . ?"

"Yes. They're not assigned to you anymore. I'll take care of them. You needn't concern yourself."

Tor turned and went out, the doors closed behind him, and the mechanic returned to his engine room. None of us spoke for a moment, and then Ross said, "While the doors were open I noticed a couple of things. From the floor there's no way up to the other loft. This one has two ladders. There are none over there." Now that he told me, even in the gloom, I could see this was so. "Another thing," he said, "the hay there in the east end is much older than the stuff over the horse stables. In good light that's plain. Also the old hay is covering something. It's been there long enough so a crosslight shows the top edges of something built underneath it."

"Big enough to be a room?"

"Oh, yes."

There was definition, but no solution. We had guessed right, but what to do? Could we seize the barn and hold it while we discovered and forced some interior stairway? And what then? How to get out? The questions answered themselves. No.

If we went down our ladders, we could get two of us up to the edge of the south loft by standing on shoulders. One man would have to come back. That wouldn't be so bad. He could cover the others. The trouble was that none of us could climb the additional fifteen feet of well-laid, vertical, slippery dried-grass.

Then the thing that had been lying out of reach in my mind began to come forward. A lifting device. In a barn like this there had to be one. A man standing on a loaded wagon, sinking a little with each forkful, couldn't pitch off by hand onto a mow that was rising twenty to twenty-five feet above his head.

It had to be at least a double-fall pulley on a track. This was something you wouldn't dismantle. Even to change rope you would pull the new through on the tail of the old. Where was it? There wasn't light enough to see the underside of the high, central crossbeam where the track should be, and even Ross hadn't looked up there when the doors were open.

I told the others what I was looking for and began climbing up the slope of hay toward the west wall. I didn't think of what we would do if the thing was stored on the other side.

When the slope eased to level, I knew I was on untouched hay. It was dark there, but there was a blacker something in front of me. That was the barn wall. I crawled toward it with one hand out in front. My fingers brushed against the stone and then my right knee came down on the edge of a squared piece of metal.

We followed the ropes to their cleats in the wall, undid them, and worked the double fork down to our first position near the middle of the barn. We needed the extra length of rope. The track under the beam made noises like a hungry cat, and we stopped twice for fear of being heard. But the engine below was running stronger and louder now. Tresk said, "It's no good to gentle it. Do it all at once—fast." We did. This time there was only a hissing whisper from above.

The fork itself was very simple, but hard to describe. It resembled two pairs of ice tongs mounted several feet apart on a common axle. The important thing for us was that there was an axle and, better than that—two: one at the point of leverage and one a bit higher at the point of suspension. The thing could be ridden and pumped.

I went back to the chute and collected the pitchfork the loft man used for the cow barn. I gave it to Tresk. He was the thrower. He hefted it and knew, as I did, that the balance of the tool said to throw it handle first, sure and easy. But he didn't. He let it go tines first, softly, in a high arch. The fork dropped straight and stood upright deep in the other loft. We needn't worry about landing on spikes.

Ross was the first to try the journey. The lifting fork, not under tension, lay jumbled at his feet like discarded parts in the back of a machine shop. He found the upper bar, stood on it, and wrapped his arms loosely around the four fall lines. I picked up the end of the long cord that was used to sway the loaded fork over a loft, pulled out my pistol, and lay down with my head just over the edge. Tresk hoisted Ross so that he swung free over the barn floor, and then higher until he was near the level of the hay in the other loft. It was a strange sight.

Ross grasped the pulley ropes and set himself to pump the ungainly swing. Then he hesitated, looked down at his feet, and stopped. For a second I thought he had vertigo, but then I recognized the trouble. We all should have seen it to begin with. The pulley ropes and their attachments were between him and his destination. He would not be able to jump off. Slowly, carefully, he changed his footing and worked his way around the ropes until he was facing us with his back to where he wanted to go. He could work the swing just as well this way, but he would have to lunge backward off it.

Just then the noise of the engine filled the barn. We all froze still. I saw Ross in mid-air staring down at the barn floor. Pushing my head over the edge, I saw the mechanic, his mouth open, gazing at the incredible thing hanging above him. He was not just astonished; he was shaken.

I managed to make him see me and the pistol, and

motioned to him to move to the middle of the floor. Then
I signaled Tresk to lower Ross. As soon as he was down,
Ross walked around the mechanic and closed the engine
room doors. Now that I could be heard, I told Tresk to go
down the ladder.

I followed him. Finally, when I was partway through
my own climb on the ladder, I awoke from my intense
preoccupation with one scheme of action and perceived
what had been looking me in the face for the last half
hour. This mechanic of Tor's was not a man to be feared
and avoided. He was to be used.

Without taking time to savor my own stupidity, I said,
"I am Isla Lang of the Frays. What is your name?"

"I am Trin of Alban."

On a long chance that could do no harm, I said, "I am
here on the advice of Hanno. Are you Tor's man? Hanno
didn't speak of you."

"I work for Tor on Hanno's orders," Trin said. "How
am I to know you come from Hanno?"

"Hanno is in the town of Shores now," I told him. "I
was with him two days ago. He lent me these." I held out
the binoculars.

He looked and nodded. "They belong to Hanno. He
gave them to you, or you took them from him. What do
you want?"

"To see Tor's guests."

Trin glanced at the collapsed machine on the floor and
then up at the loft. He understood and began to smile.
"Tor thought of everything but that. Yes. It would work."

"But you can make it much easier," I said.

"Not only can," he said looking at the gun, "but must.
All right. I've been thinking about doing it myself anyway."
He took a key out of his pocket and led the way to a
small, heavy, almost invisible door let into the southwest
wall.

✠

After the first great catch at the heart, and the long,
close embrace, a reunion under pressure of this sort is
neither very emotional nor very rewarding. Things are still
too tense and anxious. There is too much to decide and do.

Morana and Dorna seemed well, if pale and thin. The
room had nothing in it but two pallets and a washstand

and commode, but it was clean. A window on the east and another on the south gave light and air, but were too high to see out of. Both of them said they were almost out of their minds from physical inactivity, but neither one mentioned being bored. I already knew that their internal resources were far greater than mine.

We had one overriding question to decide that governed all others. With Tresk's help, I got us down to it. It was not going to be easy to get out of this place, and it was clear that we shouldn't try until night. What to do until then? A good case could be made for doing nothing—that is for leaving Morana and Dorna here, for putting the tools back where they were, for the three of us to hole up in the loft, and for Trin to go back to the engine room. I offered the argument, adding that the one really bad thing about it was that emotionally it was a big step in the wrong direction.

But Trin, who by some process of unnatural selection seemed now to have become one of us, spoke against it. "If you do that you'll have to trust me not to betray you. That wouldn't be wise yet. But there is much more. Something is going to happen soon and Tor is getting ready for it. Men of his are gathering now in the woods outside. I am supposed to take down the motor and generator and put them in boxes. I think he means to move Morana and Dorna. If he does, you will not know because he uses an outside door on the south to get under this loft.

"But if he comes for them and they are not here, and I am not in the engine room, he will be certain I have escaped with them because there are only two keys," and he held up his own. "We"—and he used the pronoun for the first time—"should take advantage of this. Tor will not believe I have done anything so desperate just to stay in some other part of the barn. We should all go up to the other loft."

Trin was convincing, the more so because, reversing the situation, he offered himself as hostage for what he said. His estimate might not be correct, but I couldn't see anything wrong with the probabilities nor any room for deceit. It was a pleasure to watch the eyes of the women light up and sparkle at the prospect of leaving this room now, whatever the chances.

For a long time things went just as Trin said they would. He went up an inside ladder to the south loft and recovered the fork Tresk had thrown. We all went into the engine room briefly. Ross, Tresk, and I drank water from a pump there and filled our flasks. Trin checked the engine and the fuel, and seemed satisfied that it would run the remainder of the two hours Tor wanted. Then from an adjacent tool room he brought two sheath knives and a long brush knife, each on a wide belt.

He armed himself with the brush knife, took an awl and drove new buckle holes in the other belts. These he handed to the women. Morana and Dorna took the weapons, looked at each other, at me and Ross, and buckled them on. We agreed then that in case the barn was searched we would try to keep hidden, but we would fight if discovered. I asked Tresk about his leg. He said it was stiff and sore, but not as bad as it had been or as he had thought it would be.

In the loft once more, Ross and I stowed away the lifting fork while at the other end Trin pitched a night's supply of hay down to the cow barn. He told us this was one of his regular chores and that he'd already done it for the horse barn. After this, Trin bringing the pitchfork with him, we gathered on the high, dark, untouched plateau in the southwest corner and made the best dispositions we could.

It's impossible to have any real idea of the passage of time in a case like that. I knew we all heard the motor spit, cough, and stop. That was one marker. I talked with Trin for a while about himself, Tor, and Hanno. He said Hanno sent him to Tor to begin with. Tor trusted him, but not with anything very important except the running of the generator and the security of the hostages. He didn't know what went out over the transmitter or what the frequencies were. He thought Hanno and Tor were working together somehow, but that they didn't belong to each other. Hanno had told him to run Tor's machines and take his instructions. Hanno was interested in the hostages and hadn't suggested anything about releasing them or even protecting them. Trin said this disturbed him. I had begun to like the man.

After that I think we all napped, not soundly but perhaps for a length of time.

When the door to the prison stairway burst open there was no doubt about the fury with which it was pushed. Running steps crossed the barn floor. The doors banged open into the engine room where Trin was not and the machines stood silent and still not packed. Steps came back into the barn.

Through the layers of hay in front of my face I saw Tor

very dimly, standing with a wild, enraged kind of grace, knees a little bent, arms out from his sides, head thrust forward, roaring. "Trin! Trin, I say! Where are you? This is Tor! Come here to me!" In his great anger, his powerful voice acquired a metallic keening quality, rising and falling like a siren. When there was no answer but silence, steps went toward the main door and then outside. I thought for a second Trin was completely right, but then there came two sharp blasts on a whistle.

"There'll be a search," I said. "Let's get under."

Up where we were the hay was almost a foot higher than the heavy horizontal beams separating the vertical walls from the tall, curving vault of the roof. These beams were flush with the walls on the outer surface, but projected beyond them on the inside by several inches. With Trin's fork, and our hands, we had opened six, long, narrow slits in the hay reaching under the beams. They would give concealment, breathing space, and some protection.

We worked our separate ways in, squirming down, pulling the thick, interlaced layers of dry grass over us, hoping that things would look all right on top in the dimness. I forced myself against the wall and made myself as thin under the beam as I could. Morana's niche was just beyond my head to the west. Stretching my arm up between the grass and the wall, my fingers touched her foot. I wrapped my hand around her ankle and found I was calmed and strengthened by this remote, intimate connection. In her own darkness, her own box, I knew Morana felt it, too, because she moved her free leg to touch.

We would have done better to climb in heads and hands toward each other, but we didn't think of it—how many things I didn't think of, or became obsessed with. I closed my fingers some on her anklebone. She responded with a gentle bowstring motion of the Achilles tendon of her other leg across my hand.

Listening to Tor giving orders, his voice muffled through the hay but clear enough, my worst worry was that some of us might sneeze. We had soaked handkerchiefs and cloths in water. Each of us had one to breathe through. But even so . . . Tor's instructions gave us the number of the search party, some undoubtedly called from the woods. And there would be others surrounding the building.

"We need light," he said. "Open the main doors. You two, guard them. Two men into the south storerooms. Two into the engine room side. Two men up to the south loft. That ladder's in there. Two up to the north loft. You can see the ladder." There was nothing about the stables. He must be searching them from outside.

For what seemed like fifteen or twenty minutes and probably, this once, was just that, I received no more direct intelligence. When you are thinking hard about a place you know, and about the actions and decisions someone else is being constrained to make in it, you can keep close to the clock.

In due course and by indirection, time told me two important things. The men looking for us were working as a team, not individually, and they were searching the lower part of the loft first. When a signal finally came from them, felt as much as heard, it was a repeated something that was a *chuff* with a hiss in it. This grew stronger, but slowly.

I didn't recognize the signals, and yet I knew that I knew what they were. The sounds and impacts seemed to move laterally as well as forward because they diminished regularly after each increase.

Now there was a tickle in my nose. I held my breath, counting to ten, to thirty, to sixty, to ninety, and exhaled slowly. I didn't sneeze, but I was still about to and my head was spinning. For a moment my senses all seemed to leave and move up on top of the hay to join the hunt for me. My hands, feeling as though they were grasping something, told me without doubt what the chuffing was. I didn't worry any more about sneezing.

The searchers were probing the hay with pitchforks. This was sensible of them. I should have anticipated it. I thought of the others, hoping they might not identify the sound. But they would, with the possible exception of Ross.

My connection with external time broke then. The chuffing of the forks took its place. Anyone who has experienced fear knows the indecent expedients a person uses in order to remain himself. *Suum cuique.* I abased myself in my own way in front of myself until I was able to put names to the things I was afraid of. A long, curved tine driving down through my eye or my throat was the worst. Next, and part of the other, was the fear that I, or one of us, would not be able to stick it out and would break cover.

As the search drew nearer, I began to feel the real force of the thrusts. They were driving the forks hard and deep. One man drew even with me and worked across toward me. I was on my side, my back pressed against the wall. The fork came down and the hay moved across my ribs. The next blow struck the hidden beam just above my face.

The fork rebounded, its tines singing like a tuning fork. For a moment or so the searcher stood over me speaking to himself about the stupidity of forgetting the beam and the hurt in his wrenched wrists. Then he moved on past Morana, giving the beam fair clearance by the sound of it.

From the other side of the loft there came the clash of metal on metal followed by the high, thin noise of good steel snapping. Up from the barn floor there was Tor's voice, "What do you find?"

"Nothing." A pause. "I tripped on the pulley fork. Broke a tine. Nobody's up here. We'd have pricked 'em."

And from his companion, "We've stabbed every foot of hay there is."

Tor said, "Then come down."

✠

No doubt Tor was lazy, as Tresk said, but when he was stung he didn't give up easily. Sounds of active search in the near distance came to us for hours after Tor ordered his men out of the barn. We came up from our crypts very soon, but the stars eventually told us we didn't leave the loft until well after midnight.

When things had been still for some while, and when we knew we couldn't wait any longer in any case, I said to Trin, "Do you think he's posted men to watch the barn?"

"Maybe," Trin said, "but it isn't like him. He's searched the barn. He's had men in to pack the machinery I left. He's searched everywhere he knows to look. He's done what he can. We've escaped him. There are other things to be done. With Tor there always are. When he has finished something, he doesn't go back to it." After a moment, Trin added, "But I was wrong about him before and now we are all ten years older than we should be."

I remembered that, along with the fact that we would have failed if we had done what I suggested. I remembered, too, that we couldn't go back through the woods. There was only one other way.

We went out through the side door on the south and made for the sea. Overhead, the stars had not yet begun to pale, but we saw them dimly through streaks of cirrus clouds whose lines indicated they were in the stream of a powerful north wind. On the ground the air was chilly, but almost still. After a few steps I felt something cold and damp on my fingers and then something warm and soft under my hand. Fenris was back again.

The instant joy and pleasure of this reunion, sharper than any conscious emotion I felt at finding Morana safe, shocked me without surprising me. I've seen the thing in other people and had it happen to me in lesser situations. It's something I feel ashamed of when I recognize it, but I don't really understand it. Learned explanations don't quite reach it. What I know is that Fenris lightened my heart then when I needed help.

The shore was some distance away. Trin said a mile. My guess was half of that. We were both correct. Our inclination, and the shape of the land, took us away from the barn and the house more to the east than the sea. When I arranged the party in walking order after we reached our first bit of cover, I gave Morana the rifle I had slung on me, keeping one of our two pistols.

Mostly by touch in the dark, she checked the magazine and the safe lever and then hung the piece across her back. Then for a moment she took my face between her hands, and said, "Don't worry so much about the rest of us, Jon. You just lead, we'll follow."

By the time we completed our circuit to the sea, it seemed to me the stars were beginning to dim. The surf down on the narrow beach was light for this coast at this season. Beyond the seaward line of breakers there was so little motion it was difficult to distinguish the surface of the water. We worked our way carefully down the steep land's end to the beach. I wanted no falls or broken bones at this point. Then we set off west along the inner edge of the shingle.

We didn't have far to go. The beach was about a quarter of a mile long. It is the middle section of a shallow crescent bounded on the east and west by short horns of tumbled rock rolled up there by the sea through centuries of southerly gales. In the predawn dark the footing on the beach was not bad so much as dangerously unpredictable. Pads of new kelp from some recent storm would slide on stones or cover a water hole. We had to test our steps as though we were climbing a rock face.

Two places behind me Ross misjudged. I heard the gulp of his feet going down into water and then a thudding as he fell against the bottom of land's end. The procession stopped. No sound from anyone. Then from Ross, very low, "Christ, what's here? A rope? Two? This one crosses. A cargo net."

I went back to him. He put my hands on the heavy ropes and their crossings. "All right," I said, "go up and unpeg if you can. No chances." He started up the net, and Trin with him. The rest of us kept on along the beach. Morana, Dorna, and Tresk began to press up behind me. I wanted to hurry, too, but I did not increase the pace.

The beach ended some distance from the western horn of rock. Under the lightening sky we could see its profile. It was a horn, or a fang, fifty to seventy feet high thrusting twelve times that into the sea. Between us and it stretched a grim rubble of stones, rocks, and boulders. We struggled back up the steep pitch to land's end and lay flat in the grass to get our bearings. We had come up west of the house, and near us was a patch of what looked like blueberry and beach plum bushes, an extension of one of the north-south tree-hedges. We made for it, dropped down behind it, and found Ross and Trin already there.

"It seemed the likely place," Ross said. "We dropped the cargo net down onto the beach. Things are beginning to happen." He pointed out to sea.

Good sense said we had done what we came for and should get away while we could. We didn't. I haven't talked with any of the others about this, except Morana, but I think we all had the feeling somehow that what was about to happen was more important to each of us than being hostages or redeeming them. The scale of things was changing. We wanted to be there for something bigger than the hugger-mugger of the forks in the hayloft. Something that would give a reason to that. And for all but one of us, our country was at issue.

For Ross it may have been as intense as it was for us, certainly more complicated. An American, at the height of his country's imperium, he must feel in his bones the history of Rome, Spain, and England. And here in Islandia —Transmarine Gaul in one sense and Tibet in another— there was at last the ancient east-west-north-south conflict. He was involved here, and so was his country by default or engagement.

Looking where Ross pointed, I saw first that the fog-bank had dissolved or retreated south out of sight. Next, well out on the water, I picked up several rows of dark dots. I'm not good at estimating distance at sea, but they looked faraway. Hanno's glasses turned them into four rows of powered barges, five to a row, heading toward the beach. I fixed on the leading barges and guessed they were carrying sixty to seventy men each, a first landing force of almost 1400.

Then in the improving light, hull partly down in the distance, I saw a familiar silhouette that could be the Russian trawler. Fore and aft of her were lower, sharper profiles that could be armed escort vessels, and beyond all of them were two large shapes with the high superstructures of merchant ships. Transports for men and equipment.

The escort vessels standing by the trawler were destroyers and had to be Russian because Sulliaba had nothing that big. The transports were something else. Sulliaba had a merchant marine of sorts. The long sequence of indignities old merchant ships go through before they founder, rust apart, or go to the breaker's yards does not always end in the Levant trade or the Indian Ocean. From their silhouettes, these two ships were built on the Tyne or at Fore River soon after the First World War.

This flotilla must have left Sulliaba days ago on a wide swing to the east and south. That was the only way to avoid detection. Morana touched my arm and motioned toward the tight tracery of still leafless branches that was our cover. Through the stems I began to see a confusion of running and place-taking in the grassy space between the house and the barn. Tor was forming his men to welcome the allies and brothers from the north. No doubt he would move the formation down to land's end at the dramatic moment. From the way his people were shaping up, they wouldn't impress their Sulliaban friends favorably, let alone the Russian advisers. But then, with the cargo net dumped onto the beach, and with some wading from the barges, the union at the top of land's end would be scraggly on both sides. Meanwhile the barges came on.

Suddenly I was sick and sour. I wanted to be away from here. I didn't want to watch this sloppy, skillful treason. We were in no danger now for some time. Not until the Sulliabans were ashore from the transports and began sending out patrols. Our job was to watch it and get away. But there was nothing in me to do it with except the word that it should be done. I touched Morana's hand. Her fingers wound around mine like wire.

Then there was a whisper from Tresk. "Look there." He pointed over the horn of rock to the west. Emerging from behind it, moving out into open water, were two motor torpedo boats, an Islandian version of a DE, and a seagoing tug. Looking automatically east, I saw a similar small force moving out from the other rock promontory. Six fighting craft and two tugs. This must be Islandia's entire naval establishment east of Islandia Bay on the south coast.

The formations moved slowly, MTB's in front, tugs in the middle, the DE's astern. The white water under the stern of the tug near us diminished, then vanished, and she slowed almost to a stop. A man holding a gaff leaned over the port side and brought aboard a small, gray float attached to a light line. He unhitched the float, and gave the line to a team of four who walked it down to the stern and began hauling in. It came slow and hard. Finally, dripping and snakelike, the end loop of a hawser came up out of the water. The crew worked it onto the towing bollard, and then the tug got underway to the south-south-east. As this happened, the DE turned hard east parallel to the beach. In the same moment, its sister ship turned west toward it.

I wasn't feeling disgust any longer. I don't know what I felt, except Morana's fingers twined around mine and mine around hers. This seemed to have been going on forever. I was aware of the discomfort of the grip, and for her it must have been outright pain, but neither of us released.

I didn't understand the meaning of what was happening on the water, and there was no time to work it out. From the southeast horizon, at that instant there blazed an intolerably brilliant white light. It glared at us for a moment and then began to wink. Another ship, or a group of ships, was now involved. Whatever the vessel was, its message was for us, not the Russians or the Sulliabans.

The signalman was a master of masters. He sent the message so fast I could make out only that it was in clear English, and I'm good at Morse. Then there was a repeat, and a repeat again, each a bit slower than the one before. By then I could read it: FROM: COMMANDER U.S.S. BANGOR/TO: COMMANDER ISLANDIAN FORCES AFLOAT/ THIS IS VISITING SQUADRON. AT YOUR SERVICE SHORT OF SHOOTING. ADVISE.

The Islandian DE heading eastward was barely moving and was still not quite abreast of us when its signal light lit up. It sent a two-word message repeated twice. "Dewey. Thanks." This was senseless to me, and it eluded Ross, but it didn't puzzle the American commander. Beginning seemingly at once, and thereafter minute by minute, four

American ships grew bigger in my glasses. At last Ross said, "I've got it. At the battle of Manila Bay the British moved their ships between the Germans and Admiral Dewey to keep the Germans from helping the Spanish."

"I hope it makes you feel better," I said. "Look at that."

The two DE's had now taken position off the center of the beach, their bows pointing southeast and southwest, enough of an angle so that all their guns bore on the on-coming barges and the small escort craft I could now see were with them. Our tugs and MTB's were well out on the east and west flanks of the barges and still somewhat in-shore of them. I wondered why the DE's held their fire. It was dangerously late now. I understood none of this.

Then, as I watched, queer things began to happen in the barge formation. The leading barges were breaking their lines, pinching in toward each other. And they seemed to be slowing down. One of the escort vessels on the east looked dead in the water.

Once again I lost all sense of time. Out at sea the American squadron was much nearer. It was full daylight now, and had been since I couldn't remember. A gray sky over gray, quiet water. Without glasses I could distinguish the shapes and some of the details of the cruiser and the destroyers. Many deadly things are exceedingly beautiful, and these were certainly among them. Those sinister, pow-erful ships hurling themselves smoothly up over the curve of the sea was something to make you catch your breath.

Among the barges confusion was spreading. The front rank was stopped, the boats squeezed in to within a few yards of each other. Back through the columns, some barges were drifting out of control. Others turned out of their lines to keep from ramming the ones ahead. Both the escorts on the west looked to be in trouble. Out on the flanks, the tugs and MTB's, steering south now and per-haps even converging, were seaward of all but the last rank of barges.

It was Tresk, the real seaman from Dorn Island, who finally saw what was going on. "They've laced and fouled all that water with nets," he said. "And the tugs have a line of nets strung between them on that hawser. You notice they're not moving very fast." Then I understood. Brome must have collected every fishnet on the southeast coast. Some of them, weighted at the bottom and buoyed at the top, he laid out from the beach in patterns that would turn the bows of the landing craft and then entan-gle their propellers. From the other nets he made one huge seine and strung it along the hawser which the tugs were now wrapping around the crippled barges.

The last rank of four barges, still unencumbered, turned back and headed toward the trawler and the transports. Our MTB's let them pass, and they crossed unharmed a half mile in front of the leading American destroyer. Inside the nets, under the guns of the DE's, the Sulliabans began throwing arms and ammunition into the water.

All this time Tor and his men, gathered at the edge of land's end, stood watching good plans and firm hopes turn into disaster. They kept on standing there. I could feel no sympathy for Tor, but something in me understood what must be happening in him.

Morana felt it, too. We had extricated our fingers from each other without being aware of it. She said, "It must be hard to lose when you know you're bad and know you're wrong."

One of Tor's men turned away in distress and, with no apparent purpose except to stop seeing what was happening down on the water, swung his gaze around the rest of the landscape. Something he saw in the north stopped him. He started and then stood rigid, pointing. Tor turned, everyone turned. I peered through the bushes.

Pouring out of the woods, the same woods we had used and Tor's people had used, came swarms of men. Some were gathering in rough formations and marching toward the sea. Others just kept on coming as they were in twos, and threes, and singly. An advance guard of twenty or so was already well south of the house and the barn. They weren't uniformed, but each man seemed to be wearing some item of uniform equipment that would identify him as a member of the special levy. This was no body of troops, but it was eager.

Tor stood looking for a moment. Then he bent his knees slightly and thrust his head forward in the position I had noticed in the barn. With a strange, awkward, wide-armed motion he drew a pistol and raised it. It was impossible to tell whether he intended to rally his men or shoot himself. He did neither.

Out of the corner of my eye I saw a man drop to one knee about two hundred yards away. Tor's pistol slipped from his fingers and he was falling where he stood when the sound of the shot reached us.

The marksman rose to his feet, but stayed where he was. The glasses didn't show me his face, which was turned away, but his arms were unnaturally white and remarkably bulky. His arms could be bandaged. The man could be Hanno. Hanno back in Isla Brome's good graces. Hanno was very good at talking. Good enough for that probably. And Hanno was good at shooting. That one excellent shot could save him a lot of trouble.

It was all over here. And it was all over with the rebellion. I had a feeling that it would soon be all over with the invasion in the north, but for the first time I had a sharp stab of fear that it would cost Atta's life first.

I didn't want to talk to Hanno. I didn't want to congratulate Brome right now, much as he deserved it; and particularly I did not want to go over what Brome, if I knew him at all, would refer to as the stirring events of recent days.

I collected the others by eye and touch. We moved out to the west of the beach plum and blueberry patch and up the west side of the tongue of forest toward the place where we hoped the ponies still were.

Fenris padded along just ahead and a few feet to the left.

AFTERWORD

New York City
November

When Morana and I arrived here a month ago we were taken up enthusiastically by the American press for a few days, and we drew crowds wherever we went. Now we are again anonymous in public, which is a relief, but we both suffer under the pressures of American life.

Morana tried to prepare me for it by saying that if I intensified my grandfather's descriptions ten or even twenty times I would still be short of the reality. I didn't understand what she meant until I was out of the plane and had been on the ground for two or three hours. To say that I was undergoing cultural shock, a popular term here, is true, but that is only half the experience. The rest was physical shock, and still is. People in this country not only must do more difficult things and do them faster than anywhere else, but they must also spend more physical and nervous energy to do even the simplest things. The sheer noise, rising, falling, never stopping, hour after hour, day and night—this is shattering.

There is no doubt in my mind that the Americans are a great people to survive and thrive inside this epileptic artifact, simultaneously a dynamo, a hall of spinning mirrors, and a chamber of reverberation. I expected to admire Americans, and I find I also like them. But to borrow from their idiom, they can have it. I can't take it very long.

Morana and I have adjacent suites high on the northeast corner of the splendid old Plaza Hotel. The rooms are spacious and well proportioned. The ceilings are high. Occasionally, for minutes at a time, the illusion of serenity, though never of quiet, is almost persuasive. We feel very fortunate.

The second weekend in October I went to Vermont at the invitation of a second or third cousin, I'm not sure which. His name is William Gravelle and he is a lawyer in New York. He is in his late forties, tall, spare, energetic, the gray inconspicuous in his sandy hair. He and his wife have two sons in college and an older daughter with a family of her own.

On the Friday afternoon I flew with Gravelle and his wife in their private plane to a small airfield near Woodstock. From there we drove another eight miles into the country. The sun was still two hours high, and the weather was one of those miracles autumn produces now and then in characteristic ways in the temperate zones. The country was much like parts of Islandia, great sweeps of rolling grass meadows disappearing between heavily forested mountains. In the late afternoon all the green things were rich with gold from the sun, and the foliage was even more brilliant than the magnificent displays Islandia puts on. Here there were more bright yellows and reds among the wine and russet. The house was white clapboard with straight, sharp lines, the kind I remembered my grandfather talking about.

Gravelle told me New York would have killed him years ago if he didn't have this to come to. In a sense, even now, I understand this and believe it. At the time I thought I understood completely. Vermont was as beautiful and seemed as tranquil as the Islandia in which I grew up.

But we were still inside the housing of the dynamo, and its energies and tensions reached him here intensified by the fact that they didn't belong. It goes without saying that Gravelle is intelligent. He is also friendly, conscientious, humble and witty in important ways. More than anything else he is concerned, but about what I don't quite know. Everything perhaps.

On both evenings the television brought into the house the city he had bought an airplane to get away from at will; and it brought other cities, ghettos, truncated statements and pleas, war and destruction abroad, violence and pillage at home, and interminably senseless discussions by panels of experts.

Once, during a commercial which Gravelle turned off with a remote-control switch, I said, "All this is still astounding to me. What does it do to you to see and hear this day after day? How can anyone make a policy, or live with a policy, when all you see are splinters and pieces and no shape?"

Gravelle recognized the change in tone from the cousinly to the semi-ministerial, and he didn't like the question. He didn't answer me directly, but he said something more interesting, "In New York there isn't time to keep track of what's going on. Up here we can catch up."

Saturday, Gravelle didn't get far from the house, or even out of it more than once or twice. He was expecting long-distance phone calls, and he worked on papers in the intervals. He had five calls, protracted ones. I overheard parts of his end of two of them. He was easy, instructive, authoritative, resourceful. He knew exactly what he was talking about and a great deal more. From what I heard, the subjects were important but not so urgent that he couldn't have held the same conversations from New York on Monday, or Tuesday, or Wednesday. Unless perhaps there were so many really crucial matters during a New York week that affairs of this order were scheduled for leisure time in Vermont. Or maybe professionally, and as a requirement of conscience, Gravelle himself made sure the tension never relaxed too much.

Frances Gravelle must be about the same age as her husband. Her hair is dark mahogany with some white in it. She is a beautiful woman in any time and place, and she dresses with a casual disregard of fashion that requires knowledge and self-confidence.

Her house is a skillfully simple, handsome, comfortable place. There are good books, good chairs, and nice windows. The trouble is that often you can't use them. Frances Gravelle responds to a social silence as nature does to a vacuum. She abhors it.

If you try to read in her living room when she is anywhere in the public part of the house, she will interrupt and make conversation. She doesn't do this to be rude, and it isn't. I know she considers it a friendly social obligation that rests on her. It's not that she herself loves to talk; she is more than willing to listen to others. But in her dining room or living room, talk of some kind there must be. After a good deal of annoyance, it began to penetrate my Islandian mind that there was a lot to be said for the custom. This didn't happen until quite late in the game when I discovered that it was perfectly acceptable to take a book and escape to your room with it.

Sunday morning Frances went to church. Not, she said, to hear Mr. Imry preach. He only had four sermons and she knew them all very well. But after the service she could grab him and get some answers about the Organizing Committee for next year's Street Fair. Gravelle asked me if I would like to go for a walk.

Very soon we turned off the paved road onto a narrow dirt one that wound through undulating orchard land and then climbed through steep pastures toward a pass in the high hills. The trees, like cool fire, now marched close to us, and now receded leaving stretches of meadow. A hawk circled for a while overhead. It was quiet, so quiet that the insect noises from the grass sounded like a conversation. A covey of partridge whirring out of some young poplars was an explosion.

Early in the walk, Gravelle said, "We could go up through my woods. But I think spring is the time to see woods from the inside."

For an hour and a half, until we were back on the paved road, that was all either of us said. Meanwhile we absorbed the weather, and walked the city out of our systems. The morning showed me an unexpected aspect of Gravelle, and so possibly of other Americans. It was one that I liked, and it started me thinking somewhat differently about the possibilities of my job here.

My assignment came in two parts. The first was to accredit myself as the first Islandian Minister to the United States, or any country for that matter, secure suitable quarters in Washington, and employ an American clerical and household staff. Then, in my capacity as Minister, I was to complete the formal arrangements for the Islandia Bay project and for several large generators and turbines we needed for new hydroelectric plants.

Morana also had two jobs. One was to lead me around by the hand until I got my bearings. The other was to help Lord Farrant de-fuse the Sulliaba crisis in the United Nations. Things now called for a general toning down. We didn't intend to withdraw any of our claims. For one thing, they were true. For another, this would tempt people to listen when Sulliaba said she had suffered patiently for years under intolerable Islandian provocation and that, in the event, she was invited in by the legitimate successor of the Islandian Head of State. Also, Sulliaba was saying that none of her troops had entered Islandian territory. Thanks to Atta, this was almost so. Our best course was to lower the Islandian voice by several decibels, and to avoid involving Russia. In short, the problem was to stop complaining without seeming to.

Yesterday I think was a turning point. The Washington plane put me down at La Guardia on a cold, starry evening at about six o'clock. I was feeling much cheered, and still am. It looks now as though Morana and I will be free to go home before long and turn things over to Lord Farrant in New York and a long-term representative in Washington.

I have been Minister officially now for almost three weeks. In Washington there is, physically, a Ministry with a small staff. And now I feel confident for the first time that we can contract for the modest program we want instead of the comprehensive development the Americans proposed. I thank the weekend in Vermont for letting me see that even though what the Americans suggested was what they were convinced we ought to have, they still might be sympathetic to what we actually wanted if I could reach in them the layer of Islandian sensibility I had found in Gravelle.

When I left Islandia I wasn't hopeful. Just one thing was brutally clear. If we didn't modernize and soon, we would be overrun and vanish as a nation. In that case, we would be modernized anyway by someone else and for his own purposes. It was certainly better to do it ourselves no matter what we had to pay for it. The trouble was that I could see no chance of changing at all without changing ourselves almost totally. No one was likely to help us unless we did this. But the draft agreements* I had just been over in Washington made it possible for us to stop, or pause, at a partway house of our selection. Whether we could, or would, stop there was another matter. But the good thing was that it would still be our matter.

Once in my rooms at the Plaza, I called Morana who said she had just come in herself and was about to shower off the day's accumulation of United Nations. "When you've done the same with Washington, come on over. I have our first good batch of letters from home. They came to Farrant today in the pouch. I've saved mine to read with yours."

Half an hour later in Morana's sitting room I began to make drinks. For Morana, who had fallen in with the diplomatic custom, a vodka martini. As for me, I kept on verifying my grandfather's opinion that Americans could be forgiven many sins for the invention of sour-mash bourbon.

Then we sat down to the letters, handing them back and forth, or reading passages aloud. Until now all we

* See Appendix VII: Agreement With the U.S., pp. 222–23.

had had were coded official messages and a few penciled notes saying, "Good work. Keep it up. All well here." At one point Morana had said to me in straight American, "Jon, I think they've lost their grip. The way they talk, they're here and we're there. What are we supposed to be? Their hands and fingers? I suppose that's it. But we're not. Here it's up to us. Then they can accept it or reject it."

They were pressed and busy at home, as the letters showed. Morana handed me her first one, and said, "I've ordered club sandwiches and coffee for eight-thirty."

✠

Commiter to Morana:

". . . My country plans to raise the General Consulate here to the status of a Ministry. Considering recent events and what they suggest for the future, this is a sensible decision and more than a courteous gesture of reciprocity. I may, or may not, have the honor of being the first United States Minister to Islandia. It would mean a great deal to me. At best, though, this would be a formality, because retirement is upon me within a few months. Curiously, this makes my appointment both more and less likely. More, because it would say to Islandia that America valued Islandia's approval of my activities here. Less, because it would mean upgrading me into another classification, and paying me a larger pension. My guess is that the *more* will prevail over the *less*. I hope so.

"Retirement is hard for anybody. It puts an additional question to a Foreign Service Officer, and I have given it hard thought. As a result I have asked Isla Mora and Isla Dorn if I may live in Islandia as a private citizen. An American citizen, not Islandian. I want to remain American, but it is borne in on me that the only way I may expect to do this, in any subjective sense of the word, is to stay here. If I return home, I know I will spend the rest of my life thinking, feeling, and behaving as an Islandian. You should reflect on this in case you are tempted to become a career diplomat.

"I attended those portions of the Council hearings on Hanno that were open to the public. Naturally, I have no comment on the verdict or the ultimate disposition. But Hanno interests me very much as a para-professional type.

He belongs to a brotherhood, almost a priesthood. For centuries, it seems, I have had to deal with security officers, high and low. There have been those of my own country, my host country, and sometimes others. Because they are devoted to the safety of the country—not its quality or purpose—they reverse the values most people live by. Their own treachery becomes loyalty, and a statesman's courageous good faith can be treason. I think Hanno is the purest specimen I've seen . . ."

✠

Atta to Jon

". . . When you left here, Sulliaba was still in the passes in force. One morning ten days later our patrols found nothing in front of them but mist. The enemy might never have been there. In fact, that's probably what he will say.

"Father took your seat in the Council for the Hanno hearings. The one thing I did was to get a writ from Lord Dorn and search Hanno's offices. You remember the pictures of the avalanche he showed you? I found the negatives and the record for them. They were taken two years ago. There was no avalanche on that slope last fall. The two men you saw in the pass got through to the north without any doubt . . ."

✠

Ross to Jon

". . . In another few weeks, when plans are further along, I am going home for a while on Islandian business. I hope Dorna will come with me to help, and I believe she may. Perhaps you will still be there?

"Since the war I have modified my ideas about Islandian education. I still feel that all curricula, from bottom to top, should be broadened and world oriented, but I'm now convinced that we should develop a powerful and searching program of Islandian and Karain studies within this general scheme. The problems are many and I won't insult you with the jargon that describes them. One very important question—which I'm not competent to answer although I suspect the answer is no—is whether modern mathematics and science can be taught effectively by means of the Islandian duodecimal system.

"My—our—trip to the U.S. is to make a continuing arrangement for building subject collections in the University library, and to recruit eight to ten scholars in various disciplines for one- to two-year visiting terms. I don't necessarily want them young.

"When I went to Dorn and Mora with what I had in mind, they gave me a firm and cordial authorization. It means, of course, that I will stay in Islandia for a number of years. After that, who knows? No lifework I have ever imagined for myself interests me half as much as the beginning of this reality . . ."

✠

Isla Mora to Morana

". . . In a country like this where there are few laws and many customs, a trial for treason is difficult procedurally.

"Hanno was required to explain his conduct to the Council in open session. What an extraordinary man! Ambiguous. Supple. Totally selfless and yet nothing but self. He was the most powerful man in Islandia for years, and very few even suspected it.

"There is now no doubt that he knew everything about the Tor conspiracy and Sulliaba's connection with it. In addition, there were several overt things he did to promote it. In explanation, he said perfectly correctly that he had taken no oath to support the monarchy, or the Council, or any particular form of government. His loyalty was to the country, and his duty was to do anything and everything to minimize danger to the country under any conceivable circumstances. Presumably including joining the enemy. The Council didn't like this statement, but it was difficult to take exception to it in a way that Hanno could not turn to his advantage. Some tried and had no success. I didn't like what he said, either, but I have to admit the grandeur and self-serving generosity of this philosophy of duty impressed me very much.

"Finally, it was the Lang family that caught up with him. The evidence about the avalanche pictures was damaging. Then old Isla Lang said, 'You say you did not shoot Tor to prevent him from testifying against you. Why *did* you kill him?'

" 'To bring his revolt to a quick end. As long as Tor was alive, it would have gone on. And Sulliaba would have kept fighting.'

"Lang asked, 'What if Tor's cause had still been headed for success after you inadvertently betrayed it to my son? Then what would you have done? Would you have attempted Tor's life?'

" 'The question didn't arise. This is hypothetical.'

" 'Agreed. You have been explaining your actions by hypotheses. I put it to you again. If Tor was going to win, what was your duty as Security Chief?'

" 'To be in a position to serve the country through Tor's government.'

" 'Why did you not serve the country through this government?'

" 'I did, as Isla Brome will testify.'

" 'And as Tor would if he could. On second thought, I believe you. One more question, Hanno. If Tor had won, you were prepared to be his Security Officer?'

"Hanno said, 'Yes. That, and something more. I would have been—well—a filter, a translation point between Tor and Islandia on one side and Sulliaba on the other. That would have been necessary for the country.'

"And that was all that was necessary for the Council. Ancient man? Future man? I still do not know. Hanno's manner was as important as what he said, and a clerk cannot transcribe manner. His words are there, but what he meant by them is as irrecoverable as he is. He spoke as though from a distance, dispensing to the heathen a mixture of revealed truth and self-evident first principles. He was talking to people who were lost in archaism and regional history. There could be no question of his conduct. He was above what we might consider treachery. The primitive conception was ours. The burden, if any, was ours. His wisdom was unassailable.

"Perhaps it was. The Council declared that Hanno had 'exceeded the authority of his office, and had acted with intentional irresponsibility causing grave injury to the people of Islandia as their elected representatives understood the peoples' interest.' The Council requested that the Islar

Mora and Dorn retire in order to pass sentence as the apppointed judges.

"If Hanno had been an Emperor, we could have sent him to a St. Helena. Exile and deposition are fitting retributions for conquerors. Hanno was something else. Was he guilty of futurism? Or of atavism? Clearly, he was guilty of having used a position of trust that went far beyond the terms of the grant. He may have been altruistic. He may have wanted the best for the people to come. But what he did, for everyone now alive, is still called betrayal. One would like to separate the offense from the offender, and punish only the offense. In this world it can't be done.

"Dorn and I went back to the Council, in closed session this time, and condemned Hanno to death.

"In Islandian history there are many dynastic murders and political assassinations. State executions are rare, but there are precedents. They all offer the condemned man his choice of exit.

"When we offered Hanno this option, he looked at Dorn and me, and then polled the Council in the same way. There were some who looked aside.

"He said, 'One sort of bad thing today is a good thing tomorrow. But another kind of bad thing today is a worse thing tomorrow.' Then he spoke to his judges. 'You haven't the courage of your conviction. You offer me a choice of deaths. I'd rather have a choice of executioners. I'd choose to be gutted if I could watch one of you sweating with the knife in his hand.'

"Hanno was right about me. I could not have done it, except possibly to shoot him. Dorn was magnificent. He said, 'Time will judge us both, Hanno. You believe you are a principle. I think you are a thing. If you wish to test me, I'm willing. If you want the garotte, I'll twist the cord. If you want your throat cut, I'll stick it for you. If you want to be shot, I'll hold the gun to your head and pull the trigger. I'll stand the trial of history with you unmasked. The one thing I won't do is feed you poison. You can do that for yourself. Would you like some time to think it over?'

"Hanno said he would. And he took poison . . ."

✠

Isla Dorn to Jon

". . . I think Mora was better about Hanno than I. He felt there were grounds for condemning him that couldn't later be used to hang an innocent person. Precedent is dangerous anywhere, and in Islandia it's everything. I know why Hanno shot Tor. He was too dangerous to live. So was Hanno. At the time of the sentencing I felt there were ample grounds for imprisoning or exiling him, but probably not for executing him except that he *was* too dangerous to live. That's why I spoke as Mora, or someone else, may have reported to you.

"I think I would rather take the chance of being known to history as a political murderer than as a man who fastened an unsure test of capital crime upon the future. As things have turned out, probably neither of these things will happen to me. When Hanno poisoned himself, he proved Mora right. Or rather, he completed the evidence. The laboratory people were unable to give a chemical name to what Hanno used, but they said there was no doubt it was the same substance they had been unable to identify in the death of the King. This does not mean that Hanno poisoned Tor, but it makes him at least an accessory and an accomplice.

"Hanno's department in the Civil Service is no more. Because there is a very small preponderance of opinion that no security at all is more dangerous than security, there will be a new department of sorts. It will serve the parliamentary head, or heads, of the government, and its chief will be appointed by them with approval of the Council. Its files on any subject will be open to members of the Council who have anything more than personal curiosity as a reason for seeing them. After some years this will breed its own troubles, but not I should think while your brother is managing it. Lang Atta has agreed to set up the department and run it for a maximum of two years.

"I don't need to tell you and Morana that all our possibilities ride on what you can accomplish. I think you know that I am not a cynical man, and also not an optimistic one, even though I am sanguine enough from day to day. I regard man's achievements with reverence. But the course of human progress, insupportably weighted by its by-products, has been steadily downward. Men have put an upward vector into the idea of progress that isn't in the word. For an improbable length of time, Islandia has been able to stand aside from this stream. All that is over. Now, in order not to drop suddenly into the pit, we must float along on the slow descent.

"There are others, including Mora, who see things differently, and use other comparisons. He sees the world somewhat less as a process and more as a scene of continuing conflict between Yea and Nay, good and bad, intermingled, changing their shapes and appearances of virtue, growing in strength, breeding their opposite, never prevailing. The whole constitutes an animate, impersonal demonic thing. Mora feels, I think, that if our spoon is small enough, and the handle long and curved enough, we can sup with this Devil and come away free.

"I hope so. In any case, sup with him we must. The dimensions of the spoon are what you will have to determine . . ."

✠

As usual Dorn spoke to the point. While we ate, we didn't discuss our situation. But with the coffee, Morana said, "Dorn makes a strong case. How good a spoon are you going to be able to get, Jon?"

"After what happened today, it may not be so far from what Mora and Dorn want." I told her about the draft agreements I'd just read. "I don't think I mentioned this, but I asked Gravelle's advice. Instead of that he's given me a great deal of strong, indirect help. For the last two weeks in Washington I've been seeing people who prefer to listen than talk, and seem to like a client who knows what he wants and insists on setting limits. They may not have the *Islandian layer* in them I think Gravelle has, but they speak like men who like to put measurable resources from both sides into works that can be defined and completed. I'm about convinced that we can do what's necessary without demoralizing the country. And we can keep control of it." Hearing my own voice after I stopped speaking, I didn't much like what I was saying or the words I was using. "It doesn't matter how big the spoon is, or how long the handle is. What's important is that we can break it—any time we think we're strong enough."

"Devilish perfection," Morana said. Her tone was wistful more than mocking. "How long do you think it will take, Jonno?" She set her cup down and walked across to the east window looking down on the Plaza and Fifth Avenue.

"With luck two weeks. More likely three. What about you?"

She spoke across her shoulder. "I could leave tomorrow. No, that's not so. In a week. There are still some things I ought to do for Farrant. I need to help him with a reception, for instance. But like that, they're all specific things. He's doing very well and, you know, Jonno, the old goat likes it. He'll never come home to Farrant.

"But to do him justice, he's doing a good job. And right now an able man is a much better representative in the U.N. for us than any woman. In a public forum, a man can deal with increases and decreases in tension with an urbanity that doesn't bare his teeth one moment and his soul the next. Some women can do this, more or less, but you wonder about them. The rest of us are likely to seem like Maenads, or weeping Magdalens, or just silly."

I followed her over to the window, and said, "You do want to go home."

"Yes."

"You can go next week."

"Yes."

"But no?"

"I don't want to make that trip alone again."

She leaned against my side, and I put my arm around her waist. She took my hand in both of hers, moved it up along her body, and then held it between her breasts. It had been ten days now since we had made love. The last time both of us were very tired, and anxious about what we were accomplishing. When it was over, we realized in mutual shame and anger at ourselves that we had merely been rutting, much as American writers like to say American men and women do. Tonight I knew it would be real again.

"Morana, when we get home . . . ?"

"Yes, Jon, I think so."

For a moment longer we stood at the window looking down on Fifth Avenue where the traffic was a river of white to our left and red to the right.

APPENDIXES

APPENDIX I

Historical Note

Late in the sixth decade of the twentieth century it was a fact that Islandia continued to exist as an independent, sovereign, self-contained nation. Ordinary citizens of other countries, if they had ever heard of Islandia, considered this a natural state of affairs. But it seriously puzzled diplomats, military men, and corporation executives in the course of semi-annual reviews of "presently inactive situations of potential" throughout the world. Because Islandia *was,* and because it was where it was, there was no doubt it was increasingly important. Certainly, it was underdeveloped, vulnerable, and consequently dangerous. The situation there should be kept under scrutiny and reassessed regularly.

The difficulty, as the findings regularly admitted, was that there was little hard information to scrutinize, and nothing but opinion to reassess.

For more than fifty years these men, and their predecessors, had been saying that Islandia was too innocent, too small, too ineffectual, and too rich—not to mention too arrogant—to survive. Objective evaluations had not agreed on whether this was an advanced primitive culture or a retarded advanced culture, but they all concluded that Islandia's downfall was only a matter of time.

Even some of Islandia's good and knowledgeable friends abroad have had doubts. During the early days of the Second World War, several able and well-informed Westerners expressed heartfelt misgivings, saying that Islandia's virtues would betray her. In a world of giant predators like Germany, Japan, and even Russia, a small, well-endowed but technologically antediluvian society such as Islandia would pay a fatal price for refusing association with strong and willing friends. Elmer Davis of the United States and Lord Dudley Wigmore of England were among those who were genuinely saddened by this prospect. They felt Islandia would be gobbled up. At that time the strategic leverage of nonalignment was not as evident as it has since become.

Mr. Davis went so far as to accept an unverified, and then unverifiable, Japanese propaganda claim. In 1943 he asserted that after a "heroic but brief resistance" Islandia vanished into Japan's Greater East-Asia Co-Prosperity Sphere. This seems to be uncharacteristic of Mr. Davis, both as a person and as director of the wartime American Office of Facts and Figures, later the Office of War Information. Islandians are inclined to think he was so outraged by what he felt was the stupidity of a country he loved that he was willing to believe Islandia had got what she deserved.

To do Mr. Davis and Lord Wigmore justice, however, there was little purchase for neutrality in that pre-atomic world. Their error was to suppose that all small nations almost without exception at that time must fall into the train of one or another of the greater power systems. And if their opinion was strengthened by an unformulated feeling that none had the right to escape the hurricane of his own partial and reluctant making, that certainly would have been understandable.

But Islandia did escape. The track of the storm passed far to the north, causing vicious local eddies in the tropical Karain above St. Anthony, but no more. With the help of time it is not too difficult to see why. Between 1939 and 1941 Germany and Japan made their great reaches for conquest, setting courses for themselves that could not be much altered prior to victory. After 1941 the most each could do was to attempt to advance in the directions to which it was committed. When they both found themselves fully and then finally overengaged, they retreated necessarily along the paths over which they came. It was Islandia's good fortune to lie well outside these lines of force.

Of course it is true—and Islandians know this—that if the reach of the aggressors had not exceeded their grasp, and if Islandia's powerful friends had not been quite powerful enough, then in due course Islandia would have met the fate Mr. Davis and Lord Wigmore predicted for her. This awareness is not without importance in Islandia's present time of difficulties.

The feeling among many Islandians that their country turned its back on its own destiny and survived only thanks to the courage and sacrifice of other peoples—peoples whom it declined to help—lies still at the heart of the nation's conscience. The imputation disturbs those who deny the charge as greatly as it does those who bring it. Increasingly over the past two decades this deeply felt difference over a matter that concerns both honor and vitality has exacerbated an issue historically crucial in Islandian politics: to participate with the outside world on some terms that might conceivably be kept limited or to continue to exclude it altogether.

APPENDIX II

The Frays

Before my grandfather's time, the Frays had been part of the province of Islandia, and the military responsibility for this difficult and vulnerable place had always been alarming to the Islandian Islar.* In one or another time of crisis, these Lords had tried to shift the Frays to the jurisdiction of Brome or Upper Doring. Neither of these latter provinces wished to aggrandize itself in this particular way. Both were almost as prosperous as Islandia, both had river defense problems which Islandia did not, and both were insistent that the prestige, the economic loss, and the physical dangers of caring for the nation's sacred birthplace were Islandia's true glory.

Rhetoric aside, nobody was being foolish. The Frays are, taken together, one of those things everyone loves and no one wants. The maps my grandfather drew require study, but they show clearly why this is so. Later maps, and particularly aerial photographs, make it immediately apparent.

The great Islandian Karain range crosses the continental island east and west, presenting a slightly convex face

---

* The normal Islandian way of forming plurals is to add *r* if the word ends in a vowel, or *r* plus an appropriate vowel if the ending is a consonant. There are exceptions, notably the Frays, meaning the Ledges. This is an irregular proper noun existing only in the plural; e.g., the term a *fray* would be incomprehensible. Another word designates the ordinary rock formation as such.

to an Islandian looking north. There are other mountain
systems in Islandia, and in the northern tropics of the
Karain. Mostly, they twist their way north and south as
interrupted abutments.

None of the world's major mountain ranges is a single
line of peaks with escorting foothills. Usually there are
two, or several, formations running roughly parallel. The
country in between is likely to be abnormally bad, or good,
or freakish.

The Islandian barrier range is in the two formation category, with high, tumbled, broken valleys between the
northern and southern ridges. Along the east-west crescent the southern ridge is the lesser, breaking down at
midpoint into the ledge formations of the Frays.* These
irregular shelves begin at Fraysedge and reach north for
about twenty miles, rising 2500 feet on the way. Each
ledge is different in width and slope, in the depth and
quality of its soil, and in the vertical footage between itself
and its upper and lower neighbors. Some ledges hold distance from each other throughout their length. Others
slope up and down toward each other making switch-
backs. Since The Descent in the year A.D. 800—near the
time when historical records begin—the population of the
Frays has been nonexistent officially until my grandfather
became Isla. Since then, most of its small population has
been counted.

For hundreds of years there have been no permanent
households or settlements on the high ledges. Instead, these
have become the working territory of a self-limiting, largely hereditary group of professional hunters and trappers
most of whose members come from Upper Doring and
Farrant, not from the Frays. They provide magnificent furs
and fine game meats, and the wildlife thrives. No one inter-
feres much with these people, but in recent years some
extra-professional things have been asked of them.

In the north the empty upper Frays lead directly to the
Mora and Lor passes through the barrier range. In the
northeast, though not so immediately, they give access to
the Bronclorn pass. All this is very high, extremely forbidding country. Until my grandfather's time Islandians

---

* The east-west barrier range has a political, geographical, and
historical importance that cannot be overstated. But geologically it
is arguable that the line of fault runs in a demilune SW/NE.
Some great peaks are in the SW, east of the Doring River. They
stand betwen Bannar and Doring on one side and Reeves and The
City on the other.

had given no attention to the area. On nineteenth-century military maps the Frays and the northern passes are described as naturally secure except for the "remote possibility of their use by ineffectual raiding parties." Invasions had always come by other routes.

But then geologists and surveyors of four principal nationalities, with equipment that was much better than their credentials, began to work their way up out of the breathless, steaming Karain lowlands onto the northern slopes of the barrier range. And right after them the First World War arrived. In these years Islandia accomplished an official change in its thinking.

In 1915 the Council declared the Frays a separate province. This act required a more difficult decision than the earlier one to build the Frays elevator, but it was based on the same set of facts. The outside world was encroaching from that direction. At the time the Dorn party was in control of the Council, but just barely so. Because of the prominent, courageous, and diplomatically highly improper part my grandfather had played in the border incident just after the Dorns came back to power there was some historical justification for his nomination as Isla of the new province, but the real reason for it was political necessity.

I loved my grandfather and knew him as well, I suppose, as a young organism can know an old one. He seems to me to have been seriously romantic in his attitude toward life and his adopted country, and by no means frivolous. He declared—and I can find no evidence that it was pretense as some have since claimed— that he should not be Isla of the Frays, that the post should be held by a native Islandian. He acceded finally when it became clear that the Council would not give provincial status to the Frays unless John Lang's body, so to speak, was there to be invoked. A critical number of Councillors needed an emotional pretext to vote for what they wanted and needed. "Lang, Islandia's Pulaski," as one of them said, reading into my grandfather's first coming to Islandia intentions I'm convinced he didn't have. But without this kind of legend-making they foresaw political dangers they were unwilling to risk.

My grandfather set two conditions on his willingness to cooperate, and these earn him a place in Islandian constitutional history. They also brought him a large measure of admiration from some quarters and severe criticism from others. He insisted that the Lordship of the Frays be divided into two offices with different authorizations, even though the same man might hold both of them. The Isla for civil affairs should be elected locally; the military one should be appointed by the Council.

In John Lang's letterbook there is a copy of a communication to Lord Dorn which reads, "The difficulties in the Frays in recent years have been military or submilitary, and they are the cause of proposals now under consideration by the Council. I strongly support provincial entity for the region and say also that there is no reason to suppose that security problems will obscure the natural life of the Frays through future history. It would be convenient at this time to ease matters by sending in a Proconsul. But if this is done, it will certainly be difficult later to subordinate this officer to a civilian authority. I urge therefore . . ." The result has been that my grandfather and my father have held civil and military office simultaneously. After more than fifty years the military job is still functionally much more important, but the elective civil office outranks it and confers the province's vote in the Council.

My grandfather's opponents charged that his argument was hypocritical. Under the self-deceiving facade—they must have been a little in awe of him—of generosity and abnegation they saw "the ugly reality of political power on the American model." In spite of Lang's unquestioned service to the country, it would be a danger to use separate authorities to confirm him, or any man, in two positions where one had always been customary. For "Without any appearance of it he more than doubles his power by doubling his irremovability. If he pleases his province, he can thumb his nose at the Council until it cedes him the substance of any issue. If he displeases the people of his province, he has another position from which to make them so miserable they will gladly appease him by electing him once more. He need never be in disfavor with both masters at the same time."

My own silent opinion has been that John Lang's critics had the better of the general dispute. The working out of things, however, has so far supported my grandfather. In the Frays there has naturally been no tyranny and, as a province, the small community has begun to show a spirit it didn't have when it was an appendage of Islandia. Two other border provinces, Miltain and Farrant have since adopted the two Isla system. Both are sufficiently big and complex to need a man for each Islaship. They have kept the elective-appointive and civil-military separation. It has

worked well for them. Both Islar sit on the Council, but
the elected Lord casts the vote of the province.*

APPENDIX III

Time

The coming of radio to Islandia, even in the limited form
that now exists, has brought difficulties with time and
timekeeping. To perform usefully and equitably, radio
needs a time unit of fixed duration, such as an hour of
sixty minutes. This Islandia can provide only twice a year,
once each at the vernal and autumnal equinoxes.

Like most of the rest of the world, Islandia divides its
day, one sequence of light and dark, into twenty-four
hours. The hours, again like most civil time systems, are
divided into two groups of twelve. But at this point simi-
larity ends. Islandia works on local sun time. The hours
are numbered one to twelve from sunrise to sunset, and
then again one to twelve from sunset to sunrise.

From season to season, even month to month, the Islandian hour is highly elastic. For this reason there were
no clocks or watches in the country until the advent of
radio and what is now called Radio Time. This is an ap-
proximation of Greenwich Mean Time for the longitude
and is used for nothing but radio programming.

In this narrative, for convenience, times that need to be
given with any precision are in Radio Time and not normal Islandian time.

APPENDIX IV

National Referenda

A momentous national referendum in 1908 led the Council to reject a treaty sponsored by the then Lord Mora

---

* In effect the provincial military Isla, where he exists, serves
under the two national military commanders, the Isla for the navy
and the Isla for the army. These Lords do have a vote in the
Council.

which would have opened Islandia to foreign trade and exploitation. The vote of 1908, however, was in fact a straw ballot conducted in secret, although with scrupulous fairness, by the Dorns and their adherents. In spite of its crucial effect on the vote of the Council, it was not an official and binding national mandate of the kind both Dorn and Mora are here calling for.

APPENDIX V

The Regency

The Regency began in 1280 after a disastrous war in the north against the Demiji, the Saracen tribes including the people we now call the Sulliabans. In a mountain battle in 1276, King Alwin XVII was seen to disappear into the mists totally surrounded by the enemy but still hewing and smiting with great ferocity. Alwin did not reappear but neither was there any word, verifiable or not, of his death. He merely vanished, and the country existed for four years without a King. By that time it was evident both that something had to be done and that Islandians generally did not want to confer the powers of Alwin XVII on his son. It was also clear that they didn't want to continue being governed unconditionally by the Council of Nobles which then was more arbitrary, factional, and formally hereditary than it was to be in later periods.

In 1280 the National Assembly was convoked. This body, consisting of all mature Islandians wishing to participate, has been in theory and sometimes in fact the custodian of ultimate Islandian sovereignty since the early tribes consolidated as a nation. On this occasion the Assembly met on the huge plain between the Reeves River and the Aira. The records do not show the process by which this vast gathering was enabled to formulate and express its will, nor do they name the persons who must have done the political organizing, but the whole of Islandia voted that "since the true King was absent, his son should be acting King in his place, to be crowned when news of his father's death was certain, to hold office until his father returned, and, only so long as he was chosen to that position by the Assembly, to act in lieu of his father and in trust for his father, and to be governed in all things by the advice of the Council."

Two generations later after the death of Alwina, the only reigning queen Islandia has had, the name of the dynasty changed to Tor with the accession of Alwina's son. Over the years, particularly in modern times, there has been an increasing amount of under-the-breath, unpleasant rumor and innuendo about the Tor family. The talk is never definite but it hints and suggests indecencies, aberrations, and hidden things. The overt facts are that the Tor succession has not failed and that the Kings of the line have not kicked over the traces as the Alwins did.

As far as Islandia is concerned Alwin XVII is still alive in the great mountains, coming down from the mists now and then to decapitate a Demiji. The outlying tribes attached to Sulliaba seriously agree, except that in their version he is accompanied by lightning and thunder and carries off his victims for food. Aside from legend and superstition, however, the possible continuing existence of Alwin XVII is the closest thing to a political necessity that Islandia knows. Our Constitution depends upon it. For nearly seven hundred years neither the Council nor the National Assembly, whatever that may be when it isn't assembled, has not been convinced of Alwin's death, and it doesn't seem likely that either one soon will be.

APPENDIX VI

Winder

To begin with, Winder was an independent country, contiguous with Islandia on the southwest, and stretching into the ocean long arms of spectacular and dangerous reefs, rock towers, and tidal channels. The people were of Islandian stock and spoke the same language. They were seafarers who provided the Islandian navy with equipment, men, and numbers of vessels, for a price. They also enjoyed most of the protections of Islandian citizens, without taxes or other obligations. Relations between the larger kingdom and the smaller had to be intimate, but they were usually edgy and sometimes impossible.

The final crisis between the two states began late in the thirteenth century during the time of Alwina, the granddaughter of the Alwin who is still held to be missing. History says that Alwina was not only a great monarch, but also a beautiful, passionate, and resourceful woman as well. She resolved the crisis in her own way and, in any case, seems to have wanted the man for her own. Instead of annexing Winder by armed force and setting up the indelible bitternesses that follow on a civil war, she resorted to amatory combat, subdued the Tor who was then King of Winder, married him, joined the two countries, and in the next generation gave the larger Islandia a Tor dynasty. For the most part it has been a good bargain, even at the cost of small and ugly grievances.

APPENDIX VII

Agreement With the U.S.

The final arrangement is embodied in two documents.

One, with the force of an ordinary contract, sets out the working details. Islandia is to acquire a certain number of large generators and turbines of certain specifications which Islandia will install. Islandia Bay will be developed to produce petroleum, natural gas, and sulphur. The number of Americans to be employed on the various projects will be determined by Islandia and, in general, the personnel will be restricted to engineers and highly skilled technicians. There will be no extra-territoriality, and there will be no foreign housing or other structures built in Islandia except as individually authorized by the Islandian government. American currency will not be permitted in Islandia. Wages to Americans will be paid in Islandian currency at Islandian rates for comparable work; the difference is to be deposited in dollars in America to the accounts of the employes.

On its part, Islandia agrees to solicit American firms to form a consortium for the program. Islandia will give the consortium world market rights on terms that will enable the consortium to issue thirty-year debentures. Islandia will subscribe one-third of the issue with payment in gold interest free. Production goals will be set with Islandia holding a veto on increases. When production begins, Islandia will purchase the entire product at cost until a certain volume is reached. After that Islandia's share will be above cost, but below world market by a given percentage. At maturity Islandia agrees to redeem all debentures not owned by her at a minimum rate of 110, and reserves the right to call the debentures at any time with an increase in price at least equivalent to the unpaid interest. At either time Islandia will take over operational control, as well as governance, of the installations.

The other document, with the force of a treaty, is short and simple. It commits the two governments to uphold and enforce, within their jurisdictions, all the terms of the general contract. The agreement may be terminated by either party on six months' notice, the accounts to be settled within five years.

Islandia could have made much less expensive arrangements in other ways. But the Council, the Government, and I all feel that the speed of development, the limitations on production, the protection of Islandia domestically, and the certainty of Islandian control justify the high cost.

Other SIGNET Science Fiction Titles You Will Enjoy

☐ **BY FURIES POSSESSED by Ted White.** A frightening adventure into the unknown where a manned satellite returns from a thirty year voyage into space.
(#T4275—75¢)

☐ **THE STARS AROUND US.** A Science Fiction Anthology edited by Robert Hoskins. Ten fascinating short stories by ten masters of science fiction. (#T4202—75¢)

☐ **A CIRCUS OF HELLS by Poul Anderson.** The story of a lost treasure guarded by curious monsters, of captivity in a wilderness, of a journey through reefs and shoals that could wreck a ship, and of the rivalry of empires.
(#T4250—75¢)

☐ **SWORDS AGAINST TOMORROW edited by Robert Hoskins.** An exciting science fiction anthology by such master writers as John Jakes, Lin Carter, Fritz Leiber and Poul Anderson. (#T4327—75¢)